BEHIND THE CANVAS

ALEXANDER VANCE

FEIWEL AND FRIENDS
NEW YORK

A FEIWEL AND FRIENDS BOOK
An Imprint of Macmillan

Our books may be purchased in bulk for promotional, educational, or business use. Please contact your local bookseller or the Macmillan Corporate and Premium Sales Department at (800) 221-7945 ext. 5442 or by e-mail at MacmillanSpecialMarkets@macmillan.com.

Library of Congress Cataloging-in-Publication Data

Vance, Alexander P. (Alexander Phillip), 1978– author.
Behind the canvas / Alexander Vance. — First edition.
pages cm
"A Feiwel and Friends Book an imprint of Macmillan."
Summary: Seventh-grader Claudia Miravista loves art, but socially she is always the odd girl out—but on a trip to the local art museum she sees a boy in a painting, who moves from painting to painting, and soon she embarks on an adventure behind the canvas, determined to free the boy Pim from the artistic prison he has endured for over three hundred years.
ISBN 978-1-250-02970-6 (hardcover) — ISBN 978-1-250-08025-7 (e-book)
1. Painting—Juvenile fiction.   2. Magic—Juvenile fiction.   3. Witches—Juvenile fiction.   4. Friendship—Juvenile fiction.   5. Adventure stories.   [1. Painting—Fiction.   2. Magic—Fiction.   3. Witches—Fiction.   4. Friendship—Fiction. 5. Adventure and adventurers—Fiction.]   I. Title.
PZ7.V2758Be 2016
[Fic]—dc23
2015004150

Book design by April Ward
Feiwel and Friends logo designed by Filomena Tuosto

First Edition—2016

1   3   5   7   9   10   8   6   4   2

mackids.com

For Mom and Dad
Masters in the art of life

CHAPTER 1

REMARKABLE THINGS, paintings. So different from other types of art. Drawing, after all, is just a single black line repeated over and over. Chalk has color to it, but it's flat and dusty. Sculpture is just a fancy kind of Play-Doh. And photography . . . well, there isn't anything to that at all. Just point and shoot.

But painting . . . Made up of hundreds—thousands—hundreds of thousands of tiny little brushstrokes. And layers, one color on top of another, sometimes providing depth, sometimes mixing to create a whole new color. All spread over a canvas that adds a texture of its own.

Claudia Miravista pushed her face closer to the painting on the museum wall. With her nose just inches away, she could actually see places where the paint rippled up into peaks like waves on the ocean. She could make out individual brushstrokes the artist used to—

"Ah, Miss Miravista?"

Her head snapped back as her entire sixth-grade class

turned to stare at her. Mr. Custos, the museum curator, wiggled his fingertips in her direction.

"Let's not breathe on the artwork, shall we?"

A few snickers ran through the group of students. Claudia mumbled an apology and felt her light brown cheeks start to burn pink.

"Now let's take a look at a work of art from a completely different time and place," Mr. Custos said, walking along the edge of the gallery. The class trudged behind him.

Claudia had mixed feelings about coming on a field trip to the Florence Museum of Arts and Culture. On one hand, she loved art. She'd been to the museum a dozen times before. It wasn't the largest art museum in Illinois, but she could walk to it from her house. She also checked out books from the public library on art history—the big ones that would break all five toes if you dropped one on your foot. Even now, sandwiched between her notebooks, she carried her own mini art encyclopedia, *Dr. Buckhardt's Art History for the Enthusiast and the Ignorant.*

On the other hand, she *secretly* loved art. It was hard enough trying to fit in at school without everyone knowing that she spent her free time reading about paintings and artists who had been dead for hundreds of years.

"This painting was created by a follower of Caravaggio," Mr. Custos continued, gesturing at a painting of an angel and a man in a way-too-bright orange robe. "Caravaggio[1] was known

---

1. CARAVAGGIO (1571–1610). Italian Baroque painter known for his realistic paintings promoting a prominent practice of chiaroscuro (or a bold contrast between light and dark). They say he was a bit of a party animal, complete with brawls and swaggering in the streets. He certainly had a flair for the dramatic—it seems like people are

for his masterful application of chiaroscuro, which refers to a dramatic use of light and dark in the scene."

Chiaroscuro. It sounded like a fancy Italian dessert. Claudia whispered the word to herself. *Chiaroscuro.* It was fun to say, the way it filled up her mouth. If she ever convinced her parents to let her get a dog, perhaps she would name it Chiaroscuro. Or maybe Rembrandt.

Mrs. McCoy, her sixth-grade teacher, stepped up next to Mr. Custos. "Class, what do we say to Mr. Custos for taking us on a tour of his museum?"

The reply came with the enthusiasm of limp spaghetti. "Thank you, Mr. Custos."

The teacher held up a printed worksheet. "Your last assignment today is for you and a partner to find a painting and ask each other these exploratory questions about it. Write down your partner's responses and then make a sketch of the painting. This will be the foundation for your essay. And please use your museum voices!"

The mass of sixth graders suddenly sprang to life. Students pointed at each other from across the gallery. A few fist bumps passed between boys. Definitely-not-museum-voices bounced off the walls.

Claudia scanned the room, pretending to look for someone in particular but on the inside desperately wishing for someone—anyone—to tap her on the shoulder. They had taken a head count when they came into the museum. Nineteen students. That meant . . .

---

always dying or getting their heads hacked off in his paintings. In short, had he been born a few centuries later, he inevitably would have found his way to Hollywood. (Excerpted from *Dr. Buckhardt's Art History for the Enthusiast and the Ignorant.*)

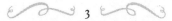

Please don't let me be the only one without a partner, she begged.

Across the room she saw Megan Connell standing alone. Megan had never said anything mean to her. She even smiled at her sometimes.

I could ask her, Claudia thought. It wouldn't be hard. All she needed to do was move her feet. One step at a time. She could do it. Here it goes. And . . . now. Take a step.

She took a step.

Then Jason Brandemeir walked up next to Megan and said something to her. She shrugged and nodded, and the two moved off toward the gallery exit.

Too late.

The crowd of students was dispersing in pairs. Claudia stood alone in the center of the gallery. She felt naked, like a blank canvas without paint and without a frame.

A tap on her shoulder. Claudia turned to see Mrs. McCoy.

"Looks like you're the odd one out today, Claudia."

Again, Claudia thought.

"You can be my partner. Would you like to choose the painting?"

Claudia nodded. She led Mrs. McCoy to the gallery exit and then through two more galleries until they came to one that was empty. At least there no one else would see her paired up with the teacher.

Rambunctious shouts came from elsewhere in the museum. Mrs. McCoy huffed and gestured to the wall. "Pick a painting, Claudia, and start your sketch. I'll be back." She hurried off.

Claudia sighed and plopped down on a purple cushy bench in the center of the gallery. She was alone. Again. Actually, she was okay with being alone. But if you do that too often, you start to get . . . well, lonely.

She liked people well enough, at least in theory. But when she actually had to start talking to them—knowing what to say, or what not to say, or how to keep people from thinking she was a total dork—her mind would go blank and her tongue would seize up and she sounded like a caveman with a stutter.

That wasn't entirely true. She could hold a conversation just fine with an adult. It was kids her own age who were the problem.

She sighed again and looked at the painting in front of her. It was a portrait of three Dutch gentlemen sitting around a table. They wore black suits with frilly white shirts and wide-brimmed hats and looked like something from a Thanksgiving play. Their swords were drawn and lying across the table or resting against a shoulder. Each had a thin mustache and a goatee. Two of them looked like they were holding back a laugh. The third looked annoyed.[2]

In the background—in the upper-left corner of the painting—was a boy, perhaps her age. Probably a servant or something, although he was in the shadows so it was hard to tell what he wore. But his eyes were a brilliant crystal blue, like marbles. His face was curious and friendly and . . . accepting.

---

2. DUTCH GOLDEN AGE OF PAINTING. During the seventeenth century, the Dutch were at the top of their game—science, trade, art, they did it all. They painted in three main categories: portraits, which often included a whole group of people loung-ing around, staring at the artist; scenes of everyday life—no doubt a prelude to reality TV; and still lifes, which required painting a table full of food or flowers. As a painting had to be created in multiple sittings, painting a still life was risky business. Think of the stink if you didn't paint the perishable products promptly. (Excerpted from *Dr. Buckhardt's Art History for the Enthusiast and the Ignorant*.)

I could be friends with a kid like that, she thought suddenly. *It wouldn't be hard.*

What would she say? That was always the tricky part. She cleared her throat. "Hey, I'm Claudia." The words echoed around the gallery and she lowered her voice. "So, do you like the museum? I know, it's a little small, right? In Florence— the real Florence, in Italy, not Illinois—they have dozens of museums. Huge ones, on every street corner. It's at the top of my places to visit someday."

Was she prattling? She was talking about herself, which was rude, right? She should at least ask the other person's name.

"So, what's your name?"

Two boys—Nate and Christian—entered the gallery, snickering over some private joke. They paused when they saw her.

"Dude, Claudia, who are you talking to?" Nate asked.

"No one," she mumbled. She grabbed her art history book and opened it up. The boys laughed quietly over something (her?) and settled on a bench on the other side of the room.

Dr. Buckhardt's book didn't have anything on the artist who painted the three Dutchmen. That didn't surprise her—it *was* a small museum.

She pulled out her notebook and pencil and began to sketch the painting.

She enjoyed drawing. She found drawing from scratch too difficult, trying to pull things out of her own imagination. So most of what she drew was like this—copying paintings or pictures she found in a book or on the wall. She thought she was pretty good at it but couldn't say for sure. She never showed her drawings to anyone except her grandpa, who knew a lot about art. He always said "¡*Qué talento!* What talent!" But then, grandpas were supposed to say that.

Her grandpa had even given her a canvas and some oil paints for her birthday several weeks ago, along with the promise to teach her a few lessons. She wasn't ready for that, though—you only get one chance with a blank canvas, and a paintbrush didn't have an eraser on top.

Her throat was dry. She hadn't finished her sketch yet, but it was time for a break.

She glanced at Nate and Christian as she left the gallery. They still hadn't done any work. Boys.

Claudia walked through the high-ceilinged atrium, lined with sculptures and purple benches. Sunlight trickled in from a crystal clear, domed skylight overhead. She paused for a moment to study it, noticing how the rays of sun highlighted the dust particles floating across the dome. She passed the gift shop and then hesitated as she approached the drinking fountain. Three girls stood next to it, talking in hushed voices out in front of the restroom.

Taking quick steps, Claudia approached the fountain and leaned in for a drink.

"I know," one of the girls said. "Jason Brandemeir has the coolest blue eyes."

The girls squealed. "I love guys with blue eyes," said another. Claudia glanced over. It was Megan Connell. "The guy I marry is totally going to have blue eyes."

The boy in the painting flashed through Claudia's mind. He had amazing blue eyes. She straightened up from the drinking fountain. She could tell them that. She could join their conversation. She had something to say!

Before she had a chance to change her mind and go back to being alone, she blurted out: "Do you want to see a boy with incredible blue eyes?"

The girls turned to look at her. "What do you mean?" asked one.

Claudia felt her tongue turning numb. "In . . . one of the paintings. Really cool eyes."

She braced herself—one of the girls looked on the verge of giggles. But Megan shrugged and said, "Sure."

Claudia felt a nervous excitement bubbling inside her. "Um. Okay. This way." She had joined a conversation! She had suggested something and they said *sure*!

She retraced her steps back to the gallery. "It's in a Dutch painting," she said over her shoulder. "With these guys and their swords and big floppy hats."

Nate and Christian were still goofing around as she entered the gallery. She ignored them and walked over to the painting of the three Dutchmen. She waited for the girls to catch up, and then she motioned to the painting with a flourish, like they do on game shows.

She watched the girls study the painting. "Which guy?" one of them finally asked.

Claudia turned. In the painting were the three Dutchmen, their hats, their swords, and the table. And nothing more.

There was no boy.

"Their eyes are all green," said another girl.

Claudia's mind whirled. "But there was a boy right there . . ."

"What are you guys staring at?" Nate asked.

"Claudia can't tell blue eyes from green ones," a girl said.

"And she thinks those old geezers in the painting are cute."
Everyone laughed, including Megan Connell.

"I'm serious," Claudia said. "He was there."

"What's going on here?" Mrs. McCoy rushed into the gallery, followed closely by Mr. Custos. "These are *not* museum voices."

Claudia snatched up her notebook. This was crazy.

"Claudia's telling lies about the paintings," a girl said.

"I am not."

Mrs. McCoy looked at her expectantly. "I thought you were supposed to be sketching."

Claudia huffed and reluctantly held up her notebook sketch. It wasn't finished, but it distinctly showed three men with wide-brimmed hats and a boy in the upper-left corner. "There was a boy in that painting earlier. A boy with blue eyes. And now he's gone."

The kids in the gallery snickered again.

Mrs. McCoy folded her arms. "Is this supposed to be funny, Claudia? No one is going to laugh when you get a zero on your assignment."

Claudia stared at her sketch, fighting back the burning in her eyes that would inevitably be followed by tears. "I'm not lying."

Mrs. McCoy clucked her tongue. "Everybody back to your paintings, right now! Get your assignments finished up." She pointed at Nate and Christian. "You two aren't even supposed to be in here. Get back to where I put you, please."

As everyone filed out of the gallery, Mrs. McCoy paused by Claudia. "I need to see how the class is doing. Just answer those questions on your own, okay?"

The questions. Who cared about the stupid assignment?

She'd made a complete fool of herself. Everyone had laughed at her. And there was the definite possibility that she was going crazy.

Claudia stood in the empty gallery and stared at the painting of the three Dutchmen. She hadn't imagined it. The image of that boy with his crystal-blue eyes was as clear in her mind as anything. She had seen it. She had *talked* to it, for crying out loud.

She took a few steps toward the painting. The patch where the boy had been was now a muddy black, unremarkable and blending in with the rest of the background. She reached her hand up toward that corner of the painting . . . and stopped.

She spun around.

Mr. Custos stood in the gallery exit, his three-piece suit immaculate, his shoes shiny. He looked at her as if she had done something completely surprising.

They stared at each other for a moment. Then he flashed her a fake toothy smile and a wave, and ducked out through the exit.

She sighed and plopped down on the cushy purple bench.

Once again, she was alone.

CHAPTER 2

THAT EVENING, after the table had been cleared, Claudia secluded herself in the large chair by the window. She pulled out her notebook sketch and added some details from memory. A few lines here, some shading there. She filled in the hat for one of the Dutchmen and strengthened the slightly annoyed look on another. She tried to ignore the boy altogether, but she had drawn his eyes in the museum, and now they stared at her relentlessly.

She needed insight. Illumination. Inspiration. Like the old man with the orange cloak and the angel in the Caravaggio painting.

As she drew, another possibility occurred to her. What if she wasn't going crazy? What if she had seen a ghost? Ghosts could appear anywhere, even in a painting. Right?

Except that she didn't believe in ghosts.

Finally she couldn't take it anymore. She flipped her pencil over and scrubbed the eraser against the face of the boy.

A hand slipped in from behind her and lifted the notebook, rescuing the boy and spilling eraser dust into her lap.

She twisted in the chair to see her grandpa studying the sketch.

"Hmmm . . ." he rumbled. "Wonderful detail. Fine shading. Perhaps even a hint of chiaroscuro. You have such a talent, *mi prodigia*."

"You always say that. Even when it looks like chicken scratch."

"This is hardly chicken scratch. You're getting better all the time. Any talent worth having takes time to develop. But I can see it in everything you draw. You have a magic all your own, Claudia."

Her ears pricked up. *Magic*. It was just a passing comment, but if anyone knew, it was her grandpa.

"Do you really believe in that, Grandpa? Magic? Ghosts? That kind of thing . . . ?"

A speck of humor leaped into her grandpa's eyes. "Ghosts? Of course I believe in ghosts. Why, when I was a *pequeñito*, we had a ghost that lived in the outhouse on our farm. He mostly hibernated during the winter, but in the summer you'd be doing your business out there, when suddenly . . ."

He paused and studied her. Perhaps he saw the disappointment in her eyes. "But that's not what you're really asking me, is it?" He sat on the edge of the sofa across from her. "You're asking me about things you can't see but that you suspect might be there. Hidden worlds. Magical powers. Beings who are completely invisible unless you know where to look."

Her eyes grew wide. She caught her breath.

Grandpa held up the notebook. "Yesterday this paper was

blank. No one knew that it contained three men with beards and swords. No one but you. *Magic*."

Claudia huffed. "That's not magic, Grandpa. That's just art."

He smiled. "You say tomato, I say *el tomate*." He placed the sketchbook in her hands and stood. "Keep up the good work, *mi prodigia*."

She rolled her eyes. So much for age and wisdom.

After a quick round of good-nights with her parents, Claudia made her way upstairs to her bedroom. She passed through the motions of her bedtime routine, thinking about ghosts in the outhouse, and ghosts in a painting, and what the heck happened to her today?

She absentmindedly organized objects on her desk—nearly all of them were birthday presents from several weeks ago. The art history book from her parents. The white canvas and tubes of oil paints from Grandpa. And a set of twenty-four colors of nail polish complete with a bonus bottle of nail polish remover from her Aunt Maggie. It was still wrapped in cellophane.

Claudia picked up Aunt Maggie's birthday card. *Hey, chica. What artist doesn't need a bazillion colors to express herself with, right? Happy birthday. I'm back in town—come visit me.* She smiled. Her aunt was the kind of person who would probably wear all twenty-four colors at the same time.

Placing the card back on her desk, she turned and climbed into bed. On the wall beside her hung the other present from her parents. A painting—real oil colors on real canvas in a real frame. It was a painting of a meadow full of brilliant wild-flowers and a blue sky. A creek cut through one corner and a willow tree stood off to the left. Her parents had brought it back for her from a trip to Canada, which made it an international work of art. It was tiny, about the length of a pencil, but it was all hers. *Her* painting on *her* wall. It meant that she wasn't just a kid who thought art was interesting. It meant that she was an art collector.

Claudia closed her eyes and pictured herself sitting in the meadow, the breeze blowing her hair, the whisper of the creek tumbling by. She breathed in and almost caught the scent of wildflowers.

Who cared about what happened at the museum? It would all be behind her tomorrow.

She lay down on her pillow and snapped off the light.

Claudia awoke with a start. Her breathing was heavy and her heart thumped against her ribs. She glanced at her clock. It was the middle of the night. Her sheets and comforter were wrapped tightly around her. But something had woken her up. She listened in the darkness. Nothing.

She slipped from bed and peered out the window. The neighborhood below was silent. Silent and dark, except for the occasional pocket of light on a front porch that somehow only accentuated the darkness. Like a scene in a Caravaggio.

She stared at the porch lights a while longer until her heart slowed to a more familiar rhythm. Maybe it was a nightmare that had woken her up. She was glad she didn't remember it.

The dark room begged her to sleep, and she was happy to oblige. She stumbled into bed and pulled up the covers, her weary eyes aimlessly searching for the outline of her painting on the wall. She found it just as her eyelids started to droop. In the back of her mind, she heard a car driving down the street. It passed, filling her room with light like a slow-motion flash from a camera.

And in an instant she was sitting up, entirely awake.

There was *someone* in her painting.

In the blaze of headlights she had seen *someone* there. She was sure of it. *Someone* in a meadow that was supposed to be empty.

She jumped out of bed and snatched a flashlight from her desk drawer. She spun around and clicked it on, her arm pointing straight out toward the painting.

The circle of light landed on the canvas. There, next to the tree, a tiny figure threw up its hands to shield its eyes from the blinding beam.

Claudia shrieked and dropped the flashlight. There wasn't just a *picture of someone* in her painting—there was a *real someone* in her painting. *Someone* who moved.

On an impulse, Claudia launched herself onto her bed. She grabbed the painting by the wooden frame and spun it around on its wire, slamming it face-first against the wall.

She stood there for a few moments, pushing against the back of the painting as though it might recoil off the wall on its own. Then she tentatively let go. The painting remained still.

Claudia snatched up the flashlight and ripped the comforter from her bed. She huddled on the far side of the room, the flashlight shining on the back of the canvas. It looked innocent and ridiculous hanging crookedly on the wall.

Her breath was ragged. What was going on? Two paintings. She had seen people now in two paintings who didn't belong there. Could she really be going crazy? But crazy is what happens to old rich people, not kids in the prime of middle school.

It was ghosts, then. She was being haunted by artistic ghosts. But who would want to haunt her? Nobody paid attention to her.

She pulled the comforter around herself in the darkness, listening to her heart pound in her ears. *I could go sleep in my parents' room,* she thought, but immediately scolded herself. *I'm not five.*

This was absurd. What was she going to do—sleep on the floor all night? Because of . . . what? Headlights flashed through her window? She imagined something in the shadows of the night?

She slowly stood up, the comforter falling to the floor. No. She had seen something. *Someone.* She raised the flashlight and took a step toward the painting.

Was it the boy? Had it been the same boy just now whom she had seen in the museum?

Another step.

She couldn't just leave the painting there with its face to the wall. The curiosity would drive her . . . well, she already might be crazy.

Another step.

What if the painting was empty? Would she need to see a shrink? Wouldn't a shrink just try to convince her that this was merely a thought followed by a daydream followed by a nightmare?

Another step. She was close enough to reach out and touch the painting.

And what if it was the boy and he was waiting for her right now in that painting? What would a ghost want with her? Maybe she should wait until her grandpa came by the next day. If he was there when she turned the painting around and they *both* saw the boy . . .

"No," whispered Claudia. "This is *my* painting."

Her chest tightened as she knelt on her bed and reached a trembling hand toward the painting. Panic inched its way to the surface. She swallowed, trying to force it down. But a strange giddiness accompanied it, too, like stepping into a haunted house on Halloween.

Her fingers tingled as she lightly touched the wooden frame. Then in a slow, methodical motion, she turned the painting on its wire.

There in the glow of her flashlight stood the willow tree, and the meadow, and the stream . . . and that was all. There was no boy. No one at all.

She closed her eyes and placed a hand on her forehead. She let out a long breath. Relief and disappointment shared a place in her otherwise empty stomach. She grabbed her comforter from off the floor and forced a laugh, a quick one, with a shake of her head. She would sleep. She would sleep and forget the whole silly thing.

She snapped off her flashlight.

"Wait!"

It was a voice, from there in her room.

Claudia's heart was in her throat as she flicked the flashlight back on.

Cheeks flushed and eyes shining, a boy stood in the painting as though he had been there all along. His tousled brown hair was in dire need of a comb, and he wore some sort of old-fashioned buttoned shirt and vest. And if he hadn't been shifting slightly from one foot to the other, she would have sworn that he had been created with the same brushstrokes as the rest of the painting.

And his eyes were crystal blue and unmistakable.

Her knees gave way and Claudia dropped to the bed.

The boy ran a hand through his hair without much result. He looked behind himself and then back at her, squinting in the beam of the flashlight. "I'm sorry. I stepped away just now because I didn't think you'd turn the painting around again so soon. But you did! They don't usually come back, not after . . . well. I didn't mean to scare you earlier. I guess I'm sorry for that, too."

Claudia inched closer to the painting, staring at the boy's tiny mouth. It actually moved as he spoke, as if repeated brushstrokes were rapidly applied and erased by some invisible artist's hand.

The boy seemed encouraged by her approach. "I don't suppose you would mind . . ." He motioned at her. "The light?"

She looked down at the flashlight. "Oh, sorry." She turned it toward the ceiling so that it cast a soft glow over the bed.

"I couldn't believe it when I saw you here in this room," the boy continued. "I mean, after seeing you in the museum. It's almost like we were meant to meet each other."

Claudia couldn't help herself. An excitement bubbled up

in her like fizz in a soda can. He seemed harmless enough. She reached out a finger and touched the canvas where the boy stood. Dried paint, nothing more.

The boy glanced at the place on the painting she had touched. "Your name is Claudia. You told me that in the museum. You asked me my name, too. It's Pim." His voice held the smallest trace of a foreign accent. Not Spanish like her grandpa. Something different.

Claudia looked at the painting as if for the first time. "Pim."

"Great work on your sketch, by the way. You have a real talent. You're still budding, of course, but you have talent."

"That's what my grandpa says, too," she mumbled.

"I wouldn't mind meeting your grandpa. He sounds like a smart fellow. I don't get to meet many people, as you can imagine."

She had no idea what to imagine.

"Hey, do you want to hear an art joke?"

"A what?"

"An art joke. Try this one: Why was the art collector in debt?"

Claudia shrugged. Was he really telling a joke?

"Because he didn't have any Monet. Get it? *Monet* sounds like *money*?"

"What are you? Are you a ghost?"

Pim laughed, a hollow sound. "No. Not a ghost. In fact I'm very much alive. Flesh and blood, just like you, but . . . well." He became silent and thoughtful for a moment before continuing. "Not a ghost. Although, I get that a lot. Once when I was

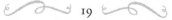

at the Louvre,[3] I scared an old woman so badly that she . . . well, anyway. Not a ghost."

"You've been to the Louvre? But that's in France, isn't it?"

"Indeed. Paris. And what a museum. There aren't words to describe it. Enormous. Gigantic. Immense. A masterpiece in every corner. Thousands upon thousands of paintings. Just when I think I've been in them all, I come across a new one I haven't seen before—at least not that I can remember."

She shook her head, trying to picture what he had just said. "So you, what? Hop around from one painting to another?"

He shrugged. "It's not quite as simple as that. I do like paintings, though. I can tell you do, too. The Louvre has some of the most famous paintings in the world. Vermeer, Delacroix, Leonardo. You know about the *Mona Lisa*, don't you?"

"Of course I do, but—"

"I've seen her many times." The boy's gaze suddenly seemed to reach past Claudia. "Taken counsel in her court. Listened to her stories . . ."

"I don't get it. You say you're not a ghost, that you're flesh and blood. But how's that possible? Where are you?"

"Ah, now that's the question, isn't it? Where am I?" Pim studied her, stroking his chin. Claudia had the feeling she was being evaluated, like those flexibility tests in gym.

---

3. THE LOUVRE MUSEUM (PARIS, FRANCE). The Louvre, located smack-dab in the middle of Paris, holds the distinction of being the most visited museum in the world. It is also one of the largest, with more than 35,000 works of art on display. That means if you were to visit the Louvre and soak in 200 works of art per day (anything more and your head starts to spin), you would need to come back for another 174 days to see it all. Hopefully you would also make some time for croissants at a French café. (Excerpted from *Dr. Buckhardt's Art History for the Enthusiast and the Ignorant*.)

"You can tell me," she encouraged. "I want to know."

He took a deep breath, his mouth twisting with indecision. Finally he said, "How many oil paintings have been created in the last five hundred years?"

She shook her head. "I don't know. Thousands. Millions."

"And how many of those were painted on canvas?"

"Well, probably most of them were."

"Yes. Oil and canvas. That is what makes up the world I live in. This wondrous and terrifying world. The world behind the canvas."

"So you live *in* the paintings?"

"Well . . . how to describe it?" The boy paced back and forth within the frame. "You go to a museum and see paintings on the wall. And to you, they appear static—people and creatures and places all frozen, never changing. But what if I told you that every painting ever created over the last five hundred years *lives*, here in the world behind the canvas."

"*Lives?* Lives how?"

"Well, if you paint a man in your world, in this world that man comes to life. Your painting will never change, but here he talks and walks and thinks and—though he'll never get a day older—he lives."

"Lives," Claudia repeated. If she hadn't been speaking to a boy whose face appeared on canvas, she would have laughed at the idea. "So if I paint a picture of a cow . . . ?"

"That same cow will appear here in this world."

"And my landscape painting I'm looking at now?"

"You will find it here as part of the great patchwork quilt of landscapes that makes up this world. Every person, every place, every creature ever painted."

"You can't really mean *every* painting. That's millions of paintings. That world would have to be huge."

"It's not small, I can promise you that," Pim said with a smile.

"And how can you show up in my painting? And the one in the museum?"

"Every painting is like a, I don't know, a window. Those windows are scattered all over the place. Through them, I can look out into your world."

A world behind the canvas. Painted people. Living people. "So you started out as a painting, then?"

"No!" Pim snapped. "I told you. I am flesh and blood. I am real. *I am real.* I—I don't belong here."

"But then . . . how did you get there?"

The boy's countenance fell. "Some stories are best left untold. You don't want to get tangled up in it." He stared at the ground, biting a fingernail.

"If you don't belong there, then . . . what? Are you stuck? Or trapped there?"

His eyes lifted to lock with hers. *Yes,* they said.

She breathed in sharply. "You're *trapped* there? How did that happen?"

But Pim only shook his head in response.

"Don't you have any friends there? Anyone to keep you company?"

"There are many people, but no one like me."

Her mind overflowed with questions, but they were pushed aside by her own memories. Pictures, as clear as a painting, of reading by herself in the corner of a crowded playground, of pretending to be busy with her backpack or homework every morning in class before the bell rang, of wishing for a party on her birthday but too afraid no one would come. She'd never been stuck in a painted world before, but she knew something about feeling out of place and all alone.

"You must be very lonely," she said.

Pim's laugh was short and bitter. "That doesn't even begin to describe my life. But . . ." His eyes met hers and they shone with a new light. "But now I have found a friend." He extended his hand toward her. "Perhaps fortune is smiling on me at last."

I could be friends with a kid like that. That's what she'd thought in the museum. Perhaps she was right.

A smile slowly spread across Claudia's face. She lifted the tip of her finger, hesitated a moment, then pressed it against Pim's hand. A tiny painted hand that belonged to a mysterious boy trapped in a world behind the canvas.

"Smiling on us both," she said.

CHAPTER 3

THE NEXT MORNING, Pim was waiting for her in the painting.

The morning after that, he was there as well.

And in the mornings that followed.

Claudia had never met anyone who was so easy to talk to. She didn't have to rack her brain for something to say, or analyze her words before they came out of her mouth in case they sounded stupid. She just said what was on her mind and he listened. And he would tell her stories or ask questions and she listened.

So this is what it's like to have a friend, she thought more than once. *I could get used to this.*

He wasn't always there. At times he excused himself, disappearing as the brushstrokes of the painted background folded over him. But when he returned—sometimes minutes, sometimes hours later—he always came with an art joke.

"What did the artist say to the dentist?"

"Hi, Pim. I don't know. What?"

"Ma*tisse* hurt."

"Why did the artist go to jail?"

"Beats me."

"Because he was *framed*."

She had always wished her painting was a little bigger. Now she was glad it was so portable. Her yellow backpack had a large mesh pocket in the front that just fit the painting, allowing Pim to look out and hear without being noticed. She took it with her everywhere, even to school. Pim was especially good at history.

"Who remembers the name of the Confederate general who surrendered at Appomattox?" asked Mrs. McCoy.

"Robert E. Lee," came a whisper from Claudia's backpack. Claudia raised her hand. "Robert E. Lee."

"Very good, Claudia. That's right."

"There's a painting of it in the Smithsonian," said the whisper.

"Did you say something else, Claudia?"

"No."

Pim loved to tour the small town of Florence—especially any place that didn't typically have paintings hanging nearby.

"You mean you've never seen inside a supermarket?" she asked.

"I've never seen the outside of a supermarket, either."

"We can fix that."

Claudia took him down to the local Food 'n' Things and walked the aisles.

On aisle seven: "Why is there a colorful bird on that box? Is that what it contains?"

"No. The bird's just there so kids will beg their parents to buy that."

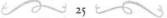

On aisle ten: "Peanut butter? You can make butter out of peanuts?"

"You've never had peanut butter? Are you kidding me? When we get home I'm totally making you a peanut butter and jam—" She stopped herself and looked at her friend in the framed painting. "Oh. Sorry."

"It's all right. I should like to try peanut butter someday."

On aisle fourteen: "Water in bottles? Why do they sell water in bottles?"

"Because people drink it."

"But don't people have sinks in their houses?"

"Yeah, most people."

"Then why would they buy water in bottles?"

Claudia thought about it but came up empty. "I guess someone thought of the idea, and people went along with it."

Pim laughed. "Pig whiskers!"

"What?"

"Pig whiskers. Where I grew up, in Haarlem, in the Netherlands, there was a man who sold pig whiskers. Just one whisker was enough to cure anything, any illness. No one really knew if they worked, but everyone had to have them. He sold a lot of pig whiskers—until the pig finally died."

She laughed, too. "Yeah, bottled water is probably the same thing. Pig whiskers." And she filed away the first piece of information Pim had revealed about his mysterious history: He was Dutch.

Because for all the talking they did and the comforting conversation that passed between them, Pim constantly deflected any questions about where he came from or how he became trapped in the world behind the canvas.

More than two weeks after Pim first appeared in her painting, on a Friday afternoon, Claudia sat with Pim in the park across the street from the Florence Museum of Arts and Culture. They stared at a shapeless bronze sculpture made up of twisty waves and bulbous blobs.

"A mother and her newborn child. That's what I see," Pim said. "It evokes the concepts of security and comfort."

"Well, I think it looks like a melted candle squished by a giant hand."

"Push aside your initial reaction to it. Look deeper."

She shook her head. "That's as deep as it gets, Pim. Melted candle. *Squish*. Poor thing never saw it coming."

"Well, I like it. It's evocative. Emotional."

"Come on. A third grader could have made that."

Pim sighed. "Well, Cubism does take some getting used to, I suppose."

"Cubism? You mean, Picasso[4] and all those guys? You don't actually like that stuff, do you?"

"I understand it. There are a thousand ways to look at the simplest object. The great artist opens her mind to them all and sees the object as it truly is."

Claudia paused to think about that. But not for long. "Okay, next week I'll take you into Mr. Griffiths's third-grade class and show you how they work with clay."

---

4. PABLO PICASSO (1881–1973). One of the most influential artists of the twentieth century and the cofounder of the Cubist movement. Picasso produced around 50,000 works of art during his career, including a four-story mural. He once said, "Art is a lie that makes us realize the truth." If that's so, then I suppose that makes this prolific painterly pundit a compulsive liar—and some of them were whoppers. (Excerpted from *Dr. Buckhardt's Art History for the Enthusiast and the Ignorant*.)

"I should like that very much," Pim said with a smile.

She held the painting in her lap and looked at her painted friend. "I wish you could. I wish you could walk with me into Mr. Griffiths's class. On your own feet, I mean. I wish you could sit right here next to me, Pim. I wish we could eat peanut butter and jam sandwiches together."

"Me, too."

"I know you don't want to talk about your past or about how you got stuck in there, but maybe we can get some help for you. There's got to be a way to get you out of there." The wish was so deep that she blinked to keep the tears at bay.

"Claudia, listen, I . . ." Pim's gaze suddenly focused on something over Claudia's shoulder. In an instant he had faded from view.

She spun around on the bench to find Mr. Custos right behind her, his immaculate three-piece suit buttoned up and free of wrinkles.

She hugged the painting to her chest.

The museum curator stared at her with wide eyes. "It would appear you have a talking boy in your painting."

The lump in Claudia's throat prevented her from either swallowing or speaking. "I—I don't know what you mean," she finally said.

Mr. Custos continued to stare. "The last time you visited, when you said there was a boy in the painting of the Dutchmen, I didn't realize . . ."

"Mr. Custos," she whispered. "What are you talking about?" Her fingers squeezed tight against the wooden frame of her painting. They would take it away from her. Scientists would poke and prod at her painting and keep Pim away forever. Mr. Custos would tell her parents. She would never see Pim again.

But Mr. Custos nodded, as though the situation had become suddenly clear. He spoke slowly now, enunciating the consonants at the ends of words as he always did. "I think, Miss Miravista, that you need to meet Granny Custos."

"What?"

"Granny Custos. Yes. She will definitely want to speak with you. Tonight. My house. Seven o'clock sharp. Both you and, uh"—he waved toward the painting—"your friend."

She had never heard of Granny Custos before, and she had no idea what Mr. Custos's grandmother might have to do with Pim. "But I . . ."

"Don't worry. Your grandfather knows where I live. He can bring you."

An elderly couple appeared on a nearby path, walking their dog.

"Seven o'clock sharp," Mr. Custos whispered. "Bring the boy." He spun around and waved at the couple as he passed. "Hello there! Gorgeous afternoon for stimulating your cultural sensitivities, isn't it?"

Claudia shoved the small painting into her backpack and tried not to break into a run as she left the park.

More than an hour passed before Pim returned to the painting, his head barely peeking around the frame. "Is it safe?" he whispered.

Claudia nodded from the place on her bed where she was sketching absentmindedly in her notebook. "We're home."

"What happened?"

"What, no joke this time?"

"I think the museum director scared them out of me. What did he say?"

"He wants us to meet his grandma."

"What?"

"I know. Weird, right?" She stood up and looked out her window at the long evening shadows. "It was like he wasn't even surprised. He was but wasn't at the same time. Instead of asking who you were or what was up with my painting, he asked me—well, told me—to come to his house tonight to meet his grandma. So strange."

"Do you know the curator well?"

"Only from visiting the museum. But my grandpa's known him for decades."

"Are you going?"

She looked back at Pim. "Well, if I go, I'm not going alone. He told me to bring you along."

"Me?" Pim looked shocked, but the expression slowly melted into a half smile. "It's been a long time since I've had an invitation to someone's home."

She pulled back her thick hair and looped it into a ponytail. "Don't get too excited. Mr. Custos isn't exactly normal. I can't imagine what Granny Custos is like."

"Who?"

"That's his grandmother's name. Granny Custos."

Pim raised his eyebrows.

"What? Have you heard of her?" she asked.

He shook his head, slowly at first and then more firmly. "No. No. Of course not. Well, I've heard the name before, but I don't remember where or when. A long time ago."

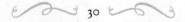

"Really? What else have you heard about her? Why would she want to talk to us? Why would she be interested in you?"

"I don't know."

"Well, think. If you heard the name somewhere, then she probably has a connection with the world behind the canvas, right?"

"I don't know. I don't know!" he snapped.

"Okay, take it easy. Just thinking out loud."

If Pim had heard that name before, and Mr. Custos thought she would be interested in Pim . . . maybe Granny Custos knew something about Pim's past. She might even know something that would help him.

"Well, I think we should go," she said. "You don't give me any answers about where you come from. Maybe she has some."

"Not all questions are meant to be answered, Claudia."

A shout came from the floor below. "Dinnertime!"

"Well, you can stay home if you want," she said. "But I'm going to see Granny Custos."

CHAPTER 4

G RANDPA, SLOW DOWN!" The cool spring breeze chilled Claudia's face as she hurried to catch up.

Grandpa glanced back at her. "You don't want to be late, do you? Didn't he say seven o'clock sharp?"

She sprinted, her yellow backpack flopping on her back, until she was even with him. He had seemed tired and reluctant to go out with her when she had asked him after dinner. But when she mentioned that Mr. Custos wanted to introduce her to his grandma, Grandpa practically pushed her out the door.

"Do you know Granny Custos?" she asked as they charged down the sidewalk.

"Know her? I should say so! She and I knew each other very well when I was younger. Very well indeed. It's been years since I've seen her, though. You know, she was quite the artist at one point in time. More talent and knowledge of art history than Sal—er, Mr. Custos—has, that's for sure. I had thought of introducing you myself one of these days. I guess Sal beat me to it. Still, you could learn a lot from her."

Breathless, she followed Grandpa up one street and down another through the neighborhoods. Eventually they came to a part of town where the architecture was tall and cramped, and the paint on many houses was peeling. Finally they stopped in front of a Victorian with steeply pitched roofs reaching toward a soaring turret. Her grandpa glanced at the outer gate and pulled a bow tie from his pocket, which he clipped onto his buttoned shirt.

"A bow tie, Grandpa?"

He paused and pursed his lips before ushering her through the gate toward the front door. Clearing his throat, he gave the door a solid knock.

She brought down the backpack from her shoulders. Her worries from the park surfaced again. What would happen when Mr. Custos pointed out the boy in her painting? Would everyone try to take it away from her?

The door opened, revealing an old woman in a thick and expansive woolen shawl. The shawl enveloped her body down to the ankles, allowing her head and arms to protrude like those of a tortoise. Her silver hair had mostly fallen out of its bun and swirled in loose wisps around her head. The woman's olive skin didn't seem nearly as wrinkled as Claudia expected of someone everybody called "Granny."

She stood upright with a slight hunch, her hand resting on the edge of the door. Her eyes were the deep brown of chocolate on candy bar commercials, melted and swirled into confectionary perfection. She stared at Claudia. Claudia shifted her feet but forced herself to return the old woman's gaze. She couldn't put her finger on it, but there was something powerful about this woman.

"*Mi estrellita*, it's so good to see you again," Grandpa said. He moved forward to give the woman a *besito* on the cheek, but she held up a hand.

"You," she said, "sit." She pointed to a swing hanging from the porch roof off to the side of the front door. "And wait."

Grandpa looked as though he was about to argue, but then his shoulders slumped and he nodded. He skulked toward the porch swing as the old woman grabbed Claudia's arm and yanked her through the door. It slammed closed behind them.

Claudia tried to turn back to the door. "But what about my—"

"*Zoot, zoot!*" Granny Custos poked Claudia in front of her and shooed her forward, as though clearing chickens from the yard. They passed down a narrow hallway and through a parlor. The room radiated a warm, inviting light. Claudia had expected to see walls filled with paintings in the home of the museum curator, but they held only knickknacks and needlepoint that matched the old-fashioned furniture.

They entered the dining room and Granny Custos silently pointed to a chair at a large mahogany table detailed with gold inlays. Claudia hesitated, not sure what to make of the pushy old woman. She relaxed a tiny bit when Mr. Custos poked his head out from what appeared to be the kitchen.

"Ah, Ms. Miravista, you made it," he said. "So glad to see that. And your grandfather?"

Claudia sat in the chair and scowled at Granny Custos. "He's waiting on the porch."

He glanced at the old woman. "Ah. I see. Well, did you bring your friend? You know, the small one?" He held his fingers an inch apart.

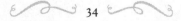

Granny Custos hissed. "Salvatore. Out you go."

Mr. Custos winced. "Yes, Granny." He nodded to Claudia. "I have to get up early and all—you understand, I'm sure." He lingered a moment longer, cleared his throat, and then ducked back into the kitchen.

Claudia's eyes widened. Both Grandpa and Mr. Custos cowered in front of this senior citizen. What was she getting herself into?

The old tortoiseshell woman lowered herself into a chair on the other side of the table.

She dug around in her shawl before surfacing with a long wooden pipe. She tapped the bowl against her hand and then set the end of the long stem between her teeth.

"Show me the boy."

Claudia stiffened at the frank command. The old woman hadn't even introduced herself yet. Claudia hadn't come here to be bossed around. But her curiosity won out, and she unzipped her backpack. She pulled the painting from within and gently propped it on the table.

Pim blinked at the sudden light of the room and then focused on the elderly woman. He bowed low. "Granny Custos, it is indeed an honor."

Granny Custos regarded him without expression, tilting her head slowly like a cat. "Are you flesh, boy, or are you paint?"

"Well . . ." Pim spread his hands. "I was born flesh, and I was flesh when I came in. I'm not sure what I am now, but I hope to be flesh again someday."

The woman chewed the stem of her pipe. *Click-clack*. "If you were flesh when you went in, then flesh you can become again. Who is your witch?"

Pim's eyes grew wide for a moment. "What do you mean? My what?"

Granny Custos gave a small smile, wrinkles forming where smooth skin lay seconds before. Wrinkles that somehow, Claudia knew, were born of secrets. "You don't just climb into the world behind the canvas on your own, boy. No door, no window, no path. If flesh you be, then it was someone what put you there. A witch is my wager. What is her name?"

Pim shook his head. "No no no no. I don't . . . I can't . . ."

The air in the room seemed to sag now with a new weight. The old woman's words buzzed in Claudia's ears. *The world behind the canvas.* In her room or around the neighborhood, having Pim in a painting almost seemed a surreal game, something she kept to herself, apart from reality. But now here was a woman who knew about that world—and probably about many other things as well. Like witches?

"Boy," said Granny Custos evenly. "I did not let you through my door to play childish games. Who is your witch?"

Fidgeting with a button on his jacket, Pim cast a long look behind him. Finally his shoulders drooped and his hands fell to his sides. "Nee Gezicht. It is—was, I mean, was—Nee Gezicht."

Granny Custos slowly took the unlit pipe from her mouth and leaned forward. "Nee Gezicht?" The pipe stem found its way back into her mouth as she thoughtfully repeated the odd name. "Nee Gezicht. How long?"

Pim sighed. "Three hundred and sixty years. Give or take a decade."

Claudia gasped. "Three hundred and—? You mean you've been around for three hundred and sixty years?"

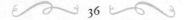

"And you probably didn't peg me for a day over twelve," Pim said with a sly smile.

"What is your name, boy?"

"Pim, mistress. My name is Pim."

Granny Custos jabbed the bit of her pipe toward his tiny image. "You, Pim, have a story to tell. And I want to hear it."

Claudia leaned in confidentially. "I've been trying to get him to tell me about his past for weeks now, but every time—"

"*Silenzio*, child," Granny Custos said. "Pim is about to tell his story."

Who is this woman? Claudia thought as they turned their heads toward Pim.

Pim looked from one pair of eyes to the other and then sighed again. He nodded and began his story.

CHAPTER 5

CLAUDIA COULDN'T believe it—she had poked and prodded Pim for more than two whole weeks to hear his story. And now he was going to tell Granny Custos only five minutes after meeting her. But then again, it seemed that no one could really say no to Granny Custos.

Pim cleared his throat and Claudia scarcely breathed. The walls around her seemed to fade away as her friend spoke.

"Haarlem, in the Netherlands. That's where I lived before it all. My father died when I was young, and I lived alone with my mother in our small home. We never had much. She was a washerwoman. Laundry. But our home did hold one magnificent possession: a painting, created by a friend of my father and given to him long before his death.

"The painting was a large but simple landscape—snowy fields and sleeping trees outside of Haarlem during the winter. My eyes and my fingers memorized that painting. How it used color, the detail of the tiny brushstrokes, the texture that the canvas added to places where the paint was thin. I wondered how something so marvelous could be created by the human hand. I wanted to find out. I wanted to create something myself.

"When I was eleven, my mother encountered my father's friend, the artist, on the streets of Haarlem. They spoke of my father, and then of me. She told him how I adored his painting, and about my ambitions to learn how to paint. Johannes Verspronck[5]—the painter—told her to send me to his workshop the following week. I went, and Master Verspronck put me to work mixing colors and preparing canvases. He must have seen some promise in me, because he took me on as an apprentice, even though I was younger than most. This was before Master Verspronck became famous, but noblemen still hired him to paint their portraits. I helped him during those visits as he captured their images on canvas."

Pim began pacing slowly back and forth in his painting, as though he were telling the story more to himself than to the others in the room.

"I apprenticed with Master Verspronck for more than a year. At that time he received a request to paint the portrait of a lady. Dame Nee Gezicht, a beautiful and wealthy woman, but also a strange one. She lived in a dark manor on the edge of the city and was rarely seen in the streets. That was how the people of Haarlem preferred it. People whispered about her in

---

5. JOHANNES VERSPRONCK (CA. 1603–1662). Portrait artist from the Dutch Golden Age. He was known for having a fine eye for detail, which required making his sorry subjects sit for days at a time. This would explain why no one is smiling in his paintings. Still, his *Portrait of a Girl Dressed in Blue* would be featured on Dutch banknotes centuries later. More than 39 million banknotes printed—not many artists can brag about that kind of circulation—nor about having their artwork squished in wallets under millions of Dutch buttocks. (Excerpted from *Dr. Buckhardt's Art History for the Enthusiast and the Ignorant*.)

the shadows. They said she was a witch with mischievous and dark magic, who spoke only in mumbled poetry. They said she had traded her left eye for power from the devil. And I believed every breath of rumor. But she promised Master Verspronck an impressive commission, and he agreed to the assignment."

Claudia squirmed at the description of Nee Gezicht and folded her arms tight across her chest.

"Unlike the estates to the north, the landscape at Nee Gezicht's manor was barren, without flowers or trees. But behind her manor stood row after row of tall, bushy tomato vines. She posed for the painting in front of those vines. When I first saw her, I didn't think she looked like a witch. Fine, modern clothes and a young face, with soft skin and rosy cheeks. She wore an embroidered patch over her left eye, but she was beautiful—certainly not the withered black creature I expected.

"Yet her smile was empty. And when she turned to look into my eyes—her watery, piercing eye locking with mine—the toes in my shoes grew cold. I knew I needed to tread very lightly in her presence, if only so she wouldn't look at me.

"We returned several times to create her portrait. She posed with the wooden staff she fancied and a bowl of tomatoes. A bowl of wretched tomatoes."

Pim stopped there for a moment. He seemed to struggle with some difficult thought. His jaw trembled, and his face flushed. Finally he looked up and cleared his throat. "On our last visit, Master Verspronck was to put the finishing touches on the portrait. I was anxious to be done with that place and that creature. As with the other visits, we arrived early to arrange the scene and prepare the paints.

"I mixed the paints on a stoneware plate, using fine colored powders and drops of linseed oil. Burnt umber and vine black, I remember the colors. I mixed them with two palette knives, the plate in my lap. A little more powder. Then a few more drops of oil. But a cry from Master Verspronck broke my concentration.

"He had already set up the easel and the painting, with a bedsheet over it for protection. But now he was frantically rummaging through the boxes. 'My badger brush, Pim, tell me you brought my badger brush!'

" 'But, Master, you took it from the box yourself only yesterday.'

"Master Verspronck rubbed his eyes and cursed under his breath. 'I shall need to fetch it.'

"I offered to go with him, though I wasn't trying to be helpful. Master Verspronck told me to stay and finish the preparations, that he wouldn't be long. He hurried back on the road we had just taken out of the city. I continued the preparations, slowly, to give my master time, but now my hands trembled as the knives rose and fell. I was scared to be alone in that place."

Pim paused, and Claudia couldn't help but urge him to continue. "And Verspronck? Did he get back before the witch arrived?"

"He hadn't returned by the time I finished mixing the paints. The sun was still mounting the sky, and I kept glancing at the road. But it was quiet, and so was the house. The scene still needed to be set, so I walked to the stairs leading up to the back porch.

"At the top of the stairs I found the chair and small table we had used on previous visits. I hauled the oak chair down the stairs and placed it in front of the tomato vines, directly over the stone we had left there to mark its position. Then I climbed the stairs once more and picked up the small table . . . and froze.

"I had never stood so close to Nee Gezicht. She was just a few feet from me in the doorway. I remember even now how she looked, tall and imposing, dressed in a regal gown. A string of black pearls adorned her neck, and a blond braid trailed down each side of her head. In one arm she held the large bowl of deep red tomatoes; the other hand held the gnarled staff."

Granny Custos had listened up to this point with her eyes closed, chewing on the stem of her pipe. But now she opened her eyes and sat forward and inch or two.

"I bowed my head and murmured a greeting," Pim continued. "She just kept staring at me with her one eye. She finally spoke in her usual odd manner, as though reciting poetry. 'The morning came; it goes much faster. Tell me, boy, where is thy master?'

"I told her and held completely still until she finally passed me to descend the stairs. Then I rushed over to place the table next to the chair as she prepared herself to sit. I took the bowl of tomatoes from her hands—so careful not to touch her white fingers—and placed it on the table. Nee Gezicht sat and arranged her gown.

"I backed away and looked down the road again, willing Master Verspronck to appear. But there was no sign of him. I could only wait. I knelt by the wooden supply boxes and pretended to busy myself by picking up the plate of mixed paints and flicking away a few dry specks of powder. I was terrified of what might happen if Master Verspronck didn't return soon.

"At that moment, as Nee Gezicht fussed with her dress, her

elbow struck the bowl of tomatoes and it crashed to the ground. I leaped up to help but immediately slipped on several tomatoes. As I fell, the plate of paint flew out of my hands.

"I landed facedown in the dirt and heard the wet rustle of taffeta. I couldn't breathe. Finally I looked up and saw the plate lying upside down in the witch's lap. Paint was smeared across her gown.

"She didn't move. It hurt to look into her fiery eye, but I had glanced into it and couldn't break her gaze. I tried to speak, apologize, offer to help, but only a soft whine came from my lips. Nee Gezicht started to mumble, words I couldn't understand and knew I didn't want to. Finally she blinked, and I dropped my eyes to the ground.

"I felt ill. I scrambled to my feet and swooned. But *home* was the only thought on my mind. I needed the safety of home. I bowed slightly to the witch, for witch she was. 'I am sorry,' I whispered, and then staggered off. I didn't follow the road to the city but cut across fields and through the undergrowth. I stumbled with every other step. My skin burned and felt clammy. I knew a fever had taken me. My vision clouded, as though looking through a dirty telescope. Finally, though I don't know how, I arrived at our home at the edge of the city.

"I staggered through the door. My mother was out delivering laundry in the city. I collapsed on a bed in the corner, underneath Verspronck's painting of the snowy fields. And there, shivering and skin burning, I left this world."

Claudia gasped. "The witch cursed you?"

Pim nodded. "By the time my mother came home the sun was already dipping below the horizon. The door was open.

The blanket on my bed was empty and tangled. My mother entered and frowned. She turned her head back to the door and called for me.

" 'Mother,' I shouted. She whirled and looked frantically around the room. Then her eyes crossed the painting that hung innocently on the wall, and she screamed.

"There I was, with tears on my cheeks, staring at her from inside the painting. I suppose I must have seemed desperately out of place in that calm, snowy canvas."

The warm glow permeating the dining room moments before seemed to have dimmed. Granny Custos continued to chew on the stem of her pipe, eyes narrowed and glued on Pim.

Claudia took a deep breath. "Whoa. All because of a little paint on her dress." The story made her heart hurt. So cruel— and so long ago. And a *witch*. If Claudia had heard this story weeks before, she would have rolled her eyes at the fairy tale. But now, looking at her friend trapped within the picture frame, just the thought of someone working magic like this made her hair stand on end.

"Indeed," Pim said. "It was a steep price to pay."

"An arduous place to be for so long, the world behind the canvas," said Granny Custos. "Do your eyes yearn for sleep?"

Pim's eyebrows shot up in surprise. "Always."

"And your stomach—teased by bread that doesn't fill?"

He placed a hand on his belly. "Yes," he said softly.

"And your mind," continued Granny Custos, "pulled like a piece of dough by time that never passes?"

Pim stared at the old lady and nodded.

"Wait a minute," Claudia said. "Do you mean that you

don't sleep in that world? You've been awake for almost four hundred years?"

"Paint and canvas his body became on that day," answered Granny Custos. "But his soul never forgets the flesh. Sleep will not come to him in such a place. Hunger will not be satiated. Time passes and yet doesn't. Weariness and pain are all that are afforded you. A wonder it is that his mind has not wandered and left him entirely. A wonder indeed."

Pim's eyes studied the table.

Claudia tried to imagine what it would be like not to sleep for hundreds of years. Or to always be hungry. She looked to Granny Custos. "How do you know so much about that place? Have you been there?"

The old woman smiled a secretive smile and turned back to Pim

"What is your greatest desire, boy?" Granny Custos asked.

"To leave this painted prison. To escape."

"And what would you risk for it? Your body? Your existence?" Granny Custos shot a glance toward Claudia. "Your friends?"

"My body was stolen centuries ago," Pim replied. "My existence is only misery. My friends . . ." He, too, looked at Claudia. "I have but one. And, no, I wouldn't risk her."

Claudia's heart skipped a beat and she felt her cheeks turning pink. She didn't like the way they were discussing risking bodies and existence, but Pim had called her his *friend*. One he wouldn't trade for anything. Even freedom.

In the silence that followed, Claudia took a breath and then asked Granny Custos, "Do you know how to set Pim free?

Because if you do, and if I can help, I will. I mean, I don't have any special skills or anything, but I'll do whatever I can to get him out of there."

The chocolate eyes of Granny Custos were suddenly lost in a nest of wrinkles as she grinned and let out a cackle of laughter. At first Claudia thought the old woman was laughing at her pitiful offer to help. But as Granny Custos pushed back her chair and rose carefully to her feet, she patted Claudia on the shoulder and muttered, "Good, good, good."

Granny Custos padded through the kitchen doorway. Her voice trailed back with the sounds of bottles and dishes and rustling paper. "There are many ways to enter the world behind the canvas. But fewer ways to exit. And when a person enters with a curse . . ." She made a clicking sound in her cheek.

Finally she reemerged from the kitchen, hefting a serving tray laden with tins, bottles, bowls, and a dozen other items. It looked like she was getting ready to make soup or a salad dressing or—

Claudia felt a tingling in her fingertips, just as when she had turned over the painting that faced her bedroom wall. "You do know, don't you, Granny Custos? You know how to get Pim out of there."

"*Naturalmente*," the woman replied. "Of course. Of course." She turned to Claudia with yet another secretive smile. "Who do you think created the world behind the canvas? Built it up? Raised it from the ground?" She leaned in close, poking Claudia with her pipe stem. "Granny Custos, that's who."

CHAPTER 6

For a moment, the room was silent, except for *clicks* and *tinks* as Granny Custos unloaded her tray.

"What do you mean you created the world behind the canvas?" Claudia asked. "That's impossible. Pim's lived there for hundreds of years."

Granny Custos shot her a warning glance with one squinty eye. "Not old enough for you, am I? I was mixing colors and dabbing palettes when his mother was a *bambina*." She gestured at Pim, who stared at her with wide eyes. "Speaking of colors . . ." She looked around at her collection on the table, harrumphed, and then turned the corner of the dining room. She was back in a moment with a long wooden case in her hands and a book half tucked into her shawl. She unfolded a sheet of aged but blank white paper and placed it on the table in front of Claudia with the wooden case.

"Paint something, child," she commanded.

Paint something? Now? Claudia reached forward and opened the case. It was filled with small tubes of watercolor paint and several brushes. She looked up at Granny Custos. "I don't want to paint anything. I want to know how you're going to help Pim get home."

Granny Custos set a small bowl of water and a stoneware plate next to the paper. "Then you'd best get started." She gestured to the paper. "And make it a good one. *Paint*."

The old woman projected an aura that left no room for argument. Claudia wasn't sure yet what to think of her. Granny Custos seemed to know a lot about the witch who had trapped Pim. She could just as easily be a witch herself. Then again, wasn't that the type of person who would be able to help Pim?

She reluctantly picked up one of the brushes. "What do I paint?"

"Whatever comes to you. Courage, perhaps. One can always use more courage."

Pim had been staring in wonder at Granny Custos since her declaration about creating the world Pim was in. He fidgeted with his hands, looking desperate to ask a question. Finally he asked it. "If you created the world behind the canvas, then you must be an *Artisti*." Understanding settled on his astonished face. "A Renaissance[6] *Artisti*."

---

6. THE RENAISSANCE. When scholars speak of the Renaissance, they are usually referring to a period roughly from the fourteenth to the sixteenth centuries in which citizens became tired of the stupidity of the Dark Ages and decided to become a more progressively prosperous people. You will find, however, that scholars disagree on what truly caused the Renaissance. Allow me to enlighten you. The Renaissance began in the Italian city of Florence, the birthplace of what is known as Italian cuisine. As the incredible food found on Florentine tables improved, so did the city's artistic talent, which in turn had its influence on politics, literature, science, etc. (Leonardo da Vinci's mother, for example, was an excellent cook.) Don't let academia tell you differently—the Renaissance was brought about by one thing: an astoundingly good plate of spaghetti. (Excerpted from *Dr. Buckhardt's Art History for the Enthusiast and the Ignorant*.)

"What's an *Artisti*?" asked Claudia.

"Patience, child," Granny Custos mumbled. "Paint." She sat and opened the book she had tucked under her arm. The leather cover was worn beyond reading and the yellowed pages were whisper-thin. She flipped through them delicately with nimble fingers.

Claudia picked up a tube of orange paint and squeezed a dab onto the plate, followed by a dab of yellow, then red. While she'd never had the guts to try oil painting, she had played a bit with watercolor. But she had no clue what to paint as she dipped her brush into the water, and even less of an idea why she was painting in the first place. *What does courage look like?* Suddenly an image came to mind—something she had seen in an art book in the library.

"Aha!" cried Granny Custos. Claudia jumped. The old woman jabbed her finger at a page in the book. She studied it for a moment before reaching for a bottle on the table. Claudia leaned over to see the title of the page: *Unguento di Attreversarse la Tela.* Flowery, illegible Italian streamed in rows and columns, but Claudia had seen the inside of her mom's cookbooks often enough to know a recipe when she saw one.

I'm painting and she's cooking. Next she's going to ask Pim to tap-dance. She mixed the paint on the stoneware palette.

Granny Custos poured some of the contents of the bottle into a tablespoon, tipping the measured liquid into the green plastic bowl in front of her. "Art is magic. Always has been. And all artists, magicians. At least in part. But not all of them know it. Most do not."

Claudia looked up, her brush a breath away from the paper. "All artists are magicians? What does that mean?"

Granny Custos flicked her fingers at Claudia. "Paint, paint! Don't ask your silly questions. Let me talk." She dug a teaspoon into a can and sprinkled tiny seeds into her bowl. "To create beauty from nothing, that alone is magic. But art has stronger ties to the cords of magic than anything else. Cave paintings? Ha!—magic runes. Greek sculpture? Ha!—powerful talismans. Egyptian reliefs? Ha!—spells to make buildings strong and enemies weak."

The old woman thumped the book in front of her. "As paper and ink let us access thought, the substance of art lets us access magic. Any artist with talent can learn. But only *Artisti* can master it."

"What's an *Artisti*?" Claudia asked a second time. She thought the old woman would scold her again for asking a question, but Granny Custos stared at Claudia, looking as though she had a question of her own.

"Every generation produces a handful of *Artisti*. Incredible talent with brush or pen or chisel. But more so, they are born with a deep connection to the magic behind the art. It is no coincidence that when a civilization rises, art is its hallmark. That is because the *Artisti* are pillars of civilization. To be an *Artisti* is to lead culture, influence peoples, change the world. When the *Artisti* grow strong and flourish, civilization advances."

She paused, looking beyond Claudia and Pim and the walls of the room. "Since ancient times have the *Artisti* practiced their art. But a period came when the *Artisti* slipped into a well of greed. Selfishness. Fighting. Death. Those few who remained turned to the darker use of *Artisti* magic and faded into obscurity. The pillars of civilization were knocked away, and fall it did. The Dark Ages, historians call it. There were no *Artisti* to bring light. They were born, yes, they were born. But they lived not knowing who they were."

"And then the Renaissance came," Pim said.

"The Renaissance did not just come," Granny Custos said sternly. "It was built. It was ushered in. A young *Artisti*, a Spaniard, learned of the *Artisti* from a historian. He discovered his gifts, studied his craft, knew his mission. He went forth to find other *Artisti*—for there are ways to recognize them. Across Europe, he brought us together. Seven of us, there were. We learned side by side. We started in Italy, and through our work we influenced and enlightened in ways only *Artisti* can. It caught fire and spread slowly across the continent. As the *Artisti* art flourished, so did philosophy, trade, music, architecture, medicine. Civilization was lifted up again. The pillars were replaced."

Claudia could feel the look of disbelief on her face. "The Renaissance happened because of the *Artisti*? All those great artists and thinkers—like da Vinci, Michelangelo[7]—they were great because of *you*?"

---

7. Michelangelo di Lodovico Buonarroti Simoni (1475–1564). Michelangelo (you can see why scholars shorten his name) was the Italian Renaissance contemporary of Leonardo da Vinci, and every bit the talented fellow. While there is no historical documentation on this, I don't doubt a wager existed between the two: Which one of us will be the most famous artist 500 years from now? It would probably be a toss-up.

Michelangelo's accomplishments include creating the dome on Saint Peter's Basilica, painting the ceiling of the Sistine Chapel, and sculpting *David* (who wears no clothes, so get your parents' permission before viewing). The ceiling of the Sistine Chapel alone took four years to paint—5,100 square feet of surface space. Can you imagine constantly craning your cranium up at the ceiling as paint drips in your eyes for four years? Talk about a crick in the neck. (Excerpted from *Dr. Buckhardt's Art History for the Enthusiast and the Ignorant*.)

"We lit the spark. Started the pendulum in motion. Influenced. That is how *Artisti* work. Besides, Leonardo was one of the seven."

"And so were you?" Claudia asked.

"I was."

"You realize that was, like, five hundred years ago."

"Some days, *bambina*, it feels like much more."

"And the world behind the canvas," Pim asked, "what about that?"

Granny Custos picked up a spatula and stirred the contents of her bowl thoughtfully. "It was the paint."

"The paint?" Pim echoed.

Granny Custos smiled broadly. "Ironic, no? We delved deep into *Artisti* magic. Uncovering secrets that had been lost for millennia. And yet that great discovery occurred simply with a new paint. Oil paint. Early on, we began to use oil paint instead of tempera. Van Eyck[8] saw it first—a ghost in his painting, or so he thought. Then others saw it, as well. Painted creations granted life on a plane beyond the painted surface. We found that the oils used to make the paint—linseed, walnut, saf-

---

8. JAN VAN EYCK (CA. 1390–1441). An early Dutch master masked by a modicum of mystery, little is known about the particulars of Van Eyck's life. Historians agree that he was one of the most significant Renaissance artists of the fifteenth century, with a remarkable ability to capture detail in his paintings. But it's the hints at a more complex life that really make this artist intriguing. He was employed, for example, by a powerful duke to go on many "secret" journeys. Who knows what their purpose was. Politics? Espionage? Clandestine societies? Look closely at his paintings and you will find all sorts of hidden symbols and icons, or scribblings in Latin and Greek. And the skill with which the paintings were rendered—years beyond his contemporaries. So masterful was his use of the new medium of oil paint, in fact, that some suggest he invented it. But I say that's giving one man too much credit, no matter how mysterious he is. After all, he was just a painter, not a magician. (Excerpted from *Dr. Buckhardt's Art History for the Enthusiast and the Ignorant.*)

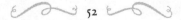

flower, poppy seed—bear strong ties to the cords of magic. When used in the powerful act of creating art, the miraculous occurs.

"But the creations we discovered were faded, erratic. Eventually we traded wooden panel for canvas—because the linen used in canvas came from the same plant as the linseed oil. That synergy of paint and canvas is all it took. A new world was established. Ah, but how to enter? That became the question. Many years of my young life were tied up in that pursuit. Theories. Experimentation. Trial and much error. And then I finally discovered a path that led straight through the canvas itself."

She tapped the fragile-looking page in front of her. "We crossed the canvas."

Claudia looked from the recipe to the bowl, and then back at Granny Custos. "And what did you do there?"

"We built that world from both sides of the canvas. We breathed life into it, painted it into existence. We crossed the canvas to give our new world structure. Order. It was a marvelous place—not simply a culture we had propped up and supported with our influence, but one created entirely by our hands, our minds. Borne of curiosity and skill. We had turned canvas into sky and pigment into grass. A place of marvel. But it was something more. It was a place that would never fall to ruin or decay. A place where the hours passed yet our bodies never aged. And when we realized this, we began to cross the canvas with more selfish intent.

"Immortality. To live forever. We thought it would house our souls and feed our bodies eternal life. We were to be gods of our own realm."

She looked down again at the bowl in front of her and snatched another bottle. "Carried away in our dreams, we became. For a time. It is a wondrous place. But not meant to house the flesh." She shot a glance at Pim. "Is it, boy?"

"Indeed not," he replied meekly.

Claudia's painting hand was on autopilot. She barely glanced down as she listened. "And that was the world behind the canvas? What happened? When you knew it wouldn't give you immortality? What did you do with it?"

Granny Custos shrugged. "Seeking immortality was a vain pursuit. We came close to losing ourselves, forgetting the true role of the *Artisti*, falling into dark places as the *Artisti* of old. But we awoke from our dream and moved on. The world we had built no longer needed us. We left it there. Went our separate ways. Found other *Artisti*. Taught them. Kept the pillars strong. But the world behind the canvas ever grows. Thousands upon thousands of hands now have constructed it. Every brush touching oil paint to canvas has made it flourish—mostly in ignorance." She tapped her finger on the page of the book. "Tarragon? Hmmm . . ." She rummaged through her stash of bottles.

"And now every painting comes to life there," Claudia said, thinking about how vast that world must be. "Not just the ones painted by *Artisti*."

"*Artisti* or artist, master or student, it makes no difference. It only matters that they paint with passion using oil paint and canvas."

"Do you still go back to visit?"

Granny Custos pursed her lips and shook her head. "I have not returned there for a very long time."

"So, how have you lived so long if you didn't find immortality in there?" Claudia asked.

She was surprised to see the old woman actually wink at her. "Story for another day."

"And the other *Artisti*," Pim said, his hands on the invisible wall that held him back. "Who were the others? Of the seven."

Again Granny Custos shrugged as she studied labels. "Dabblers and geniuses and rogues."

"Was Nee Gezicht one of them?"

Granny Custos sent a curious glance in Pim's direction. "She was. Different name, we called her then. And her black heart more hidden. But dangerous. Always dangerous."

"The witch who cursed Pim was one of you? She was an *Artisti*?" Claudia asked.

"*Artisti*, yes, because of her power. Witch, yes, because of how she uses it."

"What was her name then?" Claudia asked. "Was she a famous artist?"

"More important to ask what her name is now," Granny Custos retorted. "Nee Gezicht. Nee Gezicht. What does that mean?"

"It's Dutch," Pim replied. "It means 'one with no sight.'"

"Indeed it does. To have power without the proper vision of how to use it makes one blind. Greed makes one blind. Fear makes one blind. It is difficult to see when you walk in darkness."

"What does Nee Gezicht fear?" Pim asked.

Granny Custos stirred her thick, gelatinous mixture with

the spatula. "Van Eyck—one of the seven—died young. His death saddened all of us. But Nee Gezicht, it made her bitter. She had loved him from afar. She hated life for its frailty. She hated death for its finality. Van Eyck's death illuminated for her the human condition: that we are weak. That we will all die. And that is what she fears. Weakness. Death. Of the Renaissance *Artisti*, she worked the hardest to find a way to live forever behind the canvas. All she does is driven by those fears. Gain power. Eliminate weakness. Cheat death."

Just listening to Granny Custos talk about Nee Gezicht put a sick feeling in Claudia's stomach. "So is there any way to beat her? Or at least to break Pim's curse?"

The old woman eyed Claudia carefully before returning her attention to the concoction in front of her. "Carried a staff, she always did. All the powerful *Artisti* store magic in an object. A precious object. *La raccolta*. Gives focus to their power. If not tied down, the threads of magic start to unravel. Over time, a spell will dissipate. And so the *Artisti* creates a single *raccolta*. This keeps spells in place for hundreds of years, if needed. Like a keystone keeps an arch, or a stake keeps a tether. *La raccolta* can be anything that weathers time—a ring, perhaps. Or a pendant. Van Eyck had wooden shoes. Artemisia Gentileschi[9] used a steel sword, which she always kept sharp."

"A sword?" Claudia said.

---

9. ARTEMISIA GENTILESCHI (1593–1656). At a time when women artists were few and far between, Gentileschi established herself as one of the most accomplished painters (male or female) of the Italian Baroque period. But she wasn't content just painting what the next guy was painting. Instead, the vast majority of her fifty-seven works display dominant, daring, or defiant damsels. And did I mention swords? In fact, one of her favorite subjects was the story of Judith and Holofernes. In that ancient tale, Holofernes is the general of a conquering army and Judith lives in the city to which he's laid siege. While the general is sleeping, Judith creeps into his

"Indeed. Very fitting, had you known Missy." Granny Custos looked at Pim. "But Nee Gezicht. Nee Gezicht carried a staff. Wood from a black walnut tree. Her *raccolta*."

"Yes," Pim whispered. "I've seen it."

Granny Custos dipped the tip of her pinky into the mixture and stuck it in her mouth. She seemed to consider it a moment before spitting to the side. "After so many years, all Nee Gezicht has become is held in place by her staff. Your curse remains intact because her *raccolta* remains intact. Break the staff, break the curse." She paused as a grin spread across her face, exposing a mess of chipped and crooked teeth. "Break Nee Gezicht."

Pim beat his fist against the invisible canvas wall. "But I can't get at Nee Gezicht or her staff while I'm stuck in here."

Granny Custos tsked. "Not you. The girl helps you."

As the old woman's words registered in Claudia's mind, her heart fell. A few minutes ago she was ready to do anything to help Pim. But break the staff of a witch who was who-knows-how-old and powerful enough to create a whole new world? Well, to *help* create a whole new world. Even if it wasn't the stuff of fairy tales, it would have seemed impossible.

"That's your plan for setting Pim free?" she said faintly.

"*Sì.*"

"You're crazy."

---

tent with the help of her servant and lops off the fellow's head. City saved. End of story.

Gentileschi was a big fan of Caravaggio, and many of her paintings feature a masterful use of chiaroscuro. Most of her contemporaries and, dare I say, *ahem*, historians, couldn't get past the fact that she was a *woman* painting during this era. (Girl power! Feminism!) But that detracts from the bigger picture: Gentileschi was a darn good artist. Period. (Excerpted from *Dr. Buckhardt's Art History for the Enthusiast and the Ignorant*.)

"No," Granny Custos said as she continued to stir. "I am ancient. There's a difference."

Claudia stared at Granny Custos, expecting something more. When nothing came, she looked at Pim. His wide blue eyes locked with hers. They seemed to be more vibrant, more alive, than she had seen them before. *Alive with hope*, she thought.

It was enough for her to ask a question.

"Where is Nee Gezicht?"

The secretive smile of Granny Custos returned. She stood, not without some effort, and took the green bowl through the door to the kitchen. Claudia heard beeps followed by the familiar hum of a microwave. Granny Custos called out over the hum. "The Netherlands. So I suppose."

"Yes," Pim said. "Her estate in Haarlem remains."

Claudia looked at Pim in surprise.

"I've . . . there's a painting in her manor," Pim said, looking embarrassed. "I've gone there many times to plead with her for my release. She only laughs."

The Netherlands. The other side of the world. It was impossible. Claudia sighed in both frustration and relief. "Well, I have a holiday on Monday, but I need to be back in school by Tuesday."

"Then you will have plenty of time," Granny Custos said, ignoring the sarcasm. The microwave dinged, and she emerged balancing the green bowl in one hand and an electric blender in the other. She set both on the table.

"And this magic potion you're making is supposed to fly me to the Netherlands?" Claudia asked.

Granny Custos plugged in the blender, a puce-colored machine that Claudia guessed was older than her parents. "Not a potion. An ointment."

"An ointment?"

"And not for flying. For crossing." Granny Custos scraped the mixture from the plastic green bowl into the blender.

"Crossing? And how exactly is that supposed to work?" The riddles and impossibilities sent a throbbing through her head.

The old woman held out her hand. "Painting."

Claudia sighed and picked up her watercolor, which was still glistening. A fierce lion with a fiery mane stared back at her as she handed it over.

Granny Custos regarded the painting and then peered at Claudia shrewdly. "I recognize this."

Claudia nodded. "It's from a painting. By Rubens, I think."

"Not, then, from your own imagination."

Claudia shook her head, not sure if that was a good thing or a bad thing.

"That will come. With time." Granny Custos looked at the painting again and nodded once. "Courage." Then she ripped it in half.

"Hey!" cried Claudia. "It wasn't that bad."

Granny Custos continued to fold and tear, fold and tear, until her gnarled fingers held a soggy mess of scraps. She unceremoniously dumped them into the blender and clamped on the lid. She leaned toward Claudia as though passing along some juicy gossip. "These new gadgets make magic so much easier."

Then she punched *Frappe*.

The scraps of paper buzzed around like angry moths before the liquid sucked them down to join the mixture. The grinding whir of the blender grated on Claudia's ears, sending her frustration level even higher.

Granny Custos counted under her breath before hitting another button on the blender. It came to an immediate stop, the goop streaking down the insides of the glass jar.

"I don't understand," Claudia said, slamming a fist on the table. "How is this supposed to help Pim?"

Granny Custos paused as she picked up a spatula and sighed. She opened her leathery hand and moved the spatula over it, as though spreading peanut butter on bread. "Place the ointment on your hand." She turned her hand over and stuck it to the table. "Place your hand on a painting. Then *zoot, zoot*—you are in the world behind the canvas."

Fear gripped Claudia's heart as she realized what the old woman meant.

"Don't worry. It dries clear," Granny Custos added.

"You—you want me to go in there? Behind the canvas? How's that going to help? What if I get stuck just like him?"

"May I?" Pim said. Granny Custos nodded. "Claudia, every painting—no matter where it hangs—acts as a window into the world behind the canvas. I can look through this painting and see you. There's another painting around the corner from me— if I look through there, I can see into the Prado. In Madrid."

"Yeah? So? You've told me about that already."

"If I understand Granny Custos correctly, you can use the ointment to enter through a painting and then use the ointment again to exit through a painting that leads into Nee Gezicht's house in the Netherlands. You can steal her staff, bring it into this world, and we'll find a way to break it. Then we both return home using the ointment. Is that right, Granny Custos?"

"Esattamente." The old woman nodded and shook her hands toward the ceiling in relief. "Break the staff. Break the curse. Break the witch."

"And even if we fail to get the staff or break it," Pim continued, "you can still use the paste to return home."

Granny Custos pulled out a plastic yellow mustard bottle with a twisty cap from her pile of things. The writing was faded and it appeared empty as she unscrewed the cap.

Claudia's head felt like a wave machine. *Magic paste.*

"And I know just the painting to get us into her estate. . . ." Pim mumbled.

Find the house of witch Nee Gezicht.

"It's in the Southern Tier, but if the painting we enter is close enough . . ."

Steal her staff.

"I think it could work. . . ."

The world behind the canvas.

Granny Custos carefully lifted the glass blender jar from the base and tipped it over. The viscous goop was the color of mashed potatoes and moved like honey. With a slurping sound that would have made the boys in Claudia's class snicker, the ointment poured into the opening of the mustard bottle. A few sticky strands missed and drizzled down the side. A spatula helped every last drop over the edge of the blender jar. Granny

Custos set it down with a satisfied sigh. She wiped a wet rag over the yellow plastic.

"Not made ointment like this for decades." She screwed on the twisty top and winked at Claudia. "But I've a good feeling about this one."

She placed the mustard bottle on the table in front of Claudia. "*Unguento di Attreversarse la Tela*. Canvas-crossing ointment."

Claudia's hand was drawn toward the yellow bottle. She picked it up. It felt like . . . a bottle of mustard. She hefted it for a moment—and then quickly set it back on the table.

"No way," she said. "Not a chance. I mean, this goop looks like something my Aunt Maggie would bring to Thanksgiving dinner. You made it in the microwave and a blender that's a hundred years old. This is ridiculous."

Granny Custos shrugged. "You're the one talking to a boy in a painting."

Fear welled up inside Claudia's chest. Of course she wanted to help Pim, but this . . . "I'm twelve years old. I've never even stolen a candy bar from a grocery store. What makes you think I can steal a witch's precious *ricola*—"

"*Raccolta*," Granny Custos corrected.

"Whatever. A witch's most valuable thing from her own house? She cursed Pim in seconds just for staining her dress. What would she do to me if she catches me there trying to steal something?"

Granny Custos shrugged under the thick shawl, then reached for her pipe and tucked it between her teeth.

Claudia turned to Pim, but he stared at the tabletop. She looked back and forth between the two, waiting for someone to say something.

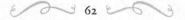

"I'm sorry, Claudia," Pim finally said, running his hand through his hair. "I got caught up in the idea for a moment. But of course you can't go. I would never ask you to. There are too many unknowns, too many perils. Nee Gezicht is evil and dangerous and should not be underestimated. I wouldn't risk my only friend in such a foolish dream."

There was that word again. *Friend*. It sent a powerful stroke of energy pumping through her veins, and she felt her face flush once more. Her frantic thoughts slowed enough for her to pick them apart and study them for a moment.

Pim needed her. When would another chance like this come along for him? "Why the staff?" she asked. "Can't I just go . . . behind the canvas . . . and give some of this goop to Pim?"

"Told you already," replied Granny Custos. "A strong curse cannot be undone. Only by breaking the magic. Breaking *la raccolta*."

Claudia nibbled at her thumbnail. She stood up from her chair and paced absentmindedly.

"Forget about it, Claudia," said Pim. "I'm not going to let you do it."

What if the witch cursed her and she ended up like Pim? What would a hundred years in that world be like? Of course, he'd suffered much longer than that. He was still suffering.

The task seemed clear enough. From there to the world behind the canvas, to the Netherlands, and back again. If they could get the staff and bring it back, Granny Custos could help them break it.

"If we did this, would you be with me the whole way?" she asked Pim.

"I . . . of course. But I'm not going to let you come here."

He would be with her. He would lead the way. With his help, she could do this. She could do this for him.

Her friend.

She picked up the painting and looked into Pim's crystal-blue eyes. "If you promise to lead the way, I'll do it."

He shook his head. "I can't let you—"

"But I want to, Pim. I can help you, and I want to help you."

He stared at her, eyes wide and a hint of a smile on his lips. "Are you sure?" whispered Pim.

Claudia smiled and slowly nodded. "We'll get you out. We'll do it together."

Pim tossed his head back and laughed in surprise and relief. His eyes shone. "All right, then. Together."

"So . . ." she breathed out. "We're going to need a painting. Can we use this one?" she asked, turning to Granny Custos.

Granny Custos wagged a finger. "Too small. You have your grandfather's head. Would get stuck in the frame."

"Gee, thanks." Claudia smoothed down her hair self-consciously.

"Do you have any paintings here?" Pim asked Granny Custos.

The old woman sat with closed eyes, arms folded within her shawls. She shook her head.

"An artist-magician like yourself and you don't have any paintings in your house?" Claudia said.

Granny Custos didn't open her eyes but smiled with the pipe protruding from her teeth. "Also a story for another time."

From the kitchen came the sound of running water and some sort of scrubbing.

"It can't be just any painting, anyway," Pim said. "The wrong painting will put us on the other side of the world behind the canvas, so to speak. We need one that places us close to the window into Nee Gezicht's house."

"Okay. Right." Claudia said. "We need options. What about the Florence museum?"

Pim nodded thoughtfully. "It has a lot of paintings. We'd at least have choices."

Hurried footsteps rushed from the kitchen and Mr. Custos burst into the dining room. His blue flannel pajamas—which looked as though they had been ironed —were complemented by fuzzy orange slippers. Claudia hid a smile behind her hand as he whipped a toothbrush out of his mouth and pointed it at the three of them.

"No, absolutely not. Not in the museum. I run a serious academic institution, not a springboard for adventurous philanthropy and vendettas. I'm sorry, kids. The world behind the canvas can be a fun place for a field trip and all, but with the"—he gestured toward the mustard bottle with his toothbrush—"the magic sludge, you never know what's going to happen. I mean, they're valuable paintings, for crying out loud!"

Claudia opened her mouth to ask what he meant about the magic sludge, but he bulldozed forward.

"Granny, you remember the Leonardo paintings, right?" He opened his arms pleadingly toward Granny Custos. "The *lost* Leonardos?[10] Don't you remember what you promised me after that?"

Granny Custos scratched her nose and then shrugged. "We need another museum," she said to Claudia, who was still worried about what Mr. Custos meant by "you never know what's going to happen."

Mr. Custos relaxed with a sigh. He wiped a spot of toothpaste foam from the side of his mouth. "Thank you, Granny. You know, the next logical option, of course, is Chicago."

Claudia perked up. "The Art Institute of Chicago!" Her parents took her there on occasion, when they got tired of her begging, and she was always anxious to return. "That would work."

Mr. Custos began wagging his toothbrush again. "As a matter of fact, the director of the AIC once came to pay me a visit and take a look at our collection. He told me that—"

"Sal," interrupted Granny Custos with a flick of her fingers. *"Zoot, ʒoot."*

"Ah . . . Right. Good night, then." Mr. Custos returned the way he had come. The water running in the kitchen turned off and then a door closed somewhere in the back of the house.

---

10. LEONARDO DA VINCI (1452–1519). Leonardo was the epitome of a Renaissance man, the perfect paragon of a polymath. He was not only a painter but also a sculptor, architect, musician, writer, scientist, mathematician, engineer, inventor, and anatomist. Imagine his response as a child to the question: What do you want to be when you grow up?

But it is as a painter that the world remembers him best. While only a handful of Leonardo's paintings survived the long journey through the centuries, his *Mona Lisa* is arguably the most recognizable work of art in the world, an achievement he probably never imagined. Of course, he also probably never imagined that his name would be given to a ninja turtle. (Excerpted from *Dr. Buckhardt's Art History for the Enthusiast and the Ignorant.*)

Pim nodded enthusiastically. "Yes, the Art Institute of Chicago will be perfect."

"Good, good!" crowed Granny Custos. "Go. Go now!"

"Now?" Claudia asked. "But it's eight thirty at night. The museum's already closed. And it's downtown."

"Small obstacles for a girl taking on Nee Gezicht," the old woman replied. She struggled to her feet, leaning hard on the table. Once she found her balance, she twisted up all of the loose strands of hair back into her bun. Then she removed the pipe from her mouth and stuck it into the bun to hold it in place.

"Perhaps you're right," she continued. "My bones are old. Time for bed. You'll find the door, and your grandfather, I suppose, where you left them." Granny Custos pulled her bulky shawl tighter around herself as she headed down the hallway. She paused for just a moment to turn and say, "Break the staff. Break the curse. Break Nee Gezicht. *Buonu fortuna.*"

Claudia watched her disappear down the hallway, wondering if Granny Custos always dismissed her guests like that. She wondered if she should shout a thank-you after the old woman. She looked at the tray of scattered ingredients and the goopy blender. She looked at the yellow mustard bottle in her hands. She looked at the boy in the painting. And she wondered what in the world had she gotten herself into.

CHAPTER 7

THREE PAIRS of underwear? Mom, I'll be gone for two nights."

"Underwear is one thing in life you can never overestimate, sweetheart." Claudia's mom stuffed the underwear next to the other clothes in her backpack.

"Okay. Sure. Great. I think I probably have everything now." Claudia pulled the zipper over the bulges.

"One more thing." Her mom grabbed the set of twenty-four colors of nail polish complete with a bonus bottle of nail polish remover and handed it to Claudia. "Take it with you. At least pretend to like your aunt's present when you visit her."

Claudia rolled her eyes. She had never been a schemer. A visit to Aunt Maggie was the best she could come up with during the late—way too late—hours of the night, but it wasn't a bad bit of scheming. She could make it to the Art Institute downtown without her parents and she would have several days to get in, get it done, and get out. (The details of that part were still a little fuzzy.)

It had taken some sweet-talking to convince her mom to let her spend the long weekend with "that sister-in-law." But in the end, in her mom's eyes it was better than Claudia's sitting alone in the library or the art museum. Claudia had called Aunt Maggie that morning, and the express bus to downtown Chicago left at noon—in less than an hour.

Claudia looked at the nail polish. "Do I have to take it?"

"Of course you do. Besides, you'll probably need it. All twenty-four colors. If there's anyone who knows how to turn things into a party, it's your Aunt Maggie."

Claudia crammed the nail polish into her backpack. "Okay. Now I have enough stuff for a trip to Africa. I think I'm good."

"Socks?"

"Three pairs. Same as the underwear."

"Toothbrush?"

"And toothpaste."

"Cell phone?"

"Check."

Her mom kissed the top of her head. "You're going to have so much fun. We leave for the bus stop in a few minutes."

As her mom headed down the hallway, Claudia took most of the clothes out of her backpack and stuffed them in her drawers. She tossed the nail polish onto her desk. She replaced them with her art history book and an assortment of sketch pads and pencils and a box of cereal bars she had snuck up from the kitchen. She had no idea what to expect, but she wanted to travel light—only the essentials. Finally she packed Pim's painting—it was empty for now—and the yellow mustard bottle.

"Mom!" she called as she headed for the front door. "Let's go!"

She especially wanted to leave before her grandpa decided to come by. The walk home last night had been awkward. He had peppered her with all sorts of questions on what she had talked about with Granny Custos—was it interesting, and did Granny Custos mention him at all? Claudia had deflected most of the questions pretty well, but he pressed for details toward the end, and she was all too happy to run up the stairs to bed when they got home.

Grandpa definitely had a thing for Granny Custos—which was just plain weird. But did he have any idea that the lady he'd crushed on from way back when was really hundreds of years old? That was just plain weirder.

Her mom came down the stairs with the set of nail polish in hand and fixed Claudia with her freeze-ray look. She pushed the nail polish toward her. "Nice try, kiddo. You're taking them."

Claudia sighed and shoved them into her backpack.

It wasn't the first time Claudia had ridden the express bus downtown by herself. She had visited her aunt before, and also her dad at his office. But this was the first time she'd taken the bus as part of a deceptive scheme to enter another world. She took a seat near the back of the bus and pulled the cell phone from her pocket, her hands shaking just a little.

"Hi. Aunt Maggie?"

"Hey, *chica*. You on your way?"

"Well, no, not exactly. Something's come up. Something important. I'm really sorry." Claudia winced with guilt as she said it. "Maybe we can do this another weekend."

"Oh. How sad. You're not dumping me for a boy, are you? Just asking . . ."

"Well, no. Not exactly. It's complicated."

"If boys are involved, it's always complicated. You owe me a rain check. Soon."

"I promise."

Claudia tucked the phone back into her pocket and unzipped her bag. The painting, with Pim next to the willow, rested on top of her things. He looked up and smiled.

"How did it go?" he asked.

She nodded. "We're on our way."

There was no doubt that if her parents found out about this whole excursion, she'd be drowning in trouble. There were so many things that could go wrong—even before she entered the world behind the canvas. What if she couldn't remember how to get to the museum? What if the museum was closed on Saturdays? What if they didn't let kids in on their own? What if Aunt Maggie called her parents?

She leaned back in the narrow seat and watched the scenery fly by like smeared paint. It was hard keeping her eyes open—she could have kicked herself for not getting more sleep the night before. The suburban streets turned into freeway and the fields became shopping centers. The Chicago skyline appeared ahead of them. It stretched its arms wider and wider before the bus and then finally embraced it.

Claudia pulled Pim's painting from the backpack, unable to resist giving him a glimpse of the towering buildings. She tilted it upward and heard him gasp.

"I've seen city streets from gallery windows," he whispered.

"But I've never looked *up* at a city." Claudia smiled. She had worried that nothing would impress her friend more than the supermarket.

The woman in the seat across from her stood up as the electric sign at the front of the bus lit up with the name of the stop.

What was the street they wanted? Claudia felt a surge of panic as her mind went blank.

What stop was it?

East. East something. Why hadn't she written it down? Her eyes bounced between the buildings they passed and the sign at the front of the bus.

EAST LAKE STREET scrolled across the sign. That didn't sound right.

EAST RANDOLPH STREET came next. *Oh, great. They're all* East *streets*. She almost jumped out of her seat, but lost the nerve when no one else stood up to exit the bus.

EAST MONROE STREET. *That's it! I think*. Claudia leaped to her feet and threw her backpack over her shoulder, clutching the painting tightly in her hand. "This is my stop," she shouted.

"No rush, darling," the driver said as Claudia bustled past. "We got plenty of time."

You might, Claudia thought. *But I only have three days*.

She stepped down to the sidewalk and was immediately swept up in a sea of people. From every direction came a roiling tide of bodies that mesmerized and disoriented her. Frantically she looked around for something familiar as she tried to picture the street map in her head. The stream of bodies broke for a moment and she saw it, half a block away: an immense white stone building stretching out parallel to the street. She recognized it immediately from the visits with her parents.

The Art Institute of Chicago.

Two bronze lions, green with age, guarded the wide stairway that led up to the building from the street. Claudia stared at the closest one as she approached. Her watercolor painting in Granny Custos's house the night before came to mind. *Courage*. That's what the old woman had told her to paint. *One can always use more courage*. Claudia wondered if her mom had left enough room in her backpack—somewhere between the nail polish and the underwear—for a hefty amount of courage.

She reached up and placed a hand lightly on a lion's paw.

"Claudia."

She jumped at the sound and lifted the painting to see Pim staring at her.

"We can do this," he said.

"We can do this," she repeated.

She swung her backpack around and zipped Pim's painting into the mesh pocket in the front so that he was looking out. Threading her arms through the straps so that the backpack rested against her chest, she glanced at the bronze lion above her. *We can do this*. Then she took a step forward.

CHAPTER 8

On THE stairs in front of the museum, Claudia pulled out the cell phone and called her mom. She kept the conversation as brief as possible, letting her mom know that she had "made it there okay." Her mom told Claudia to give Aunt Maggie a kiss for her. The pang of guilt twisted in Claudia's stomach again as she ended the call and slipped the cell phone into her pocket.

She walked through the doors of the Art Institute of Chicago[11] and joined the line of people waiting to buy tickets.

---

11. ART INSTITUTE OF CHICAGO (CHICAGO, IL, USA). When the Chicago Academy of Design was first constructed in 1870, it contained both an art gallery and an art school. As fate and a cow would have it, however, Mrs. O'Leary's heifer kicked over a lantern the following year, burning half of Chicago to the ground in a dreadfully destructive disaster known as the Great Chicago Fire. The academy's building went up in smoke, and soon thereafter the academy went bankrupt. But in true American fashion, the group sought corporate backing, renamed itself the Art Institute of Chicago, and bought its own assets at the bankruptcy auction.

Since those early years, the Art Institute of Chicago has become one of the finest art museums in the world, most famous for its collections of Impressionist, Post-Impressionist, and American paintings. It also maintains a substantial fire insurance policy. (Excerpted from *Dr. Buckhardt's Art History for the Enthusiast and the Ignorant*.)

She scanned the information board above the ticket booth. Children under fourteen were free, which was good. She didn't want to spend her return bus money on a museum ticket. But the board also said she needed to be accompanied by an adult. She didn't have one of those.

She stepped out of line and stood by the glass doors. How was this going to work without drawing attention to herself? She couldn't just ask a random grown-up to help her get in. But she needed to be with an adult to enter.

No . . . she needed the people at the ticket window to *think* she was with an adult. She started to watch the people as they entered the museum. An older man with a handlebar mustache. A few college students. A single middle-aged woman. Some tourists speaking in another language.

There. A couple approached the museum entrance, a baby strapped to the man in one of those baby backpacks. Claudia casually fell in line behind the couple as they entered. She glanced around, but no one seemed to pay her any attention.

Their spot in line came closer and closer to the ticket booth, until finally the woman was at the counter, paying for the tickets. Claudia waved at the baby, making exaggerated faces as though she played with the kid all the time. The baby cooed and reached for her with sticky hands. Claudia stayed close behind as the couple walked by the ticket booth, smiling at the ticket lady as she passed. The ticket lady smiled back and looked at the next patron.

Score a point for our team, Claudia thought as she moved through the front lobby, past the chatting patrons and the coat checks. She paused for a moment at the foot of an elegant staircase. The modern stairs marched upward, arriving proudly at a platform where they split in two separate directions. On the platform rested an ebony sculpture of a torso, lit gently by the white skylight above.

Despite her stomach tied into knots, she couldn't help but feel a little giddy. She was back in one of the great art museums of the world.

Claudia grabbed a map of the museum layout and climbed the stairs toward the second floor. The landing opened up into room after room of paintings and sculptures.

"Well, Pim," she whispered. "We have plenty to choose from. How do we decide?"

"To make that decision, you need to understand a little more about this world."

The world behind the canvas. Claudia had spent the past weeks trying to pry information out of Pim. Now she wasn't entirely sure that she wanted it.

They passed a security guard speaking with another patron as they entered a large gallery. With a nervous glance over her shoulder, she surveyed the paintings on the wall as Pim spoke quietly. "Each painting that exists here in your world also exists in my world but in reverse."

"In reverse?"

"Right. Although, it's more of a window than a painting, really. There are hundreds of thousands, even millions, of paintings in your world; there are just as many windows in mine. Each window has a specific location. If I wanted to look out of that painting there of a rainy Paris street, then I would need to leave where I am and travel—walk—to where that window resides. Does that make sense?"

Claudia shrugged. "I guess so. You told me that last night

with Granny Custos." She motioned to the painting filled with French people in long coats with black umbrellas. "And if I enter this painting, am I going to come out behind the canvas in the middle of Paris?"

"No, no. The window-paintings are usually found in random groups, hidden in out-of-the-way places. You would come out where the window-painting is physically located. Places and things are usually located in the same region as their window-paintings, but it's an enormous world. If you went through this painting, you would still have a long walk through my world before you came to this Parisian street."

"Got it. I think."

"Good," Pim continued. "Nee Gezicht keeps a painting in her attic. I know where the window-painting for it is here in this world. So right now we need to find a painting that will bring you into this world at a point close to Nee Gezicht's painting. But it also needs to be close enough to the window-painting I'm standing at now that I can travel there to meet you. Do you understand?"

It took a moment for Pim's words to register, and Claudia's heart sank. "You're going to leave me?"

"Claudia, Nee Gezicht's hand reaches far into the world behind the canvas. She has an army of spies here. She comes here on occasion herself. Once you enter this world, she will know it before too long. And once you're seen with me, she will suspect something. The less time you spend here, the better."

"An army of spies?" Her mouth went dry. "What kind of place am I going to?" She had the sick feeling that there was so much more to this adventure than she had bargained for.

"I've told you before." Pim's voice seemed distant, faint. "A place both wonderful and terrifying. Beyond imagination. No, that's not true. Everything in this world has been imagined by somebody, at least once. But not every painting is a rolling landscape or a gentle gondola ride. Many other things have been put on canvas. Violent things. Evil things."

She placed her fingers on the edges of the frame in her backpack, wishing she could hold Pim's hand. "And those things . . . are there, too? And Nee Gezicht's spies?"

"Yes."

Claudia felt a tap on the shoulder. "Hey, kid."

She jumped and spun around to face a chunky man in a bright blue suit coat and tie. Her eyes were just level with the patch on his coat that read ART INSTITUTE OF CHICAGO— SECURITY. In the center of the patch was a lion head, reared and roaring. She took a step backward. This was it. She was busted. Toast. However they found out, it was over.

The security guard pointed at her backpack. "Backpacks and large purses need to be left in the checkrooms."

"Backpack?" she stammered, looking down as though she hadn't noticed the large yellow bulge on her stomach. "Oh. Right. Thanks. I'll go tell my mom." She left the gallery as quickly as possible without running. She didn't look back but could feel the security guard's eyes on her the whole time.

Even with the close call, Claudia knew she couldn't leave her backpack in the checkroom. The ointment, Pim's painting, her food. She needed it with her. So when she reached the main stairs, she headed up to the third floor.

Another guard stood at the entrance to the next gallery. Claudia turned away from the guard and pretended to study her map. And study it. And study it.

Maybe she should look for a gallery without a guard. The place was crawling with them.

Finally another patron approached the guard with a question. Claudia dived into the gallery, map spread open over her backpack. No voice called from behind as she walked along a wall full of artwork.

"All right, Pim," she whispered. "Let's find my painting."

Haystacks. Lilies in the water. A Sunday picnic made of dots. An orange bed in a blue room. A bald farmer with a pitchfork and his wife.

After walking in and out of galleries for nearly an hour, Claudia's head swam. At each painting she stopped and waited for Pim to make his judgment call. Sometimes he gave an immediate no. Sometimes it took longer as he mumbled to himself over the distance from one window to another. One of the paintings he said was a possibility. Others he simply didn't recall or couldn't remember where they were located.

He amazed Claudia with his familiarity with the hundreds of paintings they passed. *He really has spent centuries lost in these paintings.*

Eventually they came to a gallery that was more ornate than the others. Richly carved wood trimmed the ceiling and the floor. The room spanned twenty yards from one end to the other. A plaque on the wall said it was reserved for paintings on loan from other museums.

Claudia was thrilled to see a painting by Rubens, his rich scene depicting a man—Saint George—fighting a dragon. The serpentine creature writhed and twisted and reached for the muscular knight as he raised his sword to hack at the dragon's head. A woman stood in the background, calmly watching the action.[12]

As they crossed the wide gallery to the corner opposite the Rubens, Pim let out a sudden gasp. "*Eureka*. Not right next door as I'd hoped, but we probably won't find one any closer. Yes . . . it should do. This is your painting, Claudia. The Dalí, on the right."

Claudia stared at the painting next to the gallery exit, entirely unimpressed. So many of the paintings they had passed used bold brushstrokes to tell fascinating stories. But this one was flat and ominous. A pair of brown stone statues rose up out of a barren wasteland. They vaguely resembled two people with heads bowed toward each other. The sky was gray and dreary, letting through just enough light for the statues to cast haunting shadows across the landscape. Tiny birds of prey hovered

---

12. SAINT GEORGE AND THE DRAGON. This is one of the more oft-painted subjects in art history, which is completely understandable—everyone likes dragons. The story goes like this. Next to the ancient kingdom of Silene there was a lake where a dragon made its home. The diet of dragons, of course, is primarily meat, which is hard to come by on a large scale. So the dragon made a deal with the kingdom that if they would feed him several sheep and a woman every day, he would curb his appetite and not eat the entire population in a gluttonous, fiery barbecue. The town chose the tasty woman each day by lottery. One day the princess of Silene "won" the lottery, much to the dismay of her father, the king. But the rules were rules, and so they dressed her up, splashed her with marinade, and sent her out to a lakeside dinner with the sheep.

Enter Saint George the warrior. This holy hero on horseback charged the dragon, fiercely skewering him in the side with a lance. Then he called on the princess to throw her girdle around the dragon's neck. She did so, and the wounded dragon instantly followed her around like a puppy on a leash. Saint George and the princess took the dragon back to Silene, where Saint George offered to slay the dragon if they all agreed to come to church. An offer they couldn't refuse—they were quickly running out of sacrificial women—the people agreed. The kingdom of Silene did decide to keep the concept of a lottery, however, and has used it ever since to part a fool from his money and to fund public education. (Excerpted from *Dr. Buckhardt's Art History for the Enthusiast and the Ignorant*.)

above it all as though waiting for something to sink their talons into.

It was depressing. Just looking at it made Claudia want to lie down and give up. But it was also kinda . . . weird. The plaque beside the painting read, ARCHEOLOGICAL REMINISCENCE OF MILLET'S "ANGELUS" BY SALVADOR DALÍ.[13]

"Not very cheerful, is it?" she said.

"No, but that's common for the Southern Tier. Listen, Claudia, I should go. Now. It will take me several hours to get there. You'll need to wait until you see me in the painting before you use the ointment to cross the canvas."

"Several hours?" She glanced over at the security guard standing by the gallery entrance. "The museum closes in an hour. I'll have to find some place to hide. Then I'll come out when everything is empty."

"Perfect. Claudia . . ."

She took off her backpack and turned it around to see Pim through the mesh fabric. "You've given me hope," he said. "No one has ever given that to me before."

A lump formed in her throat. She couldn't think of anything to say.

"I'll be in that painting in two hours. Be ready," Pim said. Then he disappeared.

---

13. SALVADOR DALÍ (1904–1989). One of the chief artists of the Surrealist movement. Some people claim Surrealism is ridiculous nonsense; others believe it to be the most honest form of art. It originated in the 1920s, stemming from a movement called Dadaism (literally meaning *nothing*). Surrealist works range from Magritte's quizzical men with bowler hats to Dalí's melting clocks to even more grotesque or confounding images. Dalí and these frustratingly Freudian figures believed in using the imaginative forces of the unconscious mind to attain a dreamlike state that is more true than reality itself. Of course, their predecessors also made water fountains out of urinals. (Excerpted from *Dr. Buckhardt's Art History for the Enthusiast and the Ignorant*.)

"Excuse me, miss."

Claudia jumped at the voice and spun around, once again coming face-to-face with the stitched lion on a security guard's blazer. The owner of the blazer, a woman with tight black curls and tight red lips, looked over her glasses.

"You need to take that backpack of yours down to a check-room and leave it there. It's not allowed up here."

"Okay. Sorry." She walked quickly from the gallery. Alone.

She finally paused when she reached an empty foyer with elevators lining the walls and a set of stairs leading downward. She couldn't keep wandering around with her backpack—eventually they would either take it from her or kick her out. She also needed to stay close to that creepy painting. And she needed to hide for two hours while the museum shut down.

"Yeah, right," she mumbled to herself. The place had more security guards than a bank. Would they leave when the museum closed? Which would scare her worse—being completely alone in a dark museum or being alone in a museum full of security guards?

An elevator opened and two men stepped into the foyer. They wore matching blue uniforms, and the shorter man pushed a custodial cart loaded with rolls of paper towels and cleaning supplies.

"Did you get the toilets up here?" asked the taller one.

"Nah. Let the morning crew take care of those. I'm outta here."

The taller one pulled a set of keys from his belt and opened a narrow door tucked in the corner of the foyer. He held it open while the other pushed the cart in. It clattered forward and stopped with a thud. The two men turned and walked around the corner, not even glancing at Claudia.

And the door to the custodial closet slowly pulled back into place.

Claudia leaped across the foyer and stuck her foot in just before the door pulled tight. She made sure she was alone and then peeked into the door crack.

A large closet, lined with shelves and boxes and enough toilet paper to supply her downstairs bathroom for a year. And there was plenty of room to hide. She turned the knob. The door could open from the inside.

The cleaning guys had mentioned "the morning crew." That probably meant no one would bother with the closet until morning.

The elevator dinged, ready to open.

Claudia slipped inside the custodial closet and pulled the door tight behind her. Darkness and the smell of clean bathrooms. She fumbled along the doorjamb until she found what felt like a light switch and flicked it on. A dim yellow light appeared that barely reached the surrounding shelves. Somehow it made her claustrophobic where the darkness hadn't.

Her breathing was rapid. She cleared a spot to sit on a stack of paper towel boxes and tried to calm herself. She was hungry. She opened her cereal bars and tore into several in quick succession. The chewy sweetness took the edge off her hunger but didn't touch another sensation in the pit of her stomach. The sinking feeling that what she was doing was somehow . . . wrong.

Illegal.

Criminal.

She had lied to her mom, lied to her aunt, sneaked into a major museum, and was right this moment hiding so she could slap a goopy hand against an ugly but priceless Dalí painting. If that wasn't criminal, what was?

She leaned back against the boxes and closed her eyes, trying not to think about what she would tell her mom if someone found her here. She played through various scenarios, none of them turning out well. Finally she began to trace a painting in her head. The three Dutchmen from the Florence museum. A line here. Deep shading there. The darks and the lights. The form and the substance.

The stuffy warmth of the closet settled on her like dust, and the lack of sleep from the night before tugged her downward.

Footsteps.

Clicking footsteps that echoed in the distance.

Claudia jolted awake and nearly tumbled from the paper towel box. She glanced around the closet, but everything in the dingy light still looked the same as when she—

She'd fallen asleep. *Dangit!* What time was it? She needed to find a clock somewhere in the museum.

No, her cell phone. She pulled it from her pocket and clicked on the screen. Three hours. Nearly three hours had passed since Pim left. She was supposed to have met him after two.

She pulled out the yellow mustard bottle and zipped up her pack. It was showtime. *Past showtime.* Hopefully Pim was still waiting for her.

Slowly, so slowly she wondered if she was even moving, she turned the knob and inched the door open. The foyer was empty. And silent. She stepped hesitantly forward and left the safety of the custodial closet.

The halls and galleries had changed from day to night. The normal lights in the ceiling and above the paintings were dark, replaced by scattered secondary lights that deposited shadows in every corner and in pockets along the walls. She crept to the corner of the first hallway leading out of the foyer, trying to re-call the exact path to the Dalí painting.

The evening sounds of Chicago played in the distance. Traffic. Crowds of people. Air hissed through the vents and ducts in the ceiling like the breath of a monster. And . . . footsteps. Again. Softer, muffled, clicking against the wooden floor of the galleries. Claudia glanced back at the custodial closet, the door pulled tight. *Now or never.*

She moved into the hallway, placing her feet quickly. Quietly.

Right turn down another hallway. Nothing looked the same in the dim light.

Left turn through a gallery and out the other side.

She paused, listening to the footsteps, trying to decide where they came from, where they were headed. *Stick close to the walls where the shadows are thickest.*

Right turn down the hallway. Dead end. Backtrack.

Left turn down the hallway.

The footsteps now sounded close, growing louder. She ducked into a gallery and pushed herself against the wall.

Just outside the entrance, the footsteps approached. She felt the presence of another person. And then the footsteps trailed off.

She crossed the gallery, keeping her head down. She passed

into another and stopped. The gallery with the wood trim. This was the one. Just in front of her was the Rubens with the knight and the dragon. That meant on the opposite wall at the other end, by the gallery exit—

A familiar strain of Beethoven's piano sonata played loud and clear, its electronic tones echoing like thunder in the silent museum.

Her phone!

She smacked her hand against her pocket in disbelief. She poked and jabbed at the phone through her jeans until something she hit finally silenced it.

"Who's there?"

A man's voice rang through the third floor. Claudia couldn't quite tell where it came from or how far away. *Stupid!* Why didn't she think of turning off the phone?

She needed to work fast; she had only seconds. Twisting the cap on the mustard bottle, she squeezed the paste out onto her hand, hastily outlining each finger and her palm. She tensed her legs, ready to dash across the gallery toward the Dalí.

A security guard stepped into the room. Claudia ducked under the railing that separated patrons from the paintings and threw herself against the wall under the Rubens. She froze there, mid-squeeze, hoping she was masked by the shadows.

The portly guard in the blue blazer pointed his flashlight quickly around the room. Claudia felt the piercing eyes of the lion on his patch tracking her in the darkness. She crouched lower, waiting for the bright beam to fall on her.

But instead it swung around as the guard hurried from the gallery.

Yes! Now was her chance.

Then her moist fingers slipped on the smooth yellow plastic of the bottle. The tension released and the sides of the bottle sprang back to their natural shape, sucking in air with a *slurp*.

The guard reappeared in the gallery entrance. His beam of light trained on Claudia in an instant.

"What the . . . ?" He took a few steps forward, placing himself squarely in front of the Dalí. "You're the kid with the backpack."

Tears sprang to her eyes as she crouched beneath the Rubens. Past the blinding light, past the security guard, she could see the Dalí painting on the other side of the room. It was too dark to make out details, but Pim was probably in the painting, watching her right now.

She had come so close.

Too close. Too close to give up now.

The guard charged toward her. Like a mousetrap, Claudia's legs released, springing her upward. She spun around as she rose. And with a silent apology to Rubens, she slapped her goopy hand against the painting.

CHAPTER 9

APPARENTLY GRANNY Custos knew her stuff. The moment Claudia slapped her ointment-smeared hand to the paint-smoothed canvas, it felt warm, like touching an oven door with cookies baking inside. The warmth exploded through her body in an instant as an invisible force tugged her arm toward the canvas. It pulled harder and harder and she felt warmer and warmer until finally in the middle of that instant she was soaring and falling and turning and tumbling through paint and canvas. Then at the very long end of that instant her feet again touched the ground, in a place both near and far.

As though breaching the surface of water, she gasped for breath and spun around, finding herself nose-to-nose with the museum guard. She jumped back as the pudgy face stared at her, eyes wide, from behind a pane of glass. And etched on that pane of glass was a translucent version of Rubens's *Saint George Battles the Dragon*. In reverse.

She stared at the guard and took a few more steps backward. The guard's eyes followed her. What did he see? Probably a tiny dark-haired girl in Rubens's painting, the same way Pim appeared in her landscape. The guard reached up to touch the canvas, hesitated, and dropped his hand. He looked around the side of the frame, tilted it upward, and looked behind the painting. He turned his flashlight on it, blinding Claudia. He clicked it on and off several times. Then he staggered backward and dropped to the gallery bench, where he sat facing the Rubens.

Her hand trembling, Claudia reached up and stroked the glass window-painting. Somehow it still had the gentle, rough texture of canvas but looked as though it would shatter if she rapped her knuckles on it. She stepped back and saw that, instead of a frame, the window was embedded in a rough wall of stone. She followed the curvature of the gray stone up and around . . . and was awestruck.

She stood in a wide stone tunnel—no, a cave—with a shallow ceiling. The floor and walls were uneven but smooth, as though worn down with time. The paths to the right and to the left curved around so that she couldn't see where they went. Woven throughout the walls like spiderwebs were veins of crystal—thin in some places but as thick as her arm in others. And just as the walls of the Art Institute had been crowded with paintings, the walls of the cave were peppered with glassy, translucent paintings in reverse.

Claudia approached another window. The portrait of a woman, a queen, maybe. The window looked out into an extravagant bedroom, colored with lush carpet and a velvety bed. The room was empty. She moved to another window, a painting of a square golden building sitting on the banks of a canal. Beyond the painting was another large gallery, this one filled with people. A tour guide discussed a painting on the adjacent wall with a large group, speaking in another language, maybe Italian. No one seemed to notice Claudia at all.

She moved from one window to the next, looking in at museums, galleries, homes, castles, and churches. Each window led to a new place and new peoples. The cave was filled with the distant, echoing hum of environments and conversations. She passed dozens and dozens of windows, astounded to think that the corners of the world—her world—were connected in that very cave.

And then, finally, she found herself standing in blinding sunlight at the cave's wide, round entrance. As her eyes adjusted, she saw a grassy field spread out before her and a forest beyond that. She stowed the mustard bottle and took a few cautious steps out of the cave.

The scenery pulsed with color. The grass. The trees. The sky—so blue it was unreal. *Azure, isn't that what you call a really blue sky?* The color surrounding her was almost too rich and too deep, like someone had messed with the settings on a computer monitor.

She walked farther into the field, the tall, wispy grass brushing against her fingertips. All of this had been a painting. Or several paintings. And now she stood in the middle of it, as if she were part of a painting herself. *Wait until I show this to Pim. . . .*

Pim. She had to get back. Pim was probably still waiting. He wouldn't leave her. She could put more paste on her hand and touch the Rubens painting again. She would have to wait until the guard left the gallery, but once she was back in the museum, she could enter the Dalí like she was supposed to.

She spun around, back toward the cave entrance.

Something wasn't right. She had a feeling. The same feeling you get when you know someone else is in a room with you even before you hear a sound.

She scanned the field, the trees. The saturated colors suddenly seemed sinister. And then she saw them.

Two large yellow eyes stared at her from the tall grass. Her heart leaped into her throat.

The eyes, already immense, widened even more. The creature that owned them moved up out of its crouch. Wide jaws with dagger teeth. Wrinkled folds of brown beaded skin. Flaps on the side of its head that moved in and out like the gills of a fish. A long snakelike body. And hands and feet that looked like human hands, but clawed and gnarled and powerful.

The dragon from the Rubens painting.

The creature stood between her and the cave. It watched her, daring her to run. But she couldn't leave the cave. It was the only way back home, the only way back to Pim. This couldn't be happening.

With a snarl, it moved—slinking—toward her. A pants-wetting terror filled Claudia and she launched herself in the only direction available—into the forest. Immediately behind her came the violent rustling of grass. Panic surged through her veins, making it hard to get control of her body. She stumbled through the undergrowth. She slipped on a mossy stone and nearly collided with the ground. Finally she got her legs under her and she ran.

Branches tugged at her hair and scraped her face, leaving behind the scent of oil paint and fear. The savage growl of the dragon followed her. She crashed through bushes and branches for what seemed like forever. Over roots and under limbs, she pushed her legs to move until they hurt. The dragon was toying with her. Its powerful legs. The quick movements of its body. It could have caught her in the first ten seconds of the chase. The snarls behind her suddenly sounded like wicked laughter. She pressed on, even though her legs felt like jelly and her lungs burned. Her eyes stung with tears that swept away into her hair as she ran.

She burst into a clearing littered with boulders and stones, and her legs gave way altogether and she tumbled to the ground. She braced herself for steely jaws closing over her head. But nothing happened. She opened her eyes and looked around. The clearing was empty except for a swarm of gnats passing above her. Everything else was complete silence.

But the silence was just as frightening as the sounds of the dragon's pursuit. She rose to her feet, trying to look in all directions at once, her heart beating like the piston of a locomotive. The open space made her feel exposed and vulnerable, and she cautiously stepped backward until she found herself against a tree. Her head was spinning. She had no idea which way she had come from, which way would take her back to the window-cave. The motionless forest around her offered no clue, no hint.

She pressed herself against the thick tree trunk, the paint-smooth surface bringing an odd comfort. An unexpected breeze fell on her from above. It was warm and smelled like decay. She forced her eyes upward and saw the dragon climbing down toward her headfirst.

Claudia pushed off from the tree and leaped forward, but the dragon did the same. It flew over her head and landed in her path, turning to confront her in one fluid motion. Its yellow eyes shone with hunger. It was done playing with her. She was about to be consumed, from head to sneakers, by a painted dragon. Alone. Without a friend. And no one at home would even know.

CHAPTER 10

THE DRAGON snarled and crouched, its fingered feet digging into the earth. Scaly lips pulled back to reveal jagged teeth. Its rapid breathing fell into sync with Claudia's. It was joined by the steady rhythm of galloping hooves.

Galloping hooves?

Death must arrive on horseback in this world.

The dragon's head snapped up. A low growl tumbled from its throat, and it reversed its crouch as though it was ready to leap in defense from some invisible attacker.

An immense dark horse and a rider dressed in black shot from the trees. Claudia threw herself backward just before the hooves hit the ground where she had stood. The rider drew a rapier and extended it toward the dragon as he rode past. A second rider burst through the trees, followed by a third. Like a flock of birds, they wordlessly changed course and formed a galloping circle around the dragon. All three pointed their swords at the beast as they drew their circle increasingly tighter. The dragon crouched lower and snarled, turning in every direction to confront the horsemen. Finally they slowed to a trot and then halted with barely a tug at the reins.

One of the riders turned to Claudia, his sword still pointing at the dragon. The white plume in his hat bounced with every movement.

He gave her a regal smile. "My dear lady, I am Cornelis, of Ghent. These are Balthasar and Hendrik"—he gestured to the other two—"of townships with very little renown, but nonetheless they are men of valor." The other riders rolled their eyes. "We have cornered this beast and now request that you throw your girdle about its neck."

The dragon snapped in Cornelis's direction. The horseman swished his sword in response.

Claudia's mouth went dry. "I—I don't have a girdle."

Cornelis flinched with surprise. "Very well, then, your sash."

"I don't have one of those, either." Who did they think she was, a princess?

"Well, do you have a scarf?"

Claudia shook her head.

"A handkerchief?"

Again.

"Hmmm . . ." Cornelis looked at the dragon, which was ready to spring, and then at his companions. "It would appear that the fate of this damsel is entirely in our hands. We must rely not on our strength but on our skill and cunning to dispatch this dragon."

The others raised their swords. "Huzzah! Dispatch the dragon!"

Whether it didn't appreciate the sentiment or simply saw its last opportunity as the swords were raised, the dragon leaped toward the horseman named Balthasar. He rolled from his horse as the dragon's claws passed overhead. The beast landed near the edge of the clearing, spun, and charged at Cornelis. Cornelis spurred his horse and took off into the trees. The dragon followed, as did Hendrik.

Balthasar gripped the saddle and pulled himself back onto his horse. "That blasted Saint George," he muttered. "Why can't he do his own job for once?" He shouted one more "Huzzah!" and charged into the trees.

Claudia looked around the empty clearing. Her heart slowly came down from her throat. She was bruised and exhausted, but she was alive.

Do I stay or run? She strained to place the distant sounds of the chase, unable to tell which direction they came from. There was the beat of hooves, the ferocious growl of the dragon, the muffled shouting of the riders. She was glad the rescuers had arrived just in time, but she also wondered if they were up to the challenge of "dispatching" a dragon.

Cornelis bounded into the clearing once again, a rope with a noose in his hand. Charging forward, he tossed the noose up and over a thick tree branch and then caught it as it fell down the other side. He held on to both ends of the rope as his horse shot forward, flinging himself into the air. The dragon leaped from the trees, bounding toward Cornelis.

The horseman's timing was perfect. He swung back around and caught the dragon square in the chest, sending it crashing to the dust.

Within seconds both man and beast were on their feet.

Cornelis grasped the noose on both sides and pulled it wider. "Come at me, you scaly snake from Vagevuur!" Before Claudia could wonder where Vagevuur was, the beast leaped straight at Cornelis. At the last instant Cornelis stepped to the side and looped the noose around the dragon's head. He grasped the other end of the rope and pulled it tight, pitching himself backward with a cry.

With the rope looped over the branch above them, the dragon roared and clawed its way toward Cornelis, even as the horseman strained to pull it back in the other direction. His boots dug trenches in the soft earth as the dragon pulled him closer. It was a tug-of-war that Cornelis would obviously lose.

Without thinking, Claudia sprang forward and grabbed the rope behind Cornelis and pulled for all she was worth. The dragon skidded backward but then roared again and lunged, snapping its jaws just a foot from Cornelis's boots. And then suddenly Balthasar was beside her, pulling the rope back toward a sturdy tree. The dragon stood on its clawed tippy-toes by the time Balthasar wrapped the rope around the trunk and tied it firm.

Hendrik rode into the clearing and dismounted as Cornelis tossed him another coil of rope. "Since you are bringing up the rear, as usual, why don't you bring up the rear?" Cornelis said, breathless.

"What?" Hendrik asked.

"The tail, man! Get the tail!"

Hendrik made a quick lasso in one end of the rope and took a few steps toward the dragon. It dangled dangerously in the noose and yet it seemed only annoyed, like a cat being held by the scruff of the neck. Its round yellow eyes watched Hendrik approach.

"That little chase reminded me of a fat boar I once—"

Without warning, the beast writhed and spun and caught Hendrik across the chest with its thick tail. Hendrik flew through the air and thudded into the undergrowth.

Claudia ran to him. She wasn't quite sure what to do, so she picked up his hat from the ground and handed it to him.

Cornelis stifled a laugh. "Well, Balthasar, what do we do with this black worm? It will wiggle itself free before long."

"Why don't we kill it?" Hendrik said, dusting off his trousers. "I've heard roasted dragon flesh is a delicacy in some parts."

"Saint George would get himself into a terrible fit if he found out," Balthasar said. "He would claim the creature was just being territorial. And hungry. No, no. The beast that holds mutton between its teeth will churn the butter when beauty beckons."

Balthasar's statement made no sense, but he said it with such dramatic flair that Claudia couldn't help but smile. The three men seemed familiar, though she had no idea why.

Cornelis turned and glared at Balthasar. "What the bloomin' tulips is that supposed to mean?"

Balthasar sighed patiently and stroked his goatee. "It means, dear fellow, that to tie up the dragon we must first tame him. And there is only one in our midst with the power to do so." The three men turned to look at Claudia with obvious expectation.

She suddenly had a hard time swallowing, as if she were the one dangling by the rope. "But I don't have a corset . . . or girdle . . . or whatever it is I'm supposed to tame it with."

"Now, my dear," Cornelis said, "surely you must have something on your person you can cast around the dragon's neck."

Claudia looked down at her sweater and jeans, and was about to let her rescuers know that girdles and sashes weren't exactly in fashion, when Balthasar exclaimed, "Her shoe latchets! They would serve, would they not?"

Claudia followed his gaze to her feet and her comfortable white-and-red sneakers, tied and double-knotted with long white shoelaces. She looked up at Cornelis. "You're kidding me, right?"

Cornelis looked confused for a moment. "Kidding? I do not believe so. But I can assure you there is no other way to tame a dragon."

Even as they spoke, Claudia felt a tingling sense of urgency return to her body. She was lost in a strange world that very likely had more frightening creatures to offer than a single dragon. She had to get back to the paintings. Pim couldn't wait there forever. She needed their help—quickly.

She bent over and undid her shoelaces. They were just for looks, anyway—her shoes fit fine without them.

"Okay, what do I do?" Claudia looked at the cloaked men, a shoelace in each hand.

"Well, I don't entirely know," Cornelis replied. "I've never seen this done before. I suppose you just toss it around the beast's neck."

"Isn't there an incantation she needs to say?" Balthasar added.

"I thought she needed a vial blessed by a priest . . ." Hendrik chimed in.

"No, that is for collecting crocodile tears. It does matter which direction she throws it in, however . . ."

"I'm certain she needs something blessed by a priest. . . ."

" 'Left to right it will give the dragon strength and fury . . .' "

"Perhaps she needs the latchets blessed by a priest. . . ."

"Oh, come now, Saint George doesn't travel with a priest every time he battles a dragon. . . ."

" '. . . but right to left will make him gentle as . . . something furry.' Or something like that . . ."

"Come to think of it, Saint George doesn't really battle dragons, does he? He gets the lady to do all the work. . . ."

"I'd think twice, man, before I start criticizing the methods of a saint."

"Perhaps she does need an incantation. . . ."

Claudia shook her head and tied the two shoelaces together. Time was slipping away. She scanned the ground for a stone and spotted one the length of her finger. She tied it to the other end of the laces. Then she looked at the dragon. Its fangs were bared and its fierce eyes followed her every motion. Its tongue flicked threateningly, and Claudia was afraid that at any moment it would twist and send its snakelike tail flying toward her. She took another step. Then another. The dragon's hind claws scraped the dirt anxiously. Soon she was close enough to smell its putrid breath. She took one more step just to be sure and then flung the shoelaces out, stone first, with the other end still in her hands, like a tetherball on the playground. They sailed up in a smooth arc and landed around the dragon's neck.

A change came over the dragon almost immediately, like flipping a switch. The yellow eyes turned cotton white. Its lips drooped down to cover its fangs, and its tongue lolled to the side as it began to pant. Even the tail wagged happily back and forth. Suddenly it was more mutt than monster.

The shoelaces draped limply around the beast's neck, threatening to fall off at any moment. *This is crazy.* She edged forward and reached for the shoelaces. She formed the laces into a neat bow, double-knotted. The dragon lunged forward and planted a wet lick on her face.

Ugh. Claudia jumped back and wiped her face on her shirt, wishing she had packed hand sanitizer.

The gentlemen with the wide-brim hats applauded. "Well done, my dear," Cornelis said. "Wonderful form for such a little lady."

From there it was quick work tying up the dragon. The men bound both pairs of feet together, like a calf at a rodeo, and left it lying in a thick bed of leaves. Throughout, the dragon looked admiringly at everyone, breath panting and tongue lolling.

When the job was complete, the three men hovered together over the dragon, critiquing their handiwork.

"That should do until Saint George can come take care of it," Balthasar said. "Assuming he gets around to it."

"This beast wasn't nearly the trouble that boar gave us last week," Cornelis remarked.

"No, but at least we got to roast the boar afterward," Hendrik said.

Balthasar breathed in deeply and gestured to Claudia. "Ah, but to remedy the peril of beauty is to enclose the image of beauty in your heart forever."

The other two men looked flatly at Balthasar.

The image of beauty. Suddenly Claudia knew who these men reminded her of. Themselves. These were the three Dutchmen from the painting hanging in the Florence art museum. The same painting where she had first seen Pim. Their beards, their cloaks, their hats, their swords, everything was identical. But now so incredibly . . . alive.

Every person, every creature, every place ever painted . . . like a patchwork quilt, Pim had said. Then something clicked in Claudia's brain. *If Pim appeared in their painting, maybe they know who he is.*

Before she had time to think about it, she blurted out, "I come from the other side of the canvas."

The gentlemen stared at her blankly. Cornelis raised an eyebrow.

Claudia tried a different approach. "I came from out of a painting."

Realization appeared on Balthasar's face. "I see. That's the name of your village. Is it far from here?"

She shook her head. "No. I came from a cave under the mountains."

Now all three men raised their eyebrows. "We don't go near those caves," Hendrik said in a cautious voice. "Only evil resides there. Dark magic."

She tucked her hair behind both ears and took a deep breath. "I'm looking for a friend of mine," she said slowly. "A Dutch boy named Pim. Do you know him?"

The faces of the three horsemen hardened like clay in a kiln. Eyes fixed on her, they took wary steps away until they surrounded her as they had the dragon. With the ringing of steel they whipped their swords from their scabbards and leveled them at Claudia.

She froze as the relief she had felt a moment ago was crushed by confusion and fear.

"If you are a friend of Pim the witch-son, then your-self must be a witch." Cornelis's voice was icy. "And in our land, witches must die."

CHAPTER 11

No—no, I'm not a witch," Claudia stammered, shifting her gaze from one sword tip to another. "And Pim's not, either. He's just a kid. A very old kid. He was trapped behind the—here in this land by a witch. But he's not a witch, really."

"Hendrik, bind her tongue," Cornelis snapped. "Before she occasions a spell on us all."

Hendrik sheathed his sword and fumbled with something before stepping up to her. A strip of cloth stretched between his hands.

"No!" she cried out, trying to break past Hendrik.

Cornelis twisted his sword and thrust it forward in warning. She froze. There was a look in the Dutchman's eye that promised to run her through if she tried to escape.

"With permission, little lady," Hendrik said. He placed the cloth in her mouth and tied the ends behind her head. It was tight and tasted like oil paint.

She tried frantically to speak though the gag, to tell them

she wasn't a witch, and neither was Pim, and they were making a terrible mistake. But every word came out muffled and unintelligible.

Hendrik pulled the backpack from her shoulders and tied her hands together in front of her with stiff rope.

Claudia's eyes stung. A tear escaped and traversed her cheek. Didn't they burn witches back in the olden days? How could this be happening?

"She is just a girl," Balthasar murmured.

Claudia nodded, eyes wide.

"And Pim the witch-son is just a boy," Cornelis replied. "But look at the mark he has made on this land."

"I have never heard of a witch-daughter," Hendrik said.

"But neither is it reason for surprise," Cornelis argued. "She claims the witch-son as a friend, she comes from the caves under the mountains—for all we know she speaks with monsters and commands the Fireside Angel itself. No. Perish she must."

Balthasar lowered his sword a fraction. "But not by our hand, Cornelis. Remember what the Master commanded us."

"Yes, of course!" Hendrik said, his voice tinged with hope. "The Master from Rijn bid us bring all witches and witch-servants to him for judgment."

Balthasar dipped his sword even lower, his gaze fixed on Cornelis. "Our place is not as executioner, my friend, notwithstanding the pain the Sightless One has caused."

Cornelis seemed to weigh something in his mind, scales that teetered this way and that.

Yes, yes, yes! Take me to the Master from Rijn, Claudia pleaded silently. She had no idea what they were talking about, but it seemed like a better option than being executed here in the forest.

Reluctantly Cornelis sheathed his sword. "Very well. We take her to the Master from Rijn."

Claudia felt Balthasar sigh and glimpsed his expression of relief as he turned away to gather the horses. She breathed her own sigh of relief, but the hopeless feeling in her stomach remained. She had narrowly escaped death twice in the same hour, but she was still a prisoner, and they still thought she was a witch.

They escorted Claudia between them as they led their horses to a stream to drink. Then they placed her on Balthasar's horse and Balthasar mounted behind her. And without further delay they set off at a trot.

Claudia's head whirled, trying to take in everything at once. Why did they call Pim the witch-son? Why were they afraid of him? Not just afraid—Cornelis seemed to hold a serious hatred for him. She couldn't imagine Pim having enemies, let alone doing something to actually deserve it. And where were they taking her? Who was this Master from Rijn?

Would he want to execute her, too?

She clutched at the horse's mane with her tied hands. She'd never ridden a horse before, and it surprised her how far up off the ground they were. She tried to take deep breaths—which wasn't easy with a gag in her mouth—and clear her head. She was every bit as terrified now as when the dragon was clawing at her heels, but at least now she had time to think. Hopefully the Master from Rijn would listen to reason.

After leaving the forest, they rode through a variety of terrain. Meadows came first, with grasses and blossoms and butterflies as thick as a flurry of snow. Next they encountered a rain forest, brief but humid and glistening. The trees formed a thick canopy above their heads as roots entangled one another across the path. Flower-growing vines punctuated the scene with brilliant colors, while the nooks and recesses off the path were dark and profound. It was like something from a dream.

No, not a dream. From a painting.

Rivers, wheat fields, a patch of desert. As Pim had suggested, it was as though the quilted landscape had been sewn together from different swatches of cloth.

And everything had an unusual sheen that reminded her of dried paint on canvas. She brought her hands up to her face and studied them. They had the same painted appearance as everything else. She could even make out tiny brushstrokes on her skin.

She was paint and canvas now, too.

Several hours passed. They began a gradual ascent through steep foothills peppered with crags and boulders. The shadows were long and ominous—late afternoon, perhaps.

They saw no one else as they traveled, only the occasional animal or bird. At one point, Claudia noticed a hawk perched low in a tree along their path, with reddish feathers and strong talons.[14] It stared at her with mismatched eyes, unabashed and

---

14. JOHN JAMES AUDUBON (1785–1851). Audubon was the rare artist who cared more about the subjects he painted than he did about the art itself. And there was only one type of subject that interested him: birds. He spent years wandering the backwoods of America to document, draw, and paint hundreds of species. They were published in his original ornithological opus, *The Birds of America*. This was no field guide but a serious volume—the type of heavy illustrated book you get your father for his birthday for him to display in the living room. While it had little impact on the art world, it did invent the never-ending demand for coffee table books. (Excerpted from *Dr. Buckhardt's Art History for the Enthusiast and the Ignorant*.)

unafraid. One eye was orange and looked like the kind you would expect on a bird. But the other was blue and bulged slightly from the bird's head, as if it didn't fit somehow. The eyes followed her as they passed.

"Beautiful landscape, is it not?" Balthasar muttered in Claudia's ear.

The question startled her. Up to that point, he had been silent as they journeyed. She nodded slightly. She craned her head to look behind them, but the bird had left its perch.

"The best is yet to come," he continued. "The Lady is not the only radiant beauty in these parts."

Claudia couldn't tell who he meant by *the Lady*. It was probably just somebody else who would want to see her executed.

"Are your bonds too tight? Are they causing you pain?" His voice was low.

The gag and the rope weren't exactly comfortable, but they didn't hurt, either. She shook her head.

"You must forgive us our roughness. Cornelis in particular. He has been wounded more than most by the Sightless One. She has great power, but I do not think you are a witch-daughter. There is a magic about you, no doubt. But no, your eyes are too fair to be a witch-daughter."

Claudia tilted her head back toward Balthasar to show she was listening. She raised her tied hands toward him.

He shook his head. "No, my lady. I may not think you a witch-daughter, but the consequences would be great if I loose the bonds to find myself mistaken. The Master from Rijn will judge you."

She sighed and dropped her hands.

"We have reason to be suspicious. It is only on occasion that the Sightless One appears in our land. And she always arrives mysteriously, magically, as you have. But she has a presence here, there is no doubt of that. Whenever she wanders through our forests or our deserts or our fields, she seeks out the strong of body but weak of mind. She preys on them. Enslaves them. Buys their meager will for a penny and makes it a part of her. Most of them are not evil creatures, but after her claws ensnare them, they become such. It was not always so, but as her interest in our land grows and her reach extends, darkness comes with it."

Claudia glanced around at the rich golden hills, as though the darkness might be something visible and apparent. Pim hadn't told her any of that about Nee Gezicht—at least she assumed the Sightless One was Nee Gezicht, since that's what her name meant. It seemed Pim hadn't told her a lot of things.

She turned her head and tried to speak around the cloth in her mouth. "An' 'im?"

Balthasar looked back at the other riders before leaning closer. "Speak again."

"An' Phim?" she enunciated as carefully as she could.

"Ah, Pim. You ask about the witch-son. You say he is a friend of yours. If that is fact and you know his true nature, then the Master of Rijn will see into your soul and send you to execution for the evil you are. If you say he is your friend, and he has deceived you, hidden his true nature, then . . . well, you would not be the first."

Anger rushed through Claudia's veins. How could he say something like that about Pim? Pim was sweet and funny and considerate—there was nothing evil about him. There couldn't be. Could there?

She had known him for a few weeks. Maybe seventeen days. Even if he hadn't been stuck in a painting, how well could you get to know someone in seventeen days? What if he had tricked her, lied to her, had some reason to—

No. Pim is my friend. And friends trust each other.

Balthasar continued. "Pim is the chief servant of the Sightless One. Her captain in these lands. He comes and he goes and may not be seen for great lengths of time, but when he appears, sorrow follows and lands upon the innocent. Like Cornelis."

Balthasar's voice lowered to a whisper. "Cornelis never speaks of it, but he had a lady. Fairer than any blossom. Emilie. It was Pim's deception that brought about her death in the name of the Sightless One. Cornelis knows he cannot fight the power of that witch, but he will do what he can to oppose her. And her servants."

Claudia took a deep breath and tried to match up the Pim she knew with the one Balthasar described. It was impossible. She wondered if Pim was still waiting by the Dalí window. If he was frantically worried about her. If he even cared. Or if somehow all of this—her little painting, their friendship, the journey behind the canvas—was some kind of trick.

But why? If—*if*—Pim was working for Nee Gezicht, what good would it do him to bring Claudia into this world? More slaves for the witch? Just to be cruel? But what about Granny Custos? She seemed to know a lot about Nee Gezicht and she didn't have a problem with Pim. And she didn't seem evil. A bit crazy, perhaps, but not evil.

Balthasar must have sensed her body tense as the thoughts

wrapped around her mind, because he began to hum a tune. He fumbled for something in his coat, and pulled out a small leather book. He flipped the pages until he found what he was looking for. His hum quickly flowed into words, sung in a deep, pleasant baritone.

"My true love said 'tis not enough to labor day by day,
But one must dream and reach aloft to wend a merry way.
Yet, methink she errors, for we do not need a star—
The love we hold, yea, truth be told, we're happy as we are."

"For pity's sake, Balthasar, sing a song with some pluck to it," called out Cornelis. Without waiting for a response he, too, burst into song. Hendrik quickly joined in and, with obvious reluctance, Balthasar did as well. The song was boisterous and bouncy with a driving beat. Even the horses seemed to pick up the pace a little.

"The sound of the cock crow at quarter past dawn,
The sight of the morning dew,
The taste of adventure that nips at your tongue,
The scent of the hunt anew.
The thrash of the boar as it beats through the brush,
The clop of the laboring steed.
The whoosh of the wind as it rushes the ears,
The huzzah of the daring deed.
The thrill of the kill at the end of the chase,
The pleasure of roasting flame,
The comfort of company: family and friends,
The love of that one special dame."

The travelers approached what appeared to be the steep crest of a hill as the song came to an end. But as they drew closer, Claudia realized that it wasn't just the top of a hill but a cliff overlooking a magnificent green valley. Soon they reached the edge, and her eyes grew wide.

The valley was similar to the patchwork-quilt landscape[15] they had passed through earlier, all of it green and lush. There were waterfalls and rivers, woods split by curving roads, and majestic mountains seated at the far edges. But most breathtaking of all were the suns.

Claudia had seen sunsets before, coloring the sky in her backyard. She had also seen sunsets in paintings, over lakes, or mountains, or a city; but always with one sun at a time. Cutting through this valley were the rays of dozens of suns. Some were large and full, while others were simply bright dots pinned above the horizon. But each sun was lighting fire to its own sunset, and together the colors melded and intertwined, creating a tapestry of woven color climbing halfway into the sky.

Hendrik rode up beside Balthasar. "The Valley of the Suns," he said dreamily. His skin glowed softly in the warm light.

---

15. LANDSCAPE. Landscape is one of the most critical creative categories found in both painting and art in general. Simply stated, landscape art depicts scenery such as mountains, valleys, trees, rivers, and forests, and usually includes a sky and a horizon. True landscape focuses on these elements alone, although landscape can often be used as a backdrop for a different artistic genre. Landscape painting is found in all cultures throughout the history of art. For example, with half a continent of undeveloped land, it was a favorite of mid-nineteenth-century American painters, most notably Thomas Cole and the Hudson River School.

Note that landscape should not be confused with the modern derivatives of seascape, riverscape, cityscape, moonscape, hardscape, inscape, escape, and Pinkscape, which was my favorite British punk band in the 1980s. (Excerpted from *Dr. Buckhardt's Art History for the Enthusiast and the Ignorant.*)

"Aye," replied Balthasar. "Where the light of a million candles melts to form an illuminated vision of splendor."

Cornelis turned to look at Balthasar. "That was almost poetic."

"Poetry requires inspiration, dear Cornelis. And since I spend all of my time with you and Hendrik, I hardly carry the blame if my eloquent words dip into mediocrity."

Cornelis smiled. "Come. Let us walk quickly in this 'vision of splendor' and perhaps the Master of Rijn can cast judgment on this creature before evening departs."

They headed down a path that hugged the side of the cliff, twisting and switching back and forth toward the floor of the valley. The drop from the side of the path was sheer. It made Claudia's head spin and she wished for a moment that they had blindfolded her as well. The descent eventually leveled out, and before long they were on a white road winding through purple light and green pastures.

The soft light of the sunsets and the peaceful terrain was by far the most beautiful thing Claudia had ever seen. But it was impossible to appreciate it with her hands tied and a gag in her mouth. They passed through it quickly, and she was glad when they came to the end of it. It wasn't fair to experience something like that and not be able to enjoy it.

The Valley of the Suns fed into a cramped canyon with high, jutting walls of red rock. The suns disappeared as the towering walls surrounded the riders. They picked their way over the stony ground in a light that was noticeably dimmer. But even after they had passed through the canyon, the light didn't change.

Dusk had fallen, and it was growing colder. The riders

picked up the pace and Cornelis led the way, craning his neck to see what was up ahead.

Wherever they were going, they were getting close. And then the Master from Rijn would decide her fate.

Claudia shivered in the cool evening air.

CHAPTER 12

S NOW BEGAN to fall in the escaping light. The ground ahead of the travelers turned gray and then white. By the time the rooftops of a village came into view, the path was covered in white drifts pocked with footprints. The air had become crisp, and Balthasar removed his cloak and draped it around Claudia's shoulders. She nodded in thanks, wishing her hands were free so she could pull it tighter.

It was clear now where they were taking her, where she might be executed.

A village ran the length of the hill before them, houses and shops and a church on one side and two great ponds on the other. The ponds were frozen over and covered with skaters whisking by in a race or sauntering hand in hand. In the distance rose a span of craggy mountains, culminating in a single sharply rising peak.

It was a Dutch village from one of Bruegel's peasant

paintings.[16] She had seen it in more than one art book, and it always seemed like a happy scene to her. A busy little town. Kids having a good time.

Not a place where they take people to be executed.

Was there a stake in the middle of this town where they burned witches? Or did the skaters move to one side while they cut a hole in the ice to toss the witches in?

A group of hunters tramped wearily in front of them on foot, surrounded by a pack of orange-and-black dogs. As the horses approached, the dogs turned and frantically nipped and yipped at the newcomers. Cornelis baited the dogs with calls and greeted a hunter who shouldered a spear. "How goes the hunt, my friend?"

The man, all grizzled beard and fierce eyes, smiled. "Slow as sap, Cornelis. The boars become lazy when a cold snow falls."

"Are there festivities in the village tonight?"

"Aye. A wedding feast. The roof may be straw and the floor dirt, but tonight we feast and dance to the jealousy of a king!"

---

16. PIETER BRUEGEL (CA. 1525–1569). Pieter Bruegel is one of the great Flemish/Dutch Renaissance masters of the sixteenth century and the head of a painting dynasty. When you hear the name Bruegel in art history, chances are it refers to this fellow. However, it also might be referring to his son Brueghel the Younger; his other son, Jan Brueghel the Elder; his grandson Jan Brueghel the Younger; his great-grandson, Abraham Brueghel; or the family cat, Felix Bruegel. (The cat was the only one to keep the original spelling of the family name.)

This Bruegel set himself apart from other painters at the time, related or otherwise, by focusing on landscapes and the poor pastoral peasant. His peasant paintings, such as *The Hunters in the Snow* and *The Peasant Wedding*, are always full of action and the hustle and bustle of everyday country life. Studying his paintings is almost enough to make one want to abandon academia and become a peasant. Almost. (Excerpted from *Dr. Buckhardt's Art History for the Enthusiast and the Ignorant*.)

Cornelis laughed as they passed the man and headed down the hill into the village. The houses lining the street were constructed of brick or stone and capped with tall, pointed roofs layered with snow. The windows shone with warm light from inside, where Dutch mothers were probably lighting candles or fires in the hearth to warm their darkening homes.

Claudia's mother would never know what happened to her.

The round face of a little girl appeared in the window of one home. Her eyes unabashedly followed Claudia as they passed through the street. Claudia nodded at her, as if trying to assure her everything would be okay. The girl quickly ducked beneath the windowsill.

They soon arrived at the town square, a large, open cobblestone space surrounded by houses and shops. At the far end of the square stood a barnlike building with a wide peaked roof that reached above its neighbors. Its doors were open and light flooded out into the square. The sounds of a celebration—music, laughter, conversation—spilled out with the light.

Cornelis led the group across the square to where it intersected another street heading back into the village. He trotted toward a building that seemed slightly out of place among the aging Dutch homes.

It was another scene that came straight out of one of the large art books from the library.

Van Gogh's café stood in front of her, a smattering of people sitting at its patio tables. Waiters casually moved across the plank flooring of the terrace, sheltered from the snow by a wide, sweeping overhang. A lamp jutted out from the wall and lit the scene with a strong yet wavering light, making the blue exterior walls of the café a flickering yellow-green.[17]

The people sitting at the tables ate and spoke with spirit, wrapped in cloaks and furs. All of them stole glances of her as the horses approached, whispering to one another, taking in the gag and the rope on her wrists. She could feel her face burn. This was so much worse than the time she had been sent to the principal's office for drawing a chalk mural on the back of the door in the gym. This time she hadn't even done anything wrong.

The injustice of it boiled inside her.

Cornelis dismounted and looped his reins around a post. He reached up to lower Claudia to the ground.

With a twist of her body, she kicked at Cornelis's face. Her sneaker connected and he staggered backward. The kick threw her off balance and she toppled over the other side of the horse, a deep bank of snow breaking her fall. She struggled to get up, to run, but Hendrik and Balthasar were already there, lifting her to her feet.

---

17. VINCENT VAN GOGH (1853–1890). Van Gogh was one of the many artists throughout history who lived a tragic life, as happiness eluded him at every turn. He battled with bouts of mental illness, was constantly on the move from one town to the next, and never seemed to be able to find that special someone. At one point in his life he famously cut off a piece of his left ear and gave it to a girl. (While I'm no expert in the game of love, I would be reluctant to try that at home.)

History knows him best for paintings with wide strokes and bold colors, and some of the world's most popular paintings came from his brush. *The Starry Night* with stars surrounded by a sumptuous swirling sky; *Café Terrace at Night* with its cobblestones and yellow-warm outdoor patio; and a multitude of sunflower still lifes. And he is probably one of the few great artists to create an entire series of works based on his local mailman. (Excerpted from *Dr. Buckhardt's Art History for the Enthusiast and the Ignorant.*)

Cornelis approached as they held her, and she was satisfied to see a red spot underneath his eye. Towering over her, he removed his riding gloves.

"Well, child, if indeed you are a witch-daughter, take this moment to say your prayers. The Master of Rijn resides here tonight. He shall be your judge." He turned and strode into the café.

She struggled again, but the Dutchmen held her arms and ushered her through the glowing doorway.

After lying in the freezing snowbank, the warmth that met her as she crossed the threshold was like a furnace. The inside of the café was painted red and green and was much larger than it appeared from the outside. Tables were scattered across the floor and partitioned booths lined two of the walls. Against one wall stood a counter, where a waiter served food and drinks to a handful of patrons. Behind the counter a door swung inward, revealing the clatter of a kitchen.

Cornelis strode toward a corner booth where an old man sat, eyes fixed on Claudia. Tufts of bushy white hair gathered around his head and trailed from under a white hat that flopped to one side like a deflated beach ball. A large, round nose sat prominently above a gray mustache, and his dark, penetrating eyes looked out from a puffy and wrinkled face.

The man's stare wasn't menacing, but it was painfully honest, as though he could read every secret hidden away in her heart and make them his own, leaving her empty and forgotten.

This was the Master from Rijn. And she knew him.

Not personally, of course, but in a way, yes. She had seen

his face staring out at her from dozens of art books. She had even drawn it once. *Rembrandt. The artist.*[18]

Cornelis leaned toward the old man, whispering low and urgently. The Master from Rijn listened, never taking his eyes off Claudia.

Could he really see inside her? Would he know she wasn't a witch-daughter? That she had come, in a way, to fight against Nee Gezicht? Did he really have the power to sentence her to death?

She couldn't stand there and let Cornelis have the only say. She stepped forward, eyes locked with the old man. Balthasar called out in surprise, but she moved quickly between the café tables until she stood just a few feet away from the Master from Rijn. Cornelis straightened.

The old man looked her up and down. He signaled behind her, and Balthasar stepped up and removed the gag. Her tongue felt like a gym sock in her mouth. She flexed her jaw. She would probably taste oil paint on her tongue for the rest of her life.

Which could be very short.

The Master from Rijn spoke. "Cornelis is a man I trust. There are so few these days. He claims you are a witch-daughter, in league with the Sightless One. How do you respond?"

---

18. REMBRANDT VAN RIJN (1606–1669). My distinguished academic peers would agree with me when I say that Rembrandt is one of the most important European artists in history, and certainly the most important Dutch artist. The subjects of Rembrandt's works vary considerably, as did his style through the years. Many of his works employ a prominent use of chiaroscuro. Rembrandt was also a fan of self-portraits; he produced almost one hundred of them throughout his life. Some may consider this an egregiously egotistical effort, but I see it for what it is: He had to have something to put on the front of his Christmas cards. (Excerpted from *Dr. Buckhardt's Art History for the Enthusiast and the Ignorant*.)

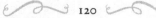

"I . . ." She couldn't swallow past the lump in her throat, and her lifeless tongue didn't help things at all. "I'm not a witch-daughter. I'm only here to help my friend. He's a prisoner of Nee . . . of the Sightless One. I'm here to free him."

The old man's eyes were fixed and impartial. "And your friend's name?"

Her eyes flicked toward Cornelis. "His name is Pim. But he's not evil, either. He's a prisoner, and I'm here to get him out of this world and back into mine."

The Master from Rijn lifted his chin slightly. "And where have you come from?"

"Illinois."

"Illinois?"

"On the other side of the canvas." This wasn't going to make sense to him, just as it hadn't to the three Dutchmen.

But he leaned forward, his eyes now probing. "And did you come by your own magic or by another's?"

That wasn't the response she had expected. "By another's."

"Whose?"

"Her name is Granny Custos."

His face didn't change, but an odd look appeared in his eye. "Custos," he repeated. "Indeed."

The Master from Rijn regarded her for a moment as he stroked at the stubble on his chin. Then he reached to a dinner plate on the table and snatched up a knife. He wiped the sharp steel clean on a napkin. Then he stood and leaned toward Claudia, knife extended.

Cornelis stepped up behind her and grabbed her arm, holding her firm.

She flinched, struggling to jump backward as the knife

flashed. But before she knew it, the rope binding her wrists fell away.

"Master—" Cornelis protested, but the old man held up a hand. Cornelis released her.

The Master from Rijn reached out and took Claudia's hand and brought it close to his face. He studied her fingertips, her palm, the back of her hand.

Finally he spoke again, slowly but with authority.

"You say you have brought me a witch-daughter, Cornelis. But I have seen past her eyes and beneath her skin and know what even she does not. A magic runs through her veins, yes. But she is not aligned with the Sightless One. She is an *Artisti*."

Claudia watched Cornelis's jaw drop—something she wouldn't have thought possible. The other Dutchmen also wore expressions of disbelief.

She knew the old man was wrong about her being an *Artisti*, but she didn't care. A thin strand of hope returned to her.

"*A-Artisti?*" Cornelis stammered. "A creator?"

"Not one of *the* Creators." The Master from Rijn dismissed the idea with a wave of his hand. "But one who creates, yes."

"But might an *Artisti* also be a witch-daughter?" Cornelis countered. "So little is known of them and their—"

"Cornelis." The Master from Rijn cut him short. "In this you will need to trust my judgment. She is not a witch-daughter. She has no allegiance to the Sightless One. If I am not mistaken, it is quite the opposite. You have done well to bring her to me, if perhaps"—he stuffed the binding ropes into Cornelis' arms—"a little roughly. It is good that she did not fall into other hands."

Cornelis stared at Claudia for a moment longer before his gaze fell to the floor. "My apologies, my lady," he mumbled.

He nodded curtly to the old man. "Master." Then he strode to the exit.

She took a deep breath and let it out slowly. It looked like there wouldn't be an execution tonight.

The old man gestured at the other two. "You may take your leave. There are stirrings that the Fireside Angel is on the move from the East. Ride with caution."

Balthasar gave a swift bow and then turned and knelt on one knee in front of Claudia. Hendrik followed suit. She felt her cheeks blush.

"My lady," said Balthasar, "we have done you wrong and beg forgiveness."

She shook her head. "No, no. I mean, you saved me from the dragon, you know, which was . . . pretty cool."

Balthasar looked into her eyes. "You are a lady of passion and purpose. You will, no doubt, succeed in your quest." With a full flourish he placed the feathered hat on his head and followed Hendrik to the exit.

She watched them go, the tension draining from her body. It was quickly replaced by uncertainty. She was so incredibly relieved, but she was still lost with no clue where to find Pim.

No one else in the café seemed to notice that Claudia had come close to being executed, nor that a *creator* stood right there in their midst, whatever that meant. The other patrons saw to their business, and the bartender lazily rubbed down a row of glasses. Nobody glanced in her direction.

Except for the old man with his penetrating eyes.

The Master from Rijn had seated himself again at the table, and he motioned for her to join him.

She sat on the bench across from him. Could he help her find—?

She was suddenly distracted by a table full of dogs playing cards.[19]

From where she sat, she could see into the adjoining room. At a green felt table in the center of the room six dogs sat upright, cards fanned out in each pair of paws. They all had a drink glass or bottle nearby, and a white bulldog crunched the stub of a cigar between his canines. The bulldog passed a playing card under the table to the dog next to him using the toes of his hind leg. The bulldog glanced up at Claudia and winked.

She tore her eyes from the bizarre card game and looked again at the old man.

He didn't say anything, so she did.

"You're Rembrandt, aren't you?"

The old man didn't blink. "It is what they called me—in another lifetime, yes."

Rembrandt continued to stare at her. She felt like a slide under a microscope. "Thank you for not executing me."

"You should know," he said, just loudly enough for her to hear, "that I lied on your behalf. You may very well be a witch-daughter—I know not. It is mostly *Artisti* who arrive through the window-caves. And the reputation of *Artisti* Custos is known to me—if you were trained at her hands, it bodes well

19. C. M. COOLIDGE (1844–1934). Coolidge worked as an artist for a marketing firm. This American is best known for his paintings of anthropomorphized dogs playing poker.

[Crass canine card sharks. Ridiculous. This isn't artwork—it's advertising! I certainly would not have included him in this book of my own volition, but my publisher forced me to. They said it would increase sales and mass market appeal. Ruddy capitalists.] (Excerpted from *Dr. Buckhardt's Art History for the Enthusiast and the Ignorant.*)

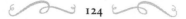

for you. But being an *Artisti* does not preclude you from being a witch-daughter. Is not the Sightless One herself an *Artisti*? And a Creator? Power does not necessarily beget honor."

Claudia set her backpack down on the bench next to her. She was tempted to tell him that she—Claudia, ultra-boring sixth grader—wasn't an *Artisti*, but thought better of it. "Why did you lie?"

"Call it the prescience of age. A hunch. You come seeking Pim, the witch-son. I do not think you come to join him in his . . . work. That means you are here to destroy him or to save him. Either way you champion a cause we have long hoped for."

She stared at him, unsure of where he was going with this. "What do you mean? What cause?"

The old man's bulbous nose shone a shade brighter. "Open war with the Sightless One. And you, child, shall strike the first blow."

CHAPTER 13

*O*PEN WAR *with the Sightless One.*

Claudia suddenly felt numb. War? That wasn't what she was there for. Was it? She'd come to steal a stupid piece of wood from some old woman. That was it. *Break the staff. Break the curse. Break Nee Gezicht.*

But everyone here seemed terrified at the thought of the Sightless One. Who was Claudia going up against?

"I don't know what you're talking about," she finally said. "I'm here to help my friend."

Rembrandt pushed aside an empty dinner plate. "What do you know about this boy Pim? Really."

Fear gnawed in her belly. Scraped at it. Is this where she would learn how Pim was an evil creature who had betrayed her?

She forced the thought away. "I know that he's been behind the . . . here . . . a very long time. I know that he was trapped here by a witch—an evil one, not just a magician or an *Artisti,* but someone really evil. I know he's a prisoner. I know I'm going to free him."

Rembrandt returned her gaze with eyes as steady as granite.

"Why?" She tried to keep her lip from quivering as she asked the question. "What do you know about Pim?"

Rembrandt scratched at his stubbled chin. "What I know is that people are not painted in black and white. They are composed of shades and hues and layers of brushstrokes, some of which never see the light of day. People are the most complex art form in existence and never complete while breath is drawn. No person is wholly evil or entirely good."

Claudia shook her head. "That doesn't help me. What is Pim? Why does everyone here seem to hate him? Why do they call him a witch-son?"

"What is Pim? You said it yourself: a prisoner. He has committed evil, and long has he suffered for his errors. There is much to pity in him. Trapped in a world where—for him, at least—time stands still, where hunger is never sated and rest is eternally elusive. Others of a lesser mettle would have fallen into madness ages ago. This world is not meant to house those of flesh and blood."

"What do you mean, he's committed evil? What has he done? Has he stolen things? Has he . . ." She lowered her voice. "Has he *killed* someone? Can people even die here?"

"While time does not age or decay in this world, death and destruction at the hand of another are possible, yes. When citizens of this world die, they do not return. All that remains are their effigies in the paintings that created them in the first place."

"Okay, but what about Pim? What has he done?" Rembrandt was answering some of her questions but not all of them. It was getting annoying.

The old man smiled sadly. "You are determined to judge people by their past, by what they have done. I prefer to judge them by their future, by what they have the *potential* to do. Your friend Pim yet has great potential to do good for this world."

He obviously wasn't going to tell her why people hated Pim so much. Had Pim really done things so terrible that Rembrandt didn't want to talk about them?

"How do you even know who Pim really is?" she asked. "Where he comes from? How do you know about my world? Those Dutch horsemen didn't seem to have a clue what I was talking about."

Rembrandt took a swig from a stein and dragged his coat sleeve across his mouth. "The nature of this world is mysterious, and there are only a handful on either side of the canvas who truly understand it. The people in your world don't know it exists. The people in mine don't know that they were created by the magic synergy found in paint and canvas."

"What's synergy?" She recalled Granny Custos using that word, as well.

"When two things combine together to create something greater than the sum of their parts. Paint is merely oil and color, and canvas is merely cloth; but together, with the touch of the talented hand, they become a café, or a countryside, or a kiss. Or an old gray artist staring into the mirror. Only the limits of the mind can determine what finds its way to canvas, and therefore what finds its way to this world."

A sudden thought came to Claudia. "You're not . . . *the* Rembrandt, are you?"

A grin spread across his face. "Never have I lived in the flesh, no. But the real Master, the one from your world, he knew of this place. Many portraits he painted of himself, each holding a different piece of his nature, perhaps even his soul. Those have been layered together in me, like sketches showing through fine vellum. Much of who Rembrandt was, I am. Like the Creators, he sought immortality. And when his flesh wasted to dust, he had achieved his aim—in a way."

Claudia nodded. She leaned her head against the wall behind the bench and closed her eyes. The Creators. That must be their name for Granny Custos and the Renaissance *Artisti* who organized this world. Flashes came to her of the dining room in Granny Custos's house. The warm light, the rich smells. Had it really been just last night? When she was so determined to help Pim? Her friend?

She opened her eyes. "You said I shouldn't judge Pim by his past, only by his potential. What does he have potential to do?"

"Like all of us, his true potential is unknown. But I believe he has the power to help in our war with the Sightless One."

"Why are you going to fight Nee Gezicht?" Claudia asked. "What has she done to you?"

"The Sightless One has remained alive for ages. Unnaturally. Long ago, she discovered the power to harness another *Artisti*'s will."

"Their will?"

"Your will is where your heart connects with your mind. It is your ability to choose for yourself. Your motivation to be and

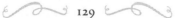

become. Your will is what truly gives you life. Now, the wills of *Artisti* can connect with the stream of magic that runs through everything. That is what makes them special. The Sightless One seeks out other *Artisti* because if she can harness their wills, they add to her own. She draws from a will's power, extending her life, until that will is depleted and cast aside like the rind of a melon."

"She sucks on other people's wills until they're dried up? Dead? And that's how she's lived so long?" This Nee Gezicht sounded more and more evil with every person Claudia spoke to.

"Indeed. Living off the wills of other *Artisti*. She has always had a presence in our lands, yet it had been distant and passing. But some time ago her interest intensified. She began gathering spies, followers, those who would do her bidding. It was once safe to travel our roads but no longer. And now rumors have surfaced that she is gathering an army to the South. She means to conquer this world, or at least as much of it as she can."

The three Dutchmen had seemed so suspicious of Claudia. That was starting to make sense. "Why would Nee Gezicht want this world? Granny Custos and Pim said it's misery for a real person to live here for very long."

"You are correct. It is not her goal to live here. She does not seek territory or land. Not really. What she wants are the inhabitants. We are a painted people, but we are alive. We also have wills, albeit wisps compared to yours. And since it is magic that gives us life, our wills are also closely connected to that magic. I believe the Sightless One has found a way to harness the wills of the people in this world. To feed off them as she does with those of the *Artisti*. But she would need many of our wills to give her life. And so she seeks to enslave us."

Whoa. This was too much for Claudia. She had come to steal a—what was the word? A *raccolta*. A staff from a cruel woman who had trapped her friend. Now she was supposed to take on the leader of armies who wanted to enslave an entire world. A world of painted people. What was she doing here?

Again, images of Granny Custos's dining room leaped to her mind. She was here for one thing.

"Listen." She pointed a finger at Rembrandt. "I don't know who you think Pim is or what he's done, but he's my friend. I'm going to help him. I don't want to strike a blow or start a war, and I sure as heck don't want to spend longer here than I have to because I've almost been killed twice and that's two times too many for me, you know?"

She paused for a breath. "But I do need your help. I need to find Pim."

"And before you came to this world, how did you expect to find him?" Rembrandt placed his chin in his hand and raised an eyebrow.

Claudia described the plan she had made with Pim in the museum, adding just enough details to explain where things had gone wrong. She looked at Rembrandt expectantly.

"Well, I certainly do not know where he is," the old man said. "This world is immense, child. You came in one window, and he waits at another. What hope do you possibly have?" He tilted his head slightly, and she detected the challenge in his statement.

Think, Claudia, think. Her stomach growled, which made thinking that much harder. "If I stay put, he definitely doesn't know where to find me. He may not even know what window I came through. But we were both going to travel to the window that leads into Nee Gezicht's home. If I head in that direction, he may have the same idea." It wasn't much, but it was a start. "Do you know where I can find a window into Nee Gezicht's house? Where she lives in the real world?"

Rembrandt leaned forward. "Most here dare not have an interest in the window-paintings. Such places are shrouded in superstition and avoided like a plague. But there are a few. And I have heard tell that an entrance to her dwelling lies to the South, in the desert. I do not know more than that."

"Is it far?"

"By some roads, yes. By others, no. But any road watched by the servants of the Sightless One makes for a long journey. It will not be without peril."

Claudia sighed. "And then if I do find Pim, that's when the real danger starts." The grueling day squeezed down on her brain, making her temples hurt. "How am I supposed to do this?" she murmured.

Rembrandt shoved his stein to the side and leaned forward. "Have you already forgotten what we've discussed this evening?" he whispered. "Synergy, my dear girl. It occurs with paint and canvas but more so with people. Therein lies the wonder of friendship. Two small insignificant beings can suddenly master the world—or at least their own troubles—when they care enough for each other."

She stared again into the granite eyes of the old man. "If Pim is a witch-son, can he really care about friendship?"

Rembrandt slowly shook his head as though she wasn't understanding. "Shades and hues and layers of brushstrokes. There is no black and white."

As she considered that, her stomach growled again. She

reached into her backpack and grabbed the box of cereal bars, but it was empty. She must have been hungrier than she thought at the museum. "Can you take me south? To the desert?"

"No. I am not a traveler, not in my old age." He thumped the table. "But I agree, your task would be easier if you had a guide."

He turned toward the table of gambling dogs in the adjacent room and called out, "Cash!"

The white bulldog snapped his head around with more annoyance on his face than Claudia could have imagined in an animal. But when the dog saw who had called, he hesitated for a moment, then put down his cards and said something to the other dogs at the table. He leaped from the chair and trotted on all fours to the booth where Claudia and Rembrandt sat. Several of the dogs watched him leave, mumbling to themselves, including a Saint Bernard with a bell around his neck. The Saint Bernard's eyes were a mismatched brown and forest green.

"What can I do for you, old-timer?" The bulldog spoke gruffly, like the elderly crossing guard near Claudia's school who practically pushed the kids across the road.

"Our friend here needs to go south," Rembrandt said. "I need you to show her the way."

Cash bent a forepaw up and removed the cigar from his mouth. "South? What the heck does a sweet little kid like this need to go south for? And how far south are we talkin'? 'Cause I ain't going *all* the way south, if you know what I mean. Them places down there give me the quivers." His body convulsed as if shaking off water.

"She's heading to the desert, past the Southern Forest."

The dog studied the cigar stub in his paw for a moment.

"I'll take her as far as the forest, but not a step more. Do I gotta bring her back, too?"

"No, she will be meeting a friend there."

Cash scratched behind his ear with a hind foot. "Yeah, I suppose I could do that. But I sure as heck ain't going into that forest. You heard what I said about the quivers." His body convulsed again. He looked at Claudia. "You carry greenbacks on you, sweetheart? 'Cause I don't accept personal checks."

Rembrandt raised a hand before she could reply. "Consider it the last installment of the debt you owe me," he said to the dog.

Cash grunted and looked at the floor but then nodded his head.

"Very well," replied Rembrandt. "When will you be ready to go?"

Cash gestured back toward the poker table. "Lenny and I are on fire tonight. You're gonna have to wait 'til tomorrow morning." Without another word the dog returned to his seat.

Rembrandt stood slowly, stretching his limbs. "I must go. You can stay here tonight—the café does not close."

Claudia gestured over to the little dog at the table. "Is that really the best we can do?"

"He knows the lay of the land. He is trustworthy."

Questions spun through Claudia's mind. There was still so much she didn't understand but felt like she should.

"Travel with caution," Rembrandt said, buttoning his brown overcoat. "You have not chosen an easy foe, my dear. And that is something we share."

He extended his hand. "Yet, in the end, I do not doubt you will succeed."

She shook his hand, feeling weary as she saw her journey grow longer and more difficult. "How do you know?"

A smile tugged at the corner of his mouth as he bowed slightly. "You forget—I am the Master from Rijn." With that he turned and scuffed through the door to the outer patio and then into the night.

Claudia crossed to the door and let her eyes follow the shuffling old master until his dark form meshed with the dark of the night. She sighed deeply, thinking over all that had happened since she and Pim arrived at the museum. Other than actually entering the world behind the canvas, none of it had brought her any closer to freeing Pim. And now doubts lingered in the back of her mind about whether she should.

On the other side of the square, the wide building burst with celebration. She was tempted to cross the snowy square and peek in through the door, but the air was cold and she was tired. She needed rest.

Inside the café, the crowd was starting to thin, although the dogs were still at it. Claudia passed by an abandoned table that had yet to be cleared and swiped a leftover hunk of brown bread. She seated herself at the corner booth and, not receiving even a glance from the waiter, made herself comfortable. She pushed her backpack to one end of the bench and laid her head on it as a pillow.

She looked at the hunk of bread in her hand, brown and coarse but still soft. Thinking hard on her conversation with Rembrandt, she bit into it and began chewing.

The bread *felt* like bread; it was coarse and became moist as she chewed it. But as she did so the wheaty-yeasty taste she expected never came. Instead the bread flooded her mouth with a strong and bitter mineral flavor.

She had once eaten an entire serving of liver and onions because her grandmother told her she couldn't have ice cream until she cleared her plate. She'd also heard about a boy at school who, on a bet, licked a wall that had just been painted.

This was worse than both of those experiences. Combined.

She sat up and spat it out, expecting to see that it had turned into something nasty in her mouth. But it simply looked like a sticky brown wad of chewed bread.

She looked at the loaf in her hand, turning it over. She gave the hard crust a tentative lick and wrinkled her nose. "It's paint." Mulling over the aftertaste in her mouth, she knew there was no way she could force it down. Not to think about what it might do to her stomach. But what if all food in this world tasted like paint?

Claudia tossed the bread onto a plate and collapsed onto her backpack. "I'm going to starve to death," she whispered. "If dragons and witches don't get me first."

CHAPTER 14

CLAUDIA SLEPT in Van Gogh's Night Café. Or rather, she lay on a bench hoping to fall asleep, but sleep never came.

At first, her mind was simply too caught up in the events of the day. She forced herself to relax and tried not to think of anything. Time passed and she was still awake. She tried making herself more comfortable, which wasn't easy to do on the hard wooden bench. She tried counting sheep, but that had never worked for her back home, either. The night dragged on, and Claudia marveled at how quickly time passes when you're asleep, and how quickly it doesn't when you're not.

At one point late in the night—or early in the morning— she pulled the art book and the nail polish and the extra underwear from her backpack and stuck her head inside as she lay down on the bench. It kept things dark, if a little stuffy, which at least helped her pretend to sleep.

When she finally emerged, she was surprised to find Cash lying on his back on the floor nearby, the brightness of day streaming in through the café windows. The bulldog's legs were spread in all directions, the cigar stub still held tightly between his jaws. His eyes were closed, his breathing slow.

"He obviously doesn't have a problem with it," she mumbled. She felt the tiredness in her eyes, the weariness in her body. She thought back to the questions Granny Custos had asked Pim when they met in her dining room.

Do your eyes yearn for sleep?

Always.

And your stomach—teased by bread that doesn't fill?

Yes.

She and Pim didn't belong in this world.

She packed up her things and hesitantly nudged Cash with her foot. He stirred but didn't wake. She nudged him again and called his name.

"King, queen, and jack," he mumbled, opening half an eye. "Don't tell me you're a morning person."

"Well, we have a long way to go today and I can't do it by myself."

Grunting, Cash stretched out his legs and his neck, then slowly lumbered to his feet and shook himself. "Spades and britches, if I ain't tired. And hungry. I'd give a full house for an Italian beef sandwich right about now."

Claudia grabbed the plate of bread from the table, sighed as she looked over the crisp crust and the chewy brown flesh, and slid it across the floor toward Cash. Her stomach grumbled. "Sorry. All we've got is bread."

They left the Dutch village on a different road than the one on which Claudia had arrived. It wasn't long before the snow on the ground became only a dusting and then disappeared altogether. They passed by meadows with thick green blades of grass and wildflowers that stretched up toward the sky. The morning sun was bright, and her surroundings were rich with detail and color, just as vibrant as she might have seen in her own world. Even more so. As she looked around, she wondered what had been real and what had been dreamed up in the artists' imagination.

When they could no longer see the spire of the village church behind them, she asked Cash, "How long will it take to get to this forest?"

"Couple of hours. Why? You in a hurry?"

"Yeah. Kinda." Because she knew Pim was waiting for her. Right?

Cash glanced up at her. "Oh, really? And what gig d'you run?"

"Gig?"

"Sure, you know, what line of work are you in?"

"I'm only twelve."

"C'mon, everybody's got a gig. Unless . . ." He glanced up at her and chuckled. "Unless, of course, you got something to hide. Maybe your gig's not quite on the up-and-up. Maybe you're on the lam, hoping not to run into any coppers. Maybe bank jobs is your thing, eh? I heard a bank got knocked over good the other day in Schaumburg." He gave Claudia a suspicious eye.

"What? I . . . No! I wouldn't even know how to rob a bank. And did I mention I'm only twelve?"

"Uh-huh. Sure. Likely story. But hey—" He glanced around as though someone might be listening. "If you're lookin' for a good wingman, I knows a guy. Done a dozen jobs, at least."

"I don't rob banks!" *Steal witches' staffs, maybe, but I don't rob banks.*

"All right. Then whaddya do?"

"I do . . . art. Drawings and things like that."

Cash wrinkled his already wrinkly nose. "Art thief, eh? I never would have pegged you for one of them. They says you can make a pretty penny or two in that, but I don't see how. Them's just pictures, after all."

Claudia rolled her eyes.

"Now, gambling," the dog continued. "There's a racket to be taken seriously. You gamble?"

"My grandpa says that having kids and gambling are the best ways to go broke fast."

"Well, if your grandpa ain't a wise man, I don't know who is. I haven't won my fortune yet and I been trying a long time. But the day's gonna come, mark my words, when fate shines a fat, golden smile in my direction. And so I keep playing."

Soon the meadows gave way to farmland, and the road cut through fields of tall yellow hay, sometimes stretching up to Claudia's chin. The fields rolled off into the distance, peaceful and innocent and simple.

"So whaddya do for fun?" Cash asked.

"Art mostly. I like to go to art museums, though I haven't been to that many. And I go to the library all the time."

Cash glanced at her and missed a step in his four-legged stride. "You must be a genuine live duck at parties."

"Oh yeah? And what do you do besides sit at a card table all night long?"

He flashed a canine grin. "Well, if you really wanna know,

when no one else is around, I——" He froze mid-stride. His nose shot upward, head turning this way, then that, nostrils flaring. Claudia glanced around at the rolling fields, which immediately lost their innocence. There was a sound nearby. Breaking glass, perhaps.

Cash's head finally snapped toward a curtain of hay on the side of the road. He barked once. "Whoever you are, come on out. I know you're in there."

She stared at the hay, waiting for something to emerge, hoping Saint George had only one dragon. She took a step backward. Finally the stalks parted as a dog stuck its head through. "Hiya, Cash."

"Get out of there, you mongrel."

The dog came out with his head down and his tail between strong legs. It was the Saint Bernard from the poker table the night before. His dual-colored eyes lingered oddly on Claudia and her arm hairs prickled. He turned back to Cash.

"Bernie, why the bankroll are you following us?" Cash asked.

The massive dog shifted from one paw to the other. "I got nothing else to do today. Thought maybe I could hoof it with you. Where you going?"

"We're chasing rabbits," Cash said, gruffer than usual.

"Sounds like fun. Lemme come."

"Bernie, you know you couldn't sneak up on a piece of cold liverwurst."

"C'mon, Cash. I really wanna go with you and your . . . friend." He glanced again at Claudia.

"Say . . . did you get your money?" Cash asked. "I left it

on the table at the Night Café. I thought you was going back there this morning."

Bernie's ears pricked up. "You got my money?"

"Yeah, yeah. I left it in one of the empty bottles on the table. You know they don't usually clean until Tuesdays. Or is it Mondays?"

Bernie turned to run back up the road but hesitated. "Promise I can come with you when I get back?"

"If you can catch up. Just don't scare the rabbits when you come lolloping back."

The Saint Bernard woofed and charged off in the direction of the village. Cash watched him go until he was out of sight. "Come on," he said. Then he turned and plunged into the field of hay. Claudia followed.

"We'll have to stay off the road," Cash said. "I don't want ol' Bernie finding us again."

"You think he's a spy for the witch?"

"Spy? Don't know what you're talking about. I owe Bernie money. I never travel with a dog I owe money."

But Claudia wasn't so sure about the Saint Bernard. That strange way he had looked at her. She didn't like the idea of leaving the certainty of the road, but she also hoped Bernie didn't find them.

"Won't he be able to track us? You know, pick up our scent?"

Cash huffed. "You been reading too many detective novels. Everyone knows Saint Bernards almost always have a head cold. Bernie couldn't smell his own supper."

"Can you see where we're going?" Claudia asked as they plunged through the wispy yellow stalks.

"Me? I'm following you."

"Bad plan. Maybe I can carry you."

A growl came from deep in Cash's throat. "I can handle my own four feet, thank you very much. You see two hills in front of us?"

"Yes." They sat prominently on the horizon.

"On the far side of the hill on the left is Colossus's digs. Bad place to be. And beyond that is L'Estaque—nice little town, great bakeries, but the viaduct is always closed for maintenance. Now, the hill on the right, that's what you aim for. At the top of that is the Lady's pavilion."

"The Lady's pavilion?" He'd said it as though there was a glow around the title.

"That's right. We can't pass this way without popping in to pay a visit to the Lady. And we can't visit the Lady without getting her cook to hand over a few of her kolaches—tastiest little morsels you'll ever sink your teeth into."

Claudia doubted that any morsel a cook dished up in this world would be the tastiest anything. "Who's the Lady?"

"Aw, just some dame. They say she knows a thing or two, but I think she's a little nuts. I usually make a beeline for the kitchen instead. You'll see."

But Claudia liked the sound of the *Lady's pavilion*. There was something powerful to it—royal wisdom and white knights and all that. Perhaps she could find more help there.

They walked in silence for a while. Claudia heard a rustling behind them and spun to see nothing but hay. "What was that?"

"You tell me. All I can see is hay and boll weevils. Bit jumpy, aren't ya?"

"I have a lot to be nervous about." She paused. Rembrandt said the dog was trustworthy, and she still had an awful lot of questions. "Do you know anything about the Sightless One?"

Cash gave her a disgusted glance from down in the hay. "The old witch? I know she's a rabble-rouser. But I don't meddle with her sort. Keep my nose where it belongs." Then he added, "You might ask the Lady, though. She'd have a thing or two to tell, I'd wager."

Claudia kept her eyes on the hill in the distance as they walked, casting a backward glance now and then at the way they had come. Cash took advantage of Claudia's nervous silence to instruct her in the fine art of poker. She listened to his monologue with only half an ear, although she found what he had to say about a "poker face" kind of interesting.

"It's all about clearing your mind, kid. Detaching yourself from your emotions. You just concentrate on your breathing. If you start thinking about what you're gonna do with the winnings—or how you're gonna have to make a run for it when the cards come down—then your face'll show it. But you gotta be consistent throughout the game. And it's not just your face— your body gives you away, too. Keep your shoulders relaxed and watch out for any nervous tics. I used to play with a dachshund who would wag his tail whenever he had a good hand. I mean, really, Sid, as if the whole table don't know what you're thinking. . . ."

Without warning, the thick forest of hay ended, opening up into a field of dry, stubbly weeds. The open pasture stretched the length of several city blocks and was crowded with dozens of haystacks. Big and little, with no apparent organization, they were scattered across the field like yellow igloos. Claudia remembered that Monet[20] had painted a few haystacks—apparently they were popular with lots of other artists, too. She stopped at the edge of the pasture.

"Ah, now that's refreshing," Cash said as he stepped out of the stalks and blinked in the sun. "Nice to see 'em break up the terrain a little."

Their surroundings were quiet. Unsettling. Claudia thought about how very still everything was just before the dragon had appeared the day before. The mounds of hay gave that same impression somehow. Like they had been waiting forever just for her to walk by. What could they be hiding?

"Nice navigating, kid," Cash said. "We're right on track."

The hill in the distance seemed closer now, and Claudia could barely make out a building on top. But to get there they would have to go through . . .

Cash looked up at her. "So. We going?"

"What do you think about those haystacks?" she asked quietly.

"What do I think? I think they grow a lot of hay around here. Gotta put it someplace."

"You don't think they look . . . dangerous?"

---

20. CLAUDE MONET (1840–1926). Monet, who painted nearly a century ago, has achieved something that would make him the envy and the scorn of his deceased contemporaries: His works have appeared on more wall calendars than any other artist in history.

Monet was one of the founders of the Impressionist movement, which focused more on the artist's perception of nature than on nature itself. Impressionistic works often appear as though the viewer is squinting, making everything look blurry and mushed together. Monet also painted several celebrated series in which he focused on the same object under different light and weather conditions. While this is an accepted tradition among artists, it does seem a tad lazy. It also makes art collectors feel jaded when they learn that just about everyone owns a "Monet haystacks." And just about everyone else owns the calendar. (Excerpted from *Dr. Buckhardt's Art History for the Enthusiast and the Ignorant*.)

Cash gave her another glance, then studied the mounds. He took the cigar from his mouth with his forepaw. "You know, now that you mention it, they do look a might sinister, don't they?"

"You think so?" Perhaps it wasn't just her imagination.

"Yeah, yeah. I mean, we could be passing by and one of them things just falls right over on us. We'd be smothered, trapped. Agricultural asphyxiation, that's what they call that."

"You're messing with me, aren't you?"

Cash grunted. "No need. You're messing with yourself pretty good. They're just haystacks, kid. And I need a kolache. C'mon." He led the way into the field.

She held back for a moment longer. Of course she was being silly. They hadn't seen a soul for hours. There was no way anyone knew where she was, much less Nee Gezicht. She followed Cash.

The haystacks closest to the edge of the field were spread apart, but quickly the distance between them began to narrow as they moved toward the center of the field. Unable to take more than a few steps in a straight line, Claudia and Cash wove in and out, her heart picking up its pace as claustrophobia crept up on her. She wiped a sweaty palm on her jeans.

Cash was ahead of her, out of sight around the edge of a haystack. A quick, sharp rustling came from his direction.

"Cash?" She hurried forward, expecting to find him around the next haystack. He wasn't there.

"Cash?" Louder now, as much to bolster her courage as anything. She ran forward, dodging the mounds of hay, but no sign of Cash. She hurried back to where she had heard the rustling—or was it over there? They all looked the same.

"Cash!" She was frantic now, visions of the leaping dragon in the forest molding her imagination. She circled the haystacks, looking for any sign of the dog but keeping her distance. She fully expected a claw or a tentacle to lash out at her.

"Help me." The voice was faint, but it was Cash's.

She froze next to a mound that towered more than a foot above her head. "Where are you?"

"Help me."

The haystack. Inside the haystack.

Without hesitating, she jumped, her shoulder plowing into the haystack. It leaned to the side and she plowed into it again. The top half of the stack toppled to the ground. She tore into the remaining hay, pushing handfuls aside, trying not to think about what creature might have pulled Cash inside. Shouting his name, she dug deeper, decimating, tearing the haystack to bits, until—yes—white fur. She grabbed a hind leg and pulled, flinging herself backward. She expected resistance, something trying to hold him tight, but Cash came freely. They tumbled to the ground, the fall softened by the scattered hay.

Claudia rolled over to look at Cash. The dog was shaking, convulsing uncontrollably. She reached out, unsure if she should touch him. And then she knew. . . .

He was laughing. Shaking and breathless, four paws in the air, but laughing with canine jaws wide open.

She sat back on her jeans pockets, breathing hard. She surveyed the mess as Cash's barking laughter continued. She felt her cheeks flush.

"Was that supposed to be funny?" she snapped.

He rolled over onto his side and gasped for a breath. "No . . . that was beyond funny." He shook again with laughter.

She glared at him.

"That was doggone hilarious," Cash roared. "Get it? Doggone . . . ?" He fell again onto his back.

She stood and grabbed an armful of hay, tossing it on top of him.

"Thanks a million," he gasped. "You just—you just saved me from that evil pile of hay!"

"Not amused, puppy dog. Next time you can find your own way out of the hay field." She turned around and stormed toward the edge of the pasture.

"Hey, c'mon, kid," Cash called after her. "Just a little fun. And who you calling a puppy dog, short stuff?"

Claudia came to the end of the pasture and plunged into another field of hay. She didn't care if Cash followed or not. Rembrandt had said the roads here were dangerous. There was nothing wrong with being a little cautious, a little suspicious.

The field grew on the side of a hill, the incline so steep that she could see only yellow hay stalks ahead of her. The field behind her rustled as Cash joined her.

"Hey, now, wait up."

She tromped ahead, rising to the top of the hill—and she froze.

The landscape plateaued into a wide plain. At one time it had probably been filled with more hay. Yellow hay that shone in the sun. A barn to store it in at harvesttime. A farmhouse in the middle of it all.

But now there was only rubble and ashes.

An area the size of a football field spread out in front of her, all of it blackened. The earth was scorched without a sign of anything living. The stone foundation of a house and barn rose

from the ground, with charred remnants of the structure still clinging to it.

Cash joined her at the crest of the hill. He took in the scene and gave a low whistle.

"I'd heard about this, but I hadn't seen it with my own eyes. Spades and britches . . ."

"What happened here?"

"You was asking about that witch. The Sightless One." He nodded at the desolation. "Some years ago her thugs came through and torched it all. Burned the house. Burned the barn. Everything. A farmer and his family lived here. Haven't been seen since."

Claudia stepped carefully toward the remains of the farmhouse, each step sending up puffs of ash. "If this happened years ago, why is everything still crispy? Why hasn't something grown back?"

"That's just the way things work around here, sweetheart. Nothing's gonna grow here again."

Rubble lay around the house, bits of iron, brick, and mortar, most of it unrecognizable. A partially burned chair and table stood in the corner of what may have been the kitchen. The lone testament that someone once lived here.

"You said the Sightless One's thugs did this," she said quietly. "Do you know who they were?"

"Naturally I don't associate myself with their kind. But I heard their captain was a Dutch kid. Name of Pim."

Claudia's heart stopped. It suddenly felt as barren as the scene surrounding her.

Pim the witch-son. Here was the proof.

CHAPTER 15

CLAUDIA STARED at the scorched earth, at the remains of the building that a farmer and his wife once called home. She couldn't believe it. There had to be a mistake. Her Pim wouldn't do this. Her Pim wouldn't even be *capable* of doing this. Something so cruel. Heartless. Maybe Nee Gezicht forced him to. Maybe the witch hypnotized him or took his will or whatever it was that evil *Artisti* did.

Or maybe Claudia had been wrong, so wrong, about him.

She placed a shaking hand over her mouth.

Then why had he brought her here? What had she gotten herself into?

Tears slipped from her eyes and coursed down her face.

She had trusted him. She had thought he needed help. She had risked herself for him.

A quiet sob escaped from under her hand.

He had deceived her.

Cash placed a paw on her leg. "Hey, kid . . . you, uh, you okay?"

She sniffed. Going forward now was useless and would probably only get her killed for nothing. There was only one thing to do.

She wiped her face with the back of her hand and licked the salty tears from her lips. "Cash, I want to go back."

"Back? Back where?"

"Back to where we started. To the Night Café. Then maybe I can find someone to show me how to get to the window-painting I came through."

"What are you talking about? The Southern Forest is just on the other side of that hill."

"I'm sorry to bring you all the way out here. But I want to go back. I want to go home."

Cash looked from her to the charred remains of the farm, confusion plain on his face. "Females," he mumbled. "Never gonna understand them."

Then to her: "Fine. I'll take you back. But first we're gonna stop at the Lady's pavilion for a breather and a bite to eat. I'm famished. Then we head back."

Claudia looked up at the building perched on top of the hill beyond the burnt farm. "Okay," she said meekly. She wasn't in a hurry anymore.

Shortly after stepping off the blackened earth, they found a barely perceptible dirt trail that led toward the hill rising in front of them. At the base of the hill it became a well-maintained stone path that lazily wove back and forth up to a large cottage on the hill's crown.

With the title of Lady (obviously with a capital *L*), Claudia had expected something grander. Perhaps even a castle large enough to house a small army. She had seen magnificent castles like that in paintings before. The cottage at the top of the hill seemed barely big enough to house her family.

But as they came closer, she saw that there was definitely something regal about it. The fine-cut stone carved with intricate patterns, the gilded windows, the charming roses climbing the walls. The building didn't give the impression of power but of importance. As though it represented something people admired.

When they came to the end of the stone path, slightly out of breath, she expected Cash to knock at the front door. Instead he skirted through the gardens on the side of the cottage and followed the sounds of talking and music into the backyard. Or rather, where a backyard might be at a normal house. Here she found a *pavilion*.

Nearly as large as the school cafeteria, the pavilion stretched across the top of the hill. Marble paving stones covered the ground. Elegant columns held up a latticework of flowering vines that filtered out the sun in some areas, leaving others open to the soft, hazy rays. A half wall at the far end partially hid the view of a sloping valley and acres of vineyards. In some places she could see fall colors and, in the not-so-far distance, a strange mound of dull browns, blues, and grays. Beyond that, stretching to the horizon, was desert.

Even from here the desert looked dismal and foreboding. At least now she wouldn't have to go there. But the thought only made her eyes burn.

A laugh tore her attention from the vista. A few ladies in delicate dresses sat near the cottage—which looked much bigger from behind. A man in velvet robes played a lute. But Claudia barely glanced at them before her eyes rested on the other person in the pavilion, seated peacefully at the far edge between two columns. The Lady.

She wore a simple green dress with a shawl draped over her shoulders. Her brown hair was parted in the middle, topped by a black mesh veil so thin it moved like air. A wispy haze surrounded her so that her features, and even the landscape behind her, looked soft. Claudia recognized her instantly as Lady Lisa. Or in old Italian, Mona Lisa.

Cash walked quickly behind the cottage toward an open doorway, Claudia trailing behind. From the corner of the pavilion, the Lady's high and subtle voice spoke. "Come."

Cash stopped mid-stride, hesitated, and turned reluctantly toward the Lady. Claudia followed. They stopped at the Lady's feet and Cash bowed his head. Claudia felt like she needed to do something, so she attempted a curtsy, which felt awkward in jeans and sneakers.

"It's, ah, it's a mighty big honor to be in your presence, my Lady," Cash said.

To Claudia's surprise, the Lady reached down, snatched up Cash, and set him on her lap. She scratched vigorously behind his ears. "There's, like, nothing cuter in the world than a talking puppy. Is there, Snookums?" One of Cash's hind legs beat up and down. She planted a kiss on top of his head, then set him on the ground again. The Lady resumed her regal visage, her back straight, her face slightly happier than neutral.

Cash blushed through his fur. He fixed his eyes on the ground and spoke hurriedly. "I was hoping to visit some of the folks in your court, my Lady."

The Lady ever so gracefully lifted her hand, palm facing the travelers. "In my court, you are most welcome."

Cash immediately turned and trotted toward the open cottage door. Claudia moved to follow when the Lady said, "Stay." The word was as gentle as a breeze and as hard to ignore as a polar bear.

Claudia turned and gave the Lady a hesitant smile. Cash had said she knew a lot, but he also said she was nuts. So far, nuts seemed more likely.

The Lady sat motionless on her stool, staring at her. Smiling.

The noise in the pavilion died down, and Claudia glanced behind her to see the lute player and ladies follow Cash into the cottage. She was alone in the pavilion with the Lady.

Who was still staring at her. Still silently smiling.

Should she say something? While she was giving up on Pim, Claudia had a million questions about the world behind the canvas and Nee Gezicht—maybe the Lady could answer them. The woman's stare was making her itch.

She cleared her throat and curtsied again. "Do you—"

"I bet you don't know how to play lily spit."

"Play what?" Claudia said.

"No. I didn't think you would." The Lady glanced to the left and right, and then jumped off her seat. "Well, come on, then." She snatched Claudia's arm and yanked her to the half wall at the back of the pavilion. The Lady leaned out over the wall and then motioned to Claudia. "Down here."

Claudia hesitated a moment and then stepped up next to the Lady. Looking down she saw that the base of the wall spread into an arch, allowing a small stream to pass through. The stream fed into a pond, large and reflective, full of scattered water lilies with blue-and-green pads. Spanning the pond was the single arc of an elegant bridge. It was a Japanese bridge, which Claudia knew only because she remembered the name of Monet's famous painting. The entire scene glowed, as though she were looking at it through a clouded window.[21]

The Lady pointed at the water twenty feet below. "The object of the game is to, like, spit on the lily pads in the pond. The ones dead below us are worth five points, those closer to the bridge are worth ten. Frogs are a twenty-point bonus and are, like, totally worth the effort. Whoever hits the most in a minute, wins. Are you ready?" A sand timer sat on the wall. Without waiting for a response, the Lady flipped it over. "Go!"

Immediately the Lady made a sound in the back of her throat like a cat with a hairball. With a *tooey*, whitish spittle sailed down and landed in the dead center of a pad directly below them. "Hah!" Within seconds she released another volley, this one arcing gracefully before hitting one of the pads farther out. The Lady glanced at Claudia. "Well, come on now!"

I am so glad no one else is here to see this.

Claudia tried to imitate the sound the Lady made in the back of her throat. She gagged and coughed. She tried clearing her throat, but there was nothing to clear. Finally she sucked on her tongue until she had enough saliva worked up. She leaned over the wall and forced it out with a single breath. The spit

---

21. IMPRESSIONISM. Through most of the nineteenth century, realistic painting was the thing in Europe. The Impressionists came along at the end of that century and raised a few eyebrows by *not* painting in a realistic style. Artists such as Renoir, Degas, Cézanne, Monet, and Manet (do not confuse the two) preferred to get out of the studio and into the fresh air and sunshine, where they could carefully capture the characteristics of natural light. Impressionistic works focus more on the artist's perception of his or her environment and often appear as though the viewer is squinting, making everything look blurry and mushed together. In an artistic way, of course. (Excerpted from *Dr. Buckhardt's Art History for the Enthusiast and the Ignorant*.)

scattered down her chin and into the air, sending tiny droplets to the pond below.

The Lady watched them fall and looked up at Claudia, who still had a string of saliva dangling from her lips. "You, like, totally hit four lily pads with one spit. So cool!" The Lady leaned over the wall, took aim again, and spit. The spittle flew through the air and landed on the edge of a lily pad beneath the bridge. She winked at Claudia and flicked the timer over with a fingertip. "But I still win."

With that, the Lady turned and glided gracefully back to her seat.

Claudia wiped spit off of her chin with the back of her hand. She had never expected this. To meet the most famous face in the history of the world—and find out she's really a loogie-hocking surfer chick. No one back home would believe it.

She followed the Lady back to her stool. The Lady arranged her skirts, head held high in a princess pose. After a moment she glanced again at Claudia as though surprised to find her there.

"Well, aren't you going to ask me any questions?"

"Questions?" Claudia repeated.

"Sure. Whenever people visit me, they always ask me questions. You know, like, what's my favorite color, or what's it like to be famous, or what makes me smile."

Maybe we can work our way up to witches, Claudia thought. "Um, okay. What's your favorite color?"

The Lady looked startled. "Oh, gee, that's a tough one. Hmm . . . blue. Definitely blue."

The novelty of meeting the real Mona Lisa was quickly wearing off. "Lady, I was wondering if you knew—"

"Well, actually, it's not strictly blue because, like, anyone could say *blue*. My favorite kind of blue is the shade of blue of bluebonnet wildflowers that you pick in the field, but not that blue exactly because that's too dark, but if you take those wild-flowers and put them into the pocket of a white blouse, and then kinda scrub that blouse in water so that the flowers get smashed into the shirt, then the shirt pocket starts to turn blue and runs all over the rest of the shirt—that blue, the runny blue, that's my favorite color."

Yep. Nuts. "Uh, right. Well, anyway, my friend Cash said—"

"That dog is, like, so adorable! Where did you ever get him? Puppies are just one of those things I get so excited about—I just can't sit still when I think about puppies, I have to go and do something. Kind of like when you're sitting with your guests and you realize that you have to tinkle. It doesn't matter that everyone is staring at your face right now wonder-ing why you're wiggling in your seat, the fact that you have to tinkle is, like, so overpowering and you just have to jump up and go find a lavatory or else you'll burst like a balloon. That's how I feel about puppies . . . and some other things in life, you know?"

Claudia glanced around. She could hardly believe she was having this conversation with *the* Mona Lisa.

The Lady shifted uncomfortably in her seat.

"Do you need to, uh, go right now?" Claudia asked. "Because that would be okay. . . ."

"Go? Go where? You just got here." The Lady's bottom lip quivered.

"I just meant we could take a break if you needed to."

"So, what? What are you saying? That you don't like talking with me? That I'm not good enough for a scrawny guest like you? Just because I can't knit underwear or cook sushi or do fancy things like that doesn't mean that I'm not an interesting person and that I don't have feelings. . . ."

As the Lady expressed herself, she began speaking faster and faster, and soon her words were flying out so quickly that Claudia had a hard time keeping hold of them.

". . . and I do have feelings-and-sometimes-they-can-get-hurt-so-you-better-watch-what-you-say-because- I-thought-you-were-being-nice-to-me-and-I-wouldn't-want-to-think-differently-about-that-becauseIlikeitwhenpeoplearenice tome. I'matotallyspecialperson,afterall."

The Lady sniffed and wiped a tear from the corner of her eye. She smoothed out her dress, checked her fingernails, and looked up at Claudia. "What were we talking about?"

Claudia resisted the urge to smack herself on the forehead. "Witches," she said instead. "What do you know about the Sightless—"

The Lady launched into another barrage of words. "I had a friend once who-wore-glasses-and-we-used-to-call-her . . ." The speed of the words increased, like a bicycle careening down a hill, until an unintelligible buzz filled the air. She went on and on, her lips moving at a bizarre pace, until it all abruptly came to a stop.

The Lady looked up at the sky and swatted at some unseen insect.

Claudia stared, dumbfounded at the flow of words, half of which were still humming in her ears.

"I have no idea what you just said. You were talking way too quickly."

"I don't think so. You were listening way too slowly."

"What?"

"You know, people usually listen at the speed they talk, when really they should listen at, like, the speed others talk. I once knew a-taxi-driver-with-bushy-eyebrows-who-could-talk-so-fast . . ." The Lady immediately catapulted into another stream of words that mashed together into a senseless noise.

This is ridiculous, Claudia thought. *I'm wasting time. There's no way you can listen to someone at a different speed.* She stared at the Lady's mouth. The words were whipping past Claudia's ears so quickly they were only a blur of sound. She concentrated harder, trying to force her ears to catch the words, but still only snatches came to her. "Pantomime . . . thoughtless fellow . . . urticating caterpillar . . ."

The monologue finally came to an end. The Lady stuck her finger in her mouth and then pulled it out. She held it up to the air as though checking for wind. "Girl," she said with her eyes closed, "we're never going to be able to have a heart-to-heart if you only focus on the words. You totally need to focus on what they mean. Open your mind. Words don't matter, meaning does."

And then she launched into another tirade of words.

"Open my mind," Claudia repeated. *Yeah, right. How can I focus on the meaning if I can't understand the words?*

But that thought brought to the surface something Pim had said in the museum in Florence.

There are a thousand ways to look at the simplest object. The great artist opens her mind to them all and sees the object as it truly is.

The Lady was a ditz, but there was something here that Claudia felt compelled to understand. Maybe it was connected to getting out of this world. Maybe it was a reluctant suspicion that Pim was right about her—that she only saw things from a limited perspective.

She closed her eyes. She forced herself to stop trying to catch every word that passed by. She let the words flow around her, envelop her. Gently, her mind probed the words, not for what they sounded like but for what they meant. What the Lady meant.

". . . and so when I have a headache—which isn't very often—I make some lemongrass tea . . ."

The meaning was coming. And the words with it.

". . . but you should never drink witch hazel tea when a stranger offers it to you 'cause it may taste so good, but you'll regret it in the end . . ."

As they continued to flow around her, it became easier for Claudia to open her mind, to make sense of everything.

". . . you probably think that the tea comes from the leaves, but it doesn't, it comes from the berries, which you can crush up in your hands and boil to make the tea and it's good for you. Kind of like bran flakes. Except that it tastes wonderfuler."

Words, phrases, sentences—and they sounded as though they were spoken normally, at the same speed Claudia herself would have spoken them.

"And speaking of witches . . ."

Claudia's eyes flashed open. The Lady was still seated, inspecting her fingernails and chewing at them here and there.

"There's a witch who visits this land all the time. They call her the witch with no sight, which isn't very politically correct, but that's what they call her. She has this total fear of death, like, completely obsessed by it. She also has this thing for tomatoes, but that's not as weird as some of the things she says. Like, she told me she's going to put together an army and, you know, take over this land and burn my cottage to the ground, which is totally crazy 'cause my cottage is made out of stone. But then she also said she's going to make us all slaves, and you know that's nuts. I mean, like, can you picture me making somebody's breakfast and scrubbing their toilet? I don't think so."

Claudia swallowed and half wished that the Lady's words were still unintelligible. She heard scraping sounds on the ground behind her and turned to see Cash licking crumbs from his lips around a cigar.

"Let's hit the road, kid," he called to Claudia.

Claudia looked up at the seated Lady, whose face had returned to its regal, enigmatic half smile. Claudia's head was still spinning from listening quickly. "I need to go. It was . . . interesting meeting you."

"Child," the Lady said serenely as Claudia turned to leave, "will you travel through the Southern Forest?"

"Well, Rembrandt said that's the quickest way to the desert. To find Pim. But—"

"Listen to what they tell you." The Lady raised an eyebrow. "And remember what I said about an open mind."

"Do they speak quickly there, too?"

The Lady giggled. "Oh, no. In the Southern Forest they, like, totally speak a different language."

Great, thought Claudia, *all the more reason not to go.* "Thank you."

"Oh, and tell Pim . . . tell him, the answer to his question is *yes.*"

The Lady knew Pim? Asking questions around her was time-consuming, but Claudia couldn't help herself. She opened her mouth to ask—

A shriek sounded in the distance, harsh and penetrating. It cut straight through to Claudia's bones, grating on them like fingernails on a chalkboard. Fear welled up inside her and she had the impulse to duck, to hide, to curl up into a ball. Even as the shriek receded, it left behind a dross in her heart that she could describe with only one word.

Despair.

Cash sprang up onto the half wall and dashed along the top until he could see into the distance, out across the field of haystacks. In a moment he bounded down and streaked past Claudia. "Fireside Angel. Time to go, kid."

Claudia looked at the Lady Lisa, whose lips twisted into a smile you might give to someone who had just dropped their ice-cream cone. "That really bites," the Lady said. "And you know he's, like, totally coming for *you.*"

CHAPTER 16

I T WAS coming for her. The Fireside Angel.

What the heck is a Fireside Angel?

There was no time to ask. Cash streaked toward the stone steps leading from the half wall to the vineyards down below. Claudia charged after him, vaguely aware of the cheerful farewell from the Lady. There was no handrail on the stairs, but Claudia took them two at a time, skidding dangerously on the loose gravel.

They were heading the wrong direction. She was supposed to be going home.

And what the heck is a Fireside Angel?

She leaped from the last steps and flew down a path that meandered past Monet's Japanese bridge. She longingly wished for a few peaceful moments to stand on that bridge and take in the artist's smooth strokes. But in a flash it was behind her. Cash plunged into the vineyard—row after lengthy row of grapevines—and Claudia followed.

Her feet pounded the muddy ground between two rows as she desperately tried to keep up with Cash. She slipped, crashing to her knees and smearing mud on her hands. She scrambled up and pushed forward.

Her lungs already burned. Vine after vine flew past. Stray branches snapped off and clutched at her face. Where was Cash? He had charged on ahead without her.

The vineyard rows were as straight as shelves in the supermarket—and just as hard for her to see over. Anything could be on the other side of those grapes.

How fast does the Fireside Angel move?

As she crested the top of the next slope, Cash charged back toward her, flinging mud into the air behind him. She eased up as he bolted past, but he immediately turned and nipped at her ankle.

"Ow!" she cried.

"You move faster or this gig is up!"

Cash snapped again and she forced her legs to stretch farther, to move harder.

She cast a hurried glance over her shoulder at the wall of the pavilion at the top of the previous slope.

Was it there? Was it coming?

"Don't look. Run!" Cash ordered.

She turned back and saw the end of the vineyard opening out into a field of cropped grass. Beyond that towered a massive wall of gray and brown and blue . . . blobs.

"Southern Forest," Cash gasped. "Look for an opening. There's only one."

They left the vineyard behind. Another shriek from the

Fireside Angel, plunging Claudia's heart into a vat of ice water. The creature sounded much closer than before.

She tried to focus at the point where the green grass met the line of the forest, but it was impossible to see straight. Each step jarred her vision and brought stars to her eyes.

The forest wasn't blobs, exactly. There were straight lines and curves and flat places that looked like cardboard. But there were also fragments and pieces and textures her eyes simply couldn't make sense of, even without the stars.

Something massive crashed through the vineyard behind them—vines snapped, leaves crushed. Claudia's legs felt like they were weighed down with cement jeans as she tried to push her tired muscles forward.

It was hopeless. The Fireside Angel would have her any second.

"There!" Cash shouted. "Hurry. It don't stay put for long."

He darted off at an angle. She followed, eyes scanning. What was he—?

Yes. A dark hole, also without any real shape, like a doorway into the otherwise impenetrable mess of dreary colors.

A burst of speed from her burning legs. Then they were there.

And Cash stopped cold at the threshold.

Claudia streaked past him into the dark opening. She spun and looked frantically back at Cash. He stared wide-eyed into the forest.

"I can't," he muttered. "I promised myself . . ."

She caught movement in the distance, just above Cash. A

creature charged toward them over the stretch of grass, loping like a gorilla with massive arms and legs.

"Cash!" Claudia screamed, not trusting her courage enough to take a second glance at the Fireside Angel.

With a growl deep in his throat and eyes squeezed tight, Cash leaped through the forest opening and onto the path. Claudia turned to charge farther down the path leading into the forest.

From behind her came a powerful crunch, like a massive fist crumpling a giant sheet of metal.

She spun around. The bright, shapeless opening into the forest was collapsing, closing in on itself. She had one last terrifying but blurred glimpse of the Fireside Angel charging toward them, shrieking, and then the light and sound from the outside was severed completely.

The crunching of the forest threshold echoed for a moment, and then silence poured over everything like a bucket of dark paint.

Claudia backed nervously up the path, staring at the place where the opening had disappeared. "Can it get through?"

"Naw," Cash panted. "There's only one way into the Southern Forest, and one way out. But it's always changing, never know where it's gonna be. Without that opening, no one gets through." He glanced up at her, his sides pumping in and out. "You could say we got lucky. Shame I didn't have any money on that little race."

Her legs felt like jelly. She leaned over, hands on her knees, sucking in lungfuls of air. Her eyes hadn't yet adjusted, and the dimness of the forest pressed in around her.

"What was that thing?"

"The Fireside Angel?[22] No good, that's what he is. Works for that witch you was asking about. Thinks he's a big ol' alpha dog."

Her skin crawled at the thought of the hulking creature barreling toward them across the field. "But what is he?"

Cash looked at the dark wall where, moments ago, they had passed through. "They say he's made out o' chaos. Out o' the desolation of war. That he's what happens when power gets hungry." He shuddered. "But I've never met the guy. I got no problem sticking my tail between my legs and making myself scarce when I need to."

Her eyes were adjusting now. The path in front of them stretched into the forest and was clearly defined, but everything else . . . wasn't. Where she expected to find trees and bushes stood large shapeless masses, similar to the outside of the forest. It was as if the forest had been drawn by a four-year-old and then cut apart and glued back together. She had the feeling that if she glanced behind the pieces, she would find that they

---

22. MAX ERNST (1891–1976). Ernst is generally clumped together with the Surrealist artists. In fact, he was one of the first leaders of that monumentally mysterious movement. Ernst's paintings vary as much in content as they do in style. Giant birds, floating hands, collages, textured paints—there is no single object or style that defines Ernst, although the adjective *unique* almost always comes up in the discussion.

Ernst served as a soldier in World War I, which had an influence on his later works. One such example is *The Fireside Angel* (1937), in which a horrid monster stalks across an abstract landscape, destroying everything in its path. The ironically named creature represents Fascism, which Ernst considered a plague spreading across Europe.

Ernst was also an avid chess player, as were many of the Surrealists, and designed his own chess pieces. He even met his wife over a game of chess. How ironic that the most impractical of art movements should be drawn to the most practical of games. But then I suppose Twister hadn't hit the market yet. (Excerpted from *Dr. Buckhardt's Art History for the Enthusiast and the Ignorant*.)

were flat, like scenery from a theater stage. But she had no desire to leave the path to find out.

And everything was in constant motion. It was subtle—like a rocking boat on calm waters—but it was all moving. Some patches of the forest were like the colorful end of a giant kaleidoscope. Fractured pieces of reality that seemed familiar but didn't hold still long enough to figure out why.

"Can't believe I'm here again," Cash muttered.

"You've been here before?"

"Once. One time too many. I was lost for days. Couldn't find that dang exit. And this is no place to be lost without a partner, let me tell you."

She sighed. "And I had just decided to go home. What do we do now?"

Cash gestured at the solid mass they had passed through. "This door ain't gonna open again for a long time. And even if it did, who knows if Ugly's gonna be waiting for us. No, we need to find the opening, wherever it's gone off to. Come on."

Cash started cautiously down the path and she followed. The dark shapes loomed tall on both sides.

"Just look at it," he said in a hushed voice. "It's spooky. Worse than spooky. Like being in a fun house that ain't no fun. And the natives here—call themselves Cubists. A bunch of nut jobs, but don't say that to their face. I knew a greyhound that came in here once on a bet—never saw the skinny fool again."

Cubists.[23] *Well, that explains it. Kind of.* Picasso and Braque

---

23. CUBISM. Artists in the Cubism movement of the early twentieth century did more than paint geometric shapes like a first grader. They wanted to answer quite the quintessential question: What would it look like if you took your favorite box of breakfast cereal, dumped out the contents, and then splayed open the cardboard at the seams

and those others who painted things that never made any sense. This looked like the kind of place they'd create.

They walked on, their footfalls disturbing the unnerving silence of the forest.

"How long do you think it'll take to find the exit?" Claudia asked.

"Your guess is as good as mine, sweetheart." A growl came from his stomach. "Don't suppose you have a bratwurst on rye stashed away in that pack of yours?"

"If I did, I promise it would be all yours."

Cash grunted. "So what did you think of the Lady?"

Claudia smiled in the dim light. "Well, where I come from—"

She jumped back with a shout. A figure appeared in front of her so quickly that she couldn't tell if it had stepped out of the shadows, sprung up from the ground, or materialized out of the air. It was taller than she was, and, like the forest, the details and texture of its body were missing, replaced with bold colors and angular shapes. Its face was divided into two colors, with simple dots for vacant eyes and lines for empty lips. It looked—vaguely—like a clown or jester.

Cash growled. Something crossed her vision to the side and Claudia spun to see another Cubist clown standing behind them.

They stared with their unsettling, dotted eyes.

"What do you want?" Claudia asked.

---

so that a three-dimensional object was now displayed in two dimensions? And what if the whole world looked like that? Cubists, you might say, thought outside the box by thinking about boxes. (Excerpted from *Dr. Buckhardt's Art History for the Enthusiast and the Ignorant*.)

No response.

"We're trying to find the way out of the forest. Can you help us?"

One of them held what might have been a guitar. "You have come," it said in a low voice.

Had they been waiting for her? Were these spies for Nee Gezicht? They were creepy enough.

"You are alone," said the second clown. It sounded disappointed. "No matter. You will follow us. The execution cannot wait."

Execution. Her hand went to her throat. "What execution?"

"The execution," the first clown said. "Planned for ages. Now it is time."

Not again. Didn't she escape an execution already? *It can't be mine,* she thought desperately, *not if they've planned it for ages. Right?*

The first clown beckoned with a stiff hand. "Come now."

"Cash?" she said out of the side of her mouth.

"They got us surrounded, kid." The dog jerked his head toward the forest.

Other figures moved in the shadows behind the tree shapes. She couldn't make them out, but they hadn't been there before. Maybe.

The rear clown poked her in the back with a stiff finger.

"Cut that out!" Claudia snapped.

"Move," the clown said. "Now."

Claudia racked her brain. She still hadn't caught her breath from their last life-threatening situation. *Think, Claudia, think.* And they were surrounded. . . . The finger poked her in the back again. "All right! I'm going."

The Cubist clown in front moved down the path. But instead of moving its legs, it seemed to break into a thousand pieces that scattered forward, like leaves in the wind. Then the pieces reassembled several yards ahead before pausing and doing it again.

Claudia followed cautiously, Cash at her side.

"Where are they taking us?" she whispered after the clowns had fallen into a steady pattern of breaking, floating, and reassembling.

"Don't know. An execution, looks like."

"What do we do?"

Cash glanced behind him. "Well, they outnumber us six to one, I figure. How are you in a brawl?"

"Not high on my list of talents."

"Then we try hightailing it outta here."

Their footsteps were the only sounds on the path through the forest. The clowns moved in complete silence, as did the creatures that guarded them from behind the trees.

If they work for the witch, then we're dead. If they don't, well, compared to Nee Gezicht there's nothing else to fear, right?

There was no exit behind them—they would have to move deeper into the forest. And they would have to be fast. Again. Her leg muscles throbbed in protest.

She eased her backpack from her shoulders and carried it in one hand. She stretched her shoulders back and forth to make it look like they might be sore. The backpack wasn't much of a weapon, but it did have Dr. Buckhardt's art encyclopedia in it, and it might at least disorient the guard.

Cash tossed a glance her way. She nodded a fraction and pointed with her chin in the direction they were walking. They would have to time it. Wait until they were close to the first clown and before it broke apart.

"Three," Claudia breathed out. "Two. One."

She leaped forward and swung the backpack around, aiming for the clown's head. Before the backpack was even halfway through its arc, the clown broke to pieces and disappeared.

She didn't have time to be surprised. Cash rushed down the path and she followed, swinging the backpack up on her shoulder. The trees became darker as Claudia and Cash plunged farther into the forest. There were no shouts, no sounds of pursuit, but also no doubt something was close behind them.

And there was a voice in her head. It was the Lady's voice, or a memory of her voice, repeating what she had said about the Cubists just moments before Claudia and Cash fled from the pavilion.

Listen to what they tell you. Listen to what they tell you. Listen to what they tell you.

Movement off to the side, deep in the trees. Clowns—or worse—breaking apart and reassembling, flanking them in the shadows.

The silence pressed against Claudia's thoughts like a juicer against an orange. Footsteps or shouts or rustling in the trees would have been more bearable.

The path split ahead of them. Cash veered toward the right, but instantly a Cubist clown reassembled in the center of that path. They spun and tore down the branch on the left.

After a dozen paces they came to another fork and again Cash veered right and again a Cubist clown appeared to block their path. Cash growled as they whirled around and charged down the other path. Claudia knew what he was thinking.

They want us to go this way.

It had to be. The figures in the shadows moved so effort-lessly and Cash had guessed there were a dozen of them. The Cubist clowns weren't chasing them. They were herding them.

And then in the dim light the ground gave way beneath them and they were slipping down a slick chute, like a twisty slide at the playground, spinning, tumbling, careening toward who-knew-what in the depths of the Cubist forest.

CHAPTER 17

THE CHUTE twisted and turned, the slope of it barreling them along at a dizzying speed. And then they burst into the open air for a brief second before sprawling across the level ground and coming to a stop, prostrate in the dirt.

Claudia's head spun but a sense of urgency pulled her upright. Cash lay on his back beside her, also scrambling to find his feet.

They were in a clearing of sorts—a wide space ringed by trees on the far side. Behind them rose a massive rock wall. There were lines up and down the wall and deep square chunks missing, as if something had cut them away. It was still Cubist and hard to define, but it reminded her of a quarry—a place where they cut stone blocks out of a pit for building. Toward the bottom of the wall was an opening where the chute must have spit them out.

The clearing glowed softly, like moonlight through fog, although it wasn't apparent where the light came from. Instead of opening up to the night sky, towering trees rose from the edges and leaned their amorphous shapes together to form a canopy that covered the clearing like a beach umbrella.

On the left side of the clearing sat a collection of chairs, set up in curved rows. Waiting for the show to begin.

Claudia whirled around, looking for options. A path they could follow, some place to hide, anything. But her heart sank. Figures emerged from the shadows. Dozens of them. All unmistakably Cubist.

"Any ideas, kid?" Cash said in a low growl.

Figures appeared right beside her—the clowns from before, flanking her now like prison guards.

She had no answer for Cash.

The figures in the clearing formed a loose ring around the prisoners, all of them keeping their distance, except for one. A portly man moved toward them   not like the clowns did, but walking with disjointed steps. He wore a blue coat that engulfed his large frame, two rows of brass buttons streaming down the front. His body, and especially his face, appeared fractured, as though Claudia was looking at him through a piece of crystal, dividing into shards that might never have made a whole to begin with.

The man stopped a few paces away and flung out his arms. "Well, well, well, what have we here? Victims? Cohorts? Vagabonds? Patrons? The possibilities are absolutely endless!" He leaned his fractured face in close to Claudia's. "Doesn't that just bolster your imagination, darling?"

She tried to take a step back but one of the clowns placed a hand on her shoulder. "Let us go," she said. "We haven't done anything to you."

The man in the blue coat stepped up next to the clown and spoke in a low voice.

"This is it, harlequins? This is all you've brought us? We can't execute with just one person."

"And a dog," said the clown. Cash growled at Claudia's feet.

"Don't look at us, Pablo," said the other split-faced clown. "The entire forest is empty."

The man in the blue suit—Pablo—scratched a fragment of his face. "Well, we can't delay any longer—everyone's anxious. We'll have to do it with just her."

"And the dog," the clown said.

"Yes, yes, and the dog." Pablo turned back to Claudia and Cash and continued speaking with the energy of a carnival barker.

"What you fine young specimens of impertinence and fur don't realize is that the second you step foot in the Forest, you relinquish all rights, privileges, and affirmations heretofore claimed by your dreary little lives. But fear not! Worry not! Here amongst our merry band you will see things never imagined. Feel emotions never yet conceived. We specialize in opening minds and abstracting angles and detaching you from your head, which is, no doubt, stuck in the lugubrious realm of inflexible boundaries and preconceived notions. The concerns of yesterday no longer concern you. You're with the Cubists now!"

Pablo bowed low and waved an arm to one side. The crowd parted, bringing the rows of chairs into view.

"Please," Claudia said. "We need to go—"

"Places everyone!" Pablo shouted. "Curtain up in two minutes!"

The crowd became a flurry of movement. Pablo jabbed a

finger at Claudia and spoke to the harlequins. "Get them in their seats and keep them there."

A hand clamped her arm like a vise. "Hey!" she cried. She jerked away, but the harlequin held firm.

The other harlequin made a whipping motion with its hand. A thin stream of brown substance flowed from it toward Cash, lashing around his neck and holding fast, forming a collar and leash.

Cash snarled and snapped, but the harlequin picked him up by his new collar and held him at arm's length.

Together the harlequins marched them forward toward the rows of chairs. Each chair was distinct and each definitely Cubist. The first chair they came to had four legs aligned in a single row beneath a seat with a steep incline. The harlequin shoved Claudia down into the second chair—a relatively level seat with three legs. Two hands remained clamped firmly on Claudia's shoulders. The other harlequin tied Cash's leash to the third chair.

Cash growled at her side. "Looks like we've stepped into some deep guano, kid. Don't see a way outta this one."

"I'm sorry, Cash."

"That's all right. My head only ever gets me into trouble. I'm probably better off without it."

The Lady's words popped into her mind again. *Listen to what they tell you.*

It was simple and could have meant anything. And it came from the Lady, who made as much sense as a helicopter with an ejection seat. But when the Lady said it, Claudia had still been listening at just the right speed, and she knew there was something there she needed to pay attention to.

But an *execution?* Maybe even hers?

The lights went out, plunging the clearing into darkness.

It only lasted a moment. Then a circle of light popped into the middle of the meadow, directly over Pablo. He spoke, his voice reverberating through the clearing. "Ladies and . . . well, canines. For some time now we have prepared and rehearsed and perfected what we consider a great work. A story of melancholy and triumph. Of remorse and wisdom. Of abstraction and beauty! You shall now be the first to witness the execution of . . . our play!"

And then there was darkness again.

Claudia held her breath, wondering if she had heard Pablo correctly.

Music. The wisps of melody were low and simple at first. She had to strain just to make them out. As they grew stronger, a section of the clearing grew brighter. Figures moved into the open space. Their movements were awkward but deliberate and rhythmic, like paper dolls doing aerobics without the help of knees or elbows. They moved in patterns and lines, interacting with one another.

They're dancing, thought Claudia, relief rushing through her veins. *The execution of their* play. *Why didn't they say so?*

"Spades and britches," Cash murmured. "You gotta be kiddin' me."

Soon figures crowded within the lights of the grassy stage. Each one looked like it had jumped right out of a Cubist painting. Some were geometric and multitoned like the clowns. Others seemed to be made out of fragments, like the man in the suit. The strangest of all were the brown and gray figures made of lines and shades that hardly looked like a human form at all.

As they moved, the individual fragments and shades shifted, like dozens of dirty playing cards lying on top of one another. Only the fact that one end stood on the ground gave a clue as to where their heads and feet might be.

Off to the right was the source of the music: a group of musicians, as strange as the figures on the stage, gathered together playing instruments. Another harlequin stood with the group, strumming its guitar. A brown "playing card" woman picked at a mandolin. And in the center of the group stood a squarish cartoonlike trio dressed in bright colors, bobbing up and down as they played their instruments. The bearded accordion player winked at Claudia, and she looked quickly away.

The panic and fear from minutes before had ebbed, leaving a syrupy puddle of frustration. This was ridiculous. She was wasting time here while the Fireside Angel—and who knew what else—was out there tracking her down. She pulled again against the hand clamped on her shoulder. The Lady was wrong. They weren't going to tell her anything useful.

And that's when they started singing.

It wasn't belting-it-out-on-Broadway kind of singing, but low and rhythmic and a hundred voices in unison. The kind of singing you snap your fingers to in a smoky café.

> *"We'll tell you a tale, as you sit in your seat*
> *That is neither objective nor true,*
> *But it's chock-full of color and wonder replete,*
> *And of fortunate Mortimer Skew."*

The words they sang were captivating. At times they seemed to be singing only in her head. In the next minute the words were almost palpable, as though she could snatch a handful and put them in her jeans pocket. And then, occasionally, random words from the song seemed to appear in the air above the singers, but it wasn't clear if they were really there or if it was a trick of the light.

> "*Mortimer Skew was a healthy young lad*
> *Who ate three bowls of bran flakes each day.*
> *But that's because that's all the grocery store had—*
> *For his world was just shades of gray.*

> "*No color, no flavor, no imagination—*
> *Not a sniff from beginning to end—*
> *No opinion, no thought, no diversification*
> *Was found between stranger and friend.*

> "*One morning as Mortimer ambled through town,*
> *With nary a thought on his mind,*
> *He happened to spot on the cold cement ground*
> *A fairly fantastical find.*

> "*Glasses—with lenses that glinted bright green,*
> *And frames of an old tarnished chrome.*
> *Then glancing around so as not to be seen,*
> *Morty snatched them and headed for home.*"

A Cubist in the center of the stage acted out the words of the song as dozens of others danced around in synchronized movements.

"Once safe in the walls of his humble abode,
He brought spectacles up to his eyes
To see everything that the glinty green showed—
And he shouted in wondrous surprise.

"Colors! In every last thing he gazed on—
Not just greens, but chartreuses and blues
And crimsons and teals and lemon chiffons,
With innumerable patterns and hues.

"And sounds! He heard sounds that were gentle and sweet,
Like the giggle and laugh of a child.
And then there were sounds that could make his heart beat,
Like his neighbor's Rottweiler gone wild.

"Curious, Morty then opened the cupboard
And gnawed on a sponge for a while.
'Ma, what a horrible taste I've discovered!'
He finally said with a smile.

"He ran out the door and he breathed the fresh air,
And he noticed a cloud in the sky.
'That looks like my math teacher, Mr. Beaufrere,'
He said to a kid passing by."

Other actors joined in the pantomime, playing other characters in the narration. A crowd slowly built around the Cubist playing Mortimer.

"He looked at the ground and he thought about ants—
'Do they call each other by names?
Is it the fashion for men ants to wear pants,
With dresses adorning the dames?

"'Oh, I see with my eyes and I hear with my ears
A place both exciting and new—
The world can be different from how it appears
Depending on my point of view.'

"A neighbor approached with a scowl on his face
And his finger was wagging with shame.
'This nonsense you spout is a horrid disgrace,
And a blemish on your family name.'

"'Your head is a square,' was young Morty's reply,
'With circles for eyes, nose, and mouth.
Your middle reminds me—now don't think I lie—
Of a hippo that's heading due south.'

"A crowd had now gathered round Mortimer Skew,
Lips pursed and with eyebrows pulled down.
'You cannot see anything more than we do—
Stop this nonsense. Quit clowning around.'

"But Morty refused to deny what he saw—
A wondrous new world complete.
The angry crowd bellowed to bring out the law,
And they strung the boy up by his feet."

 182

The Cubist playing Mortimer disappeared into the roiling crowd. One end of a rope fell from the dark ceiling, swaying as the crowd took hold of it. It snapped taut seconds later and an upside-down figure rose above the crowd, its feet attached to the rope.

It wasn't a Cubist but a regular person. A boy. His mouth was gagged and his hands tied behind his back. His crystal-blue eyes were wide with fear.

Claudia couldn't restrain the cry that leaped from her heart. "Pim!"

" 'You, Mortimer Skew, are as guilty as found
For trying to change status quo.' "

Pablo was there onstage, at the edge of the crowd. He pulled a lever protruding from a stone. A circle on the ground opened just below where Pim hung, producing an orange glow that flickered like flame. Undulating waves of heat rippled the air above it.

"So into the Furnace we must thrust you down
To pay out your sentence Below."

Claudia struggled against the hands on her shoulders, but the more she pulled, the tighter they clamped down. "Pim!"

A rough set of stairs appeared next to the dangling Pim. As the music built to a crescendo, Pablo climbed the stairs, clutching a triangular knife.

"No!" she cried, beating against the hand that held her.

Cash skittered under the chairs and sunk his teeth into the ankle of the harlequin. It cried out, loosening its grip on her shoulders.

She was out of her chair in an instant, sprinting toward the stage in the clearing. Sprinting toward Pim.

"No!" she shouted again. "Stop!"

She was a handful of paces from the crowd when the harlequins materialized on both sides of her and grabbed her arms.

The music abruptly died, notes fizzling in the air. The entire crowd onstage looked at her. The knife in Pablo's hand was pressed against the dangling rope. Pim's intense gaze drilled into hers.

A frightening grin spread across Pablo's fractured face. "Audience participation! How delightful. But you do realize you're interrupting the story's climax."

"Please," Claudia begged. "Let him go."

"We can't just release the star of our show," Pablo explained, waving the knife in the air. "He's under contract. Talent like this doesn't come along every day. You do know who this is, don't you? Pim, the witch-son? The right hand of the Sightless One? He's played in venues across the land, bringing down the house, quite literally. For years he has crept through our forest, avoiding sentries, gathering information, and always, always, always"—Pim winced as Pablo poked at him with the knife—"avoiding his adoring fans. And then today he walks right up the path to our front door. Has a question, he says. Looking for someone, he says. Now, what was he looking for . . . ? Oh, yes. A girl with raven hair."

Pablo stopped and looked at her, covering his mouth in

mock surprise. "A girl with raven hair? I don't suppose . . ." He held out his arms in question.

Claudia was speechless as her heart and mind battled. Pim had been looking for her. Why? Why had he brought her here? She had seen the burnt farm, Cornelis's hatred, even the knife in Pablo's hand. She had already made her decision—she was going home.

But to see him hanging there, helpless. She could feel the heat bursting from the pit below him. Is this really what he deserved? What if she was wrong? Could she just walk away?

No. She would always wonder. She would never stop wondering.

"I need to talk with him."

Pablo laughed. "So sorry, my dear, but you'll understand that it just isn't possible at this juncture in the story line."

"Please," she begged. She had no leverage, nothing to bargain with.

Pablo shook his head sadly and raised the knife to the rope. "The show must go on."

"No!" She struggled against the harlequin guards. "I've come all this way to find him. Even Rembrandt said I needed to find him, and I'm not going back until—"

"Rembrandt?" Pablo paused. "You spoke with Rembrandt?" He rushed down the stairs toward her, waving the guards away. He put an arm around her and drew her away from the crowd. "What did he say? Did he send a message?"

Pablo had dropped the showman facade and spoke now in serious whispers.

"He told me that I needed to find Pim," she said carefully. "That I'm to . . ." She hesitated, not sure how much to tell him.

He seemed to have a genuine respect for Rembrandt. "That I'm to strike the first blow against the Sightless One. But that I need Pim's help to do it."

Pablo studied her for a moment, scratching a fragment of his chin. Then he spun around and shouted, "Cut! Strike the set!"

The light in the clearing returned to a soft glow. The Cubists on the stage scattered like roaches. One of them pulled the lever and the opening to the Furnace rumbled closed. With a cranking sound from above, Pim was lowered to the ground.

Pablo stepped over and roughly pulled Pim to his feet, slashing the bonds with his knife. A Cubist brought two chairs over and placed them next to Claudia, facing each other.

Within twenty seconds, everything and everyone else had disappeared from the clearing, except for Cash, who was scratching at his neck where the collar had been. Pablo leaned close to Pim. "No funny business, bub. You're surrounded, and the show ain't over yet."

He bowed to Claudia. "We'll be close by." Then he disappeared into the shadows at the edge of the clearing.

She sighed. At least for the moment, no one was being executed, no one was going into the Furnace, and no one had a vise grip on her shoulder. And yet her stomach turned flip-flops as she stared at Pim. He looked just like the miniature boy in her painting, except so lifelike. And he was taller than her by a few inches—she hadn't expected that.

He took a few steps toward her. Cash bared his teeth and growled a warning, and Pim stopped short. "Thank you, Claudia," he said.

"You're welcome." She folded her arms. "Now, start talking."

CHAPTER 10

CASH'S GROWL intensified, his eyes fixed on Pim.

"It's okay, Cash," Claudia said. "This is who I was looking for. This is Pim."

Cash barked viciously. "I know who he is. This chump owes me money. Has for a long time."

Pim looked at Cash skeptically. "Your puppy dog can talk."

"Watch yourself, buddy. My bite is worse than my bark."

"I'm sure it would be if you had a step stool high enough to reach anything," Pim retorted.

Cash crouched and bared his teeth. "Listen here—"

"Cash!" Claudia snapped. "This isn't helping."

"Don't listen to anything he says, kid. He's a witch-son, this one. Can't trust him."

She couldn't trust him. That's what her mind told her, too. But her heart needed to hear what he had to say. "Why don't you give us a few minutes, Cash?"

The dog looked up at her doubtfully.

"I'll be okay," she added.

He gave one more fierce growl in Pim's direction. "This time I don't let you outta my sight 'til I collect. Right, friend?" He then retreated halfway to the edge of the clearing, where he lay down.

"I see you've made some friends," Pim said.

"I had to. You said you'd be with me the whole way. That didn't quite happen."

"No, it didn't. When I saw you enter the Rubens painting, I knew it would be difficult to find you. For you to have made it this far—I'm very impressed."

She didn't say anything.

Pim continued. "I take it . . . I assume you've heard a few things about me."

She squeezed her fists, poking her nails into her palms. It was time to find out the truth, for better or worse. "Everyone has something to say about you around here. Cornelis, Rembrandt, Cash—"

"Cornelis? You met the three Dutchmen? Well, then you must have quite the picture painted of me."

"Is it true? The things they say?"

Pim's gaze wavered, then fell to the ground.

To Claudia, his reaction was as good as an admission of guilt, and like a fist to her stomach. "Why did you lie to me?" she whispered. "Why did you bring me here?"

Pim's jaw tightened and he closed his eyes. "I did warn you, Claudia. I swear I did." He looked at her, eyes moist and wild. "I told you not to get tangled up in my story. I should never have let it happen."

"Are you my friend? Or was that all a lie?" She couldn't keep a tremble out of her voice.

"Our friendship was never a lie. Never. I only lied to you once. I tried not to. After so long . . . to be so close . . . I couldn't help it. But there are as many ways to lie as there are to mix paint. It wasn't the lie I told you that made the difference, but all the truths I didn't tell."

"What lie did you tell me?"

He ran his hands through his hair. "At Granny Custos's house. When I told you my story. I didn't actually . . ." He took a long breath and began pacing back and forth. "We were painting Nee Gezicht's portrait, Master Verspronck and I. She was a powerful woman. In her presence it felt like she could crush you with a glance. I wanted to know her secrets. If what people whispered at their windows was true—if she really could command magic then I wanted to learn.

"When we finished her painting, Master Verspronck took the money and never looked back—didn't dare. He didn't realize that she knew more about art—the deep secrets of art—than he would ever know. But *I* went back. I told her I wanted to learn from her. To be her apprentice. She kept me on for a few weeks, testing me. Then she told me I was ready to learn more. That was when she sent me here."

"You mean she trapped you here?"

"No. Not at first. I came willingly."

Claudia stared at him, trying to work through his story. "But the tomatoes . . . you tripping . . . Nee Gezicht's curse?"

Pim stopped pacing and closed his eyes. "That was my lie to you. I am sorry."

Her throat tightened. She had heard and seen too many things for it not to be true. But to hear it from Pim himself . . . She felt her face flush. Anger seethed beneath her skin. "You really do work for her, then?"

"I did for a long time, yes. But—"

"How could you do that to me?" she shouted, not caring if the whole forest heard her. "How could you trick me like that?"

"Claudia—"

"You pretended to be my friend. I cared about you. I came here to help *you*." Tears stung her eyes. "I can't believe I did that! I thought you were my friend."

"Claudia, our friendship was never a lie; I promise you that. It means everything to me."

"Oh, sure. How many times have you used that line?"

Had there been others? Had he lured others into this world, too, like a spider in a complex web?

But their friendship had seemed so real.

"Please, listen," Pim said.

She snatched up her backpack. He didn't deserve any more of her time. She took a few steps toward Cash, then paused to look back at Pim.

"You don't have anything I want to hear."

His desperate eyes pleaded with her. She had the mustard bottle in her backpack, and she was headed home. *Adiós. Au revoir.* Good riddance.

"Please," he whispered.

Why had he brought her here? Her curiosity pestered her like an unscratched itch. This would be her last chance to get some answers from him.

She dropped her backpack. "Make it quick. I have a painting to catch."

"Thank you, Claudia." He eagerly sat down. He stared at his hands for a moment, as though collecting his thoughts. "When I asked to apprentice with Nee Gezicht, she was willing to take me on because she suspected something I couldn't even fathom. That I was an *Artisti*."

She sat on the edge of the chair opposite Pim. "You? Like Granny Custos? And Nee Gezicht?"

"Not one of the Renaissance *Artisti*, but an *Artisti* nonetheless. Nee Gezicht had found a way to reap the will of an *Artisti*. Your will is—"

"Yeah. Rembrandt told me. The will is connected to magic. She can take their will and it makes her more powerful. It makes her live longer."

Pim nodded. "She had done it once before, with another *Artisti*. Reaped his will. She made the *Artisti* powerful, although he was always under her control. And to have your will in the hands of someone else—for a body of flesh and blood, it drains the life. Sucks it dry. When she finished with the young *Artisti*, he was only a hollow shell.

"But I was an experiment. She took me in, taught me secrets. Traded me power for pieces of my will. And she sent me here. I didn't know it, but she believed that if she placed an *Artisti* in this world—where a body doesn't age, doesn't corrupt— that she could live off their will forever. Never reaping all of it, always leaving some to grow, to regenerate, like seeds in a garden bed."

The hairs on Claudia's arm prickled. "She has your will. You mean she controls you?"

"If she had controlled me completely, then my heart would not be so heavy. But she had only part of my will. She had great influence over my actions, but in the end, they were my own."

"And what did you do for her?"

"When I first came here, it was still a new world, so much smaller. I brought her news of how things were growing, expanding. And I spied on people in the real world through the window-paintings. Sometimes important people, sometimes other *Artisti*, often her enemies. Nee Gezicht is not some hermit oblivious to the world around her. She has gained wealth, controlled governments, even influenced wars. And I did everything she asked of me. I only wanted to please her, to have her teach me, give me power. With that lust, it was so hard not to allow her more and more pieces of my will.

"But in time I grew tired of this place. So tired." He looked down at his hands. "There is no sleep here, you know."

"Yes," she said, remembering the night before. "And the food . . ."

He nodded. "And the food. Sleep and food aren't needed for us to survive in a painted world, but my body has never forgotten the memory of it. I am trapped here, Claudia, there was no lie in that. I can leave only by her magic, or by seeing her magic broken. And I asked to be released, many times, but she wouldn't hear of it. Instead she enticed me with power and promises of freedom and gave me other tasks. Darker tasks. Less of my time was spent spying on royals through their paintings and more of it spent focusing on this world. On conquest."

"Conquest?"

"Behind the canvas, in the Southern Lands far from here, at least at first. Nee Gezicht will rule this world entirely in the end—immense as it is. I have done terrible things, Claudia. I have stolen and bullied and hurt. I have fought battles, led armies, burned villages to the ground. I had such a command of magic that I could hurtle boulders with a mere thought. Arrows couldn't pierce me. Rivers parted at a touch. I wanted power and knowledge and immortality, and that's what Nee Gezicht gave me. But all they've done is create a monster in the painted body of a twelve-year-old boy."

She shook her head, trying to take it all in. The Dutchmen were right—he really was a witch-son. Nee Gezicht may have influenced him, but the actions were his own. And Balthasar's description had just scratched the surface. How could she trust someone like that? How could she be a friend to someone like that? Heck, why wasn't she running as fast as possible to the nearest window-painting to get away from him?

"There were other *Artisti*, as well," Pim continued. "Young ones, usually. I would find them through their paintings, and Nee Gezicht would entice them and reap their wills and send them here just like she did me. And if they wouldn't be enticed, she would capture them and take their wills by force."

"Are they still here?"

"No. Some were too weak and couldn't bear to be separated from their wills. They eventually . . . faded. The others died doing Nee Gezicht's bidding."

A thought chilled her heart. "And me? What did you want with me? Why did you bring me here? So you could hand me over to her?"

"I brought you here for recompense."

"Recompense?"

Pim rubbed his face. "Many years ago, Nee Gezicht wanted

a demonstration here in the North. Something to show her presence, to put fear in the hearts of the people. There was a gathering one night in the Lady's pavilion. A concert of sorts. Everyone in sight of her pavilion attended. While the houses were empty, we set fire to several farms. Barns, houses, fields, everything."

Claudia pictured the charred farmhouse below the Lady's cottage.

"One of the houses wasn't empty, unbeknownst to me," Pim continued. "A young woman was ill that night and didn't attend the concert. She slept in her bed. . . ."

Pim stared at his hands. "Her name was Emilie. I had seen her before in my wanderings. She was beautiful."

Claudia gasped. "Emilie? Cornelis's Emilie?"

"Yes." He nodded absentmindedly. No wonder the horseman hated Pim so much. "That night, it was as if someone held a mirror up to me. I saw what I had become. A monster worthy of Nee Gezicht's right hand. I hated that vision. I wanted to destroy myself. And I had the power to do so—but not the will. I could do nothing until my will belonged to me once more."

Pim closed his eyes. He breathed deeply, lips pursed and brow furrowed, as if in concentration. Then his chest began to glow with a bluish light just below his neck. An object followed the light, passing out of his chest and through his clothes as if the fabric was only a mirage. Pim held up his hand to catch the object, which hovered an inch above his palm.

Claudia's breath caught in her throat. She couldn't guess what the glowing object had once looked like. A glass teardrop, maybe, or a sphere the size of a golf ball. Now it was shards of broken blue glass smooshed together into a single clump, as if they were magnetically attracted to each other. Beautiful and tragic.

"It was whole once," Pim whispered. "My will. Never very strong, perhaps, but whole. I broke the pieces off by myself. Nee Gezicht took every shard I traded her and hid it here in the world behind the canvas, where it would never age, never deteriorate, but where she could draw from it always.

"After that night when Emilie died, I began searching. It took me years to find them all. And even more years to learn how to make them mine again. I started subtly at first, and she didn't notice for the longest time. Such pain. Incredible pain. And I had to sever my connection to all magic. But in the end, not long ago, I reclaimed the last piece of my will from her. It is fractured and weak, but it is mine."

Claudia studied Pim's face, illuminated softly by the glow of his will. "You mean Nee Gezicht doesn't . . . influence you . . . anymore?" A glimmer of hope kindled in her heart.

"No. Except that the very thought of her fuels my hatred."

Pim cupped his hand and pushed the shards of his will into his chest. It passed through without any resistance and disappeared.

"I cannot make complete recompense for all that I've done under her tutelage, but I can bring her down. Prevent her from committing more evil in this world or the other. And that is why I came to you."

"Me? What are you talking about?"

"I have no strength left. I can't fight her alone. Her magic still keeps me a prisoner here. And no one in this world will trust me. So I began watching through the window-paintings, searching for one person in particular."

"Who?"

"An *Artisti*."

She sat back in the chair. Rembrandt had said the same ridiculous thing about her. "But I'm not—"

"Of course you are. I had to observe you for a while, but it was very clear. I was hoping for a fully developed *Artisti*, naturally, but after getting to know you . . ." He smiled. "It's been a long time since I've made a friend, as you can imagine. I needed an *Artisti* who could help me cripple Nee Gezicht. When Granny Custos presented her plan, I knew my opportunity had come. To rob Nee Gezicht of her power. To break the thousands of spells she has intact in this world and the other. And if my freedom comes as a part of that, it will be a welcome release."

"But why would you think I'm an *Artisti*?"

"I've watched you draw, Claudia. It may not seem extraordinary to you, but you have a connection with your artwork that other artists don't have. It's easy to see and difficult to explain. But there is no doubt."

There were plenty of doubts. If she had access to magic, wouldn't she know it? If she was born with a connection to the magic behind the art, wouldn't she feel something? Wouldn't she have special powers? Wouldn't she be creating art that made people stop and stare in wonder?

She shook her head. An *Artisti*—impossible. But this wasn't about her. This was about someone she thought was her friend. Someone who had lied to her. Someone who had done evil things. Had caused a person's death here behind the canvas. Maybe more than one, who knew? How could she even trust the words he was speaking right now?

But if he *had* changed? What was it that Rembrandt said? Shades and hues and layers of brushstrokes . . .

"Claudia," he said. "I should not have deceived you. The things you have seen and heard about me since entering this world . . . I can only imagine what you must think of me. The good people of this world hate me. And they are right to. But to think I have hurt you—that pains me most. I don't deserve your help, and I will no longer ask for it."

His eyes probed hers. She wanted to trust him. But should she?

"Not everyone here hates you," she said. "Rembrandt, well, he said you weren't all bad. And the Lady—the Mona Lisa—she actually seemed to like you."

"You met the Lady?"

"Yeah, earlier today. When I was leaving, she said, well, she said to tell you that the answer to your question is *yes.*"

His face lit up. "She said that? Honestly?"

Claudia nodded. "What did you ask her?"

He jumped up and threw out his arms, laughing. "I can't believe it. My list of hurt against her pavilion is long. I visited her some time ago to ask if she would forgive me. She really said yes?"

"Really."

He laughed again. "I suddenly feel as light as air."

He looked completely different than he had moments ago. He looked like a boy. Like the boy in her painting in her bedroom. Could someone like him change completely?

But he hadn't changed. He'd lied to her to get her to come into this world to free him. Well, not to free him, really. To help make up for his mistakes.

If he had told the truth, would she have come? Probably not.

He was desperate. That was why he lied. He had no one else to turn to for help.

But that lie was tiny compared to the other things he'd done . . .

Could a person change that much? Just stop being the way he has been for so long?

Her heart told her, *Yes*.

And at the moment, that was the only thing she trusted.

She took a deep breath and stood. "All right, Pim. One more question. Is there anything else you haven't told me that you should have?"

He stepped closer to her and she didn't back away. "Only this. There is a window-painting northeast of the forest that will send you home. Allow me to escort you. I'll take you straight there."

"And you'll come home with me?"

He shook his head. "Not that way. Granny Custos is right about that. My will is my own now, but Nee Gezicht's magic keeps my body chained to this world. Her staff is the linchpin—the memory that keeps that spell and so many others in place. It must be broken before I can leave. And that is a task I will see completed, if it means my death."

"All right, then." A twinge of doubt still chafed her heart, adrenaline rushed through her veins, and a spark of hope lit in her mind. It was a strange and stirring combination. "Which way to Nee Gezicht's house?" Pim's face flooded with surprise. "But . . . you . . ."

"A friend needs my help." She shrugged. "I can't just go home."

He studied her, eyes wide. Then he leaped forward and wrapped his arms around her in a hug. She resisted for the briefest moment and then hugged him back.

It felt strange hugging a boy, even one who was almost four hundred years old. Finally they stepped back and looked at each other.

She gave him a tiny smile. "Let's go find that staff."

CHAPTER 19

WHILE THE Cubists' respect for Claudia seemed to have skyrocketed at the mention of Rembrandt, they were still reluctant to let her go.

"Have you ever considered a career in theater?" Pablo asked. "Next month we're starting work on our rendition of *Hamlet*. The entire first act will take place in a French bistro. Think of the possibilities. You'd make a smashing Ophelia." He moved uncomfortably close to Pim. "And you'd be my first choice for Hamlet's uncle. His sword fight at the end is *to die for*." Pablo grinned.

"Thanks, but we're heading south," Claudia said.

"Ah. In that case, you had better keep a careful eye on this one." Pablo gestured toward Pim. "His reputation for playing villainous characters is unparalleled."

"Show us how to get out of the forest," she said coldly. "Now."

Pablo eventually agreed, and—after several invitations to join the cast party—assigned the two harlequins to escort them to the Southern Exit. The entire group of Cubists gathered around and watched in eerie silence as she, Pim, and Cash plunged back into the forest.

The path leading out of the forest didn't look any different on the surface than the one leading in. But it *felt* different somehow. Less scary. Less hidden. Less . . . weird.

No, it's still weird. But maybe that's not such a bad thing.

They arrived at the edge of the forest much sooner than she expected. The shapeless opening was as bright as the sun on water and she had to squint as they approached. But as her eyes adjusted to the glaring daylight, her excitement at leaving the forest plummeted.

Desert.

Of course it was a desert—she knew that's what they were heading for. She'd even glimpsed it from the Lady's pavilion. But this . . . It filled her with the same taste of despair as the Fireside Angel's shriek, only more slowly.

Like a well-manicured lawn, the forest ended in a razor-straight line to the left and right as far as she could see. The desert started immediately—patches of dry, cracked earth intermixed with dunes of sand. Boulder gardens, some rising far above her head, dotted the landscape. Toward the horizon, a tower rose into the sky.

Claudia turned back to the harlequins. "Thank you . . ."

They were gone.

"Not much for good-byes, eh?" said Cash.

"They may seem like a ridiculous group of thespians," Pim said. "But they're actually the main intelligence branch of the underground resistance. They funnel all their information back to Rembrandt. That's why I came to them. They had a better chance of knowing where you were, Claudia, than anyone else."

Cash harrumphed. "Everyone's got a conspiracy theory."

Claudia took a hesitant step onto the crusty ground of the desert and looked over the barren scene. She fought at the hopelessness encroaching on her mind. Pim stepped up beside her.

"Hey . . . What did the painter say to his canvas?"

"What?"

"I got you covered."

"What's a pirate's favorite subject in school?" she asked.

"I don't know."

"Arrrrrrt."

They looked at each other and smiled.

"What is this, comedy hour?" Cash said. "We gonna stand here yukking it up, or are we gonna move?"

Pim pointed to the horizon.

"Those towers in the distance. That's where we're going."

Claudia nodded. It looked so far.

"Please tell me there's a beach on the other side of all this sand," Cash said. He looked as unsettled by the desert as Claudia felt.

She knelt down next to him. "You've already got a lot more out of today than you bargained for. Why don't you go back through the forest before it closes? I'm sure they'll help you through to the other side."

"Nah." He shook his head. "You may have buddied up to those crazies, but the feeling ain't mutual. I don't fancy the desert, but I sure don't want to get myself lost in that forest again. Besides, I can't leave a little lady alone out here with questionable company." His eyes flashed to Pim.

"All right, then," she said before Pim could respond. "Let's go."

"I got sand stuck between my toes. Do you know how uncomfortable that is?" Cash shuffled his feet, trying to wiggle his toes and walk at the same time.

Claudia had shoes on but agreed with the sentiment. It hadn't taken long for the desert to wear on her nerves. The great open expanse, the cracked earth, the stretches of sand that made her leg muscles burn.

"Nobody asked you to come along, puppy dog," Pim said with a glare.

"Oh, I'm sure you don't want me here," Cash retorted. "It's hard to keep company with a fella you owe money to. Where was it you lost all that dough to me? Phillies, wasn't it? And then your buddies showed up and—"

"So what are we going to find out there?" Claudia interrupted. Their bickering was as irritating as the sand.

"In that tower," Pim said, "we'll find the window into Nee Gezicht's manor home."

"Charming," Cash mumbled.

The dog was right—from here it didn't look like much, and what it did look like wasn't inviting. A thin building or a branchless tree, she couldn't tell.

They trudged through sandy terrain. The sun pounded on them, heating the air until it felt like they were baking inside a kiln. She wiped the sweat from her face with her shirtsleeve. Hopefully they would arrive at their destination before they became too crispy.

And as they walked through the heat, a single word rolled

over and over again in her mind. The name Pim had called her. *Artisti. Artisti. Artisti.* Finally it worked its way into a question.

"So, Pim, what do the *Artisti* actually do? I mean, Granny Custos talked about pillars and all that, but what do they *do?*"

"Well, that's hard for me to answer, since I've only really been an *Artisti* in this world. Here it manifests itself very differently. But even in the real world, it is distinct for every *Artisti*. For example, have you heard of the artist Mary Cassatt?"[24]

"I think so. Didn't she paint kids and moms and things like that?"

"Yes. She's the one. Nineteenth century. There's a story about her that goes like this. Cassatt was American, but she lived in Paris for much of her life. She had a good friend there whose little daughter became ill. At one point, the child's condition worsened, and the doctor said she wouldn't live through the week. When Cassatt heard that, she rushed to her studio and locked herself away. She painted furiously, weaving magic into a single painting. She emerged two days later, sleepless and weary, but she went straight to the home of her friend. She found the mother with her daughter—overjoyed. The girl was

---

24. MARY CASSATT (1844–1926). Mothers. Children. Mothers and children. Children and mothers. That's what most people think of when they hear the name Mary Cassatt. Do they think about the fact that she was an integral member of the Impressionist cadre in Paris? No. Do they consider that she had a longtime professional collaboration with Degas himself? Probably not. Do they even know that she was an influential figure in the women's suffrage movement? Unlikely. The focus is relentlessly on the latter part of her career, in which she almost exclusively painted scenes of a mother and child.

And yet that attraction makes sense. Cassatt was never a mother herself, but she captures beautifully the innocence of childhood and the necessary nurturing nature of mothers. It is a universal part of the human experience. Sentimental, perhaps, but it's enough to make even a stodgy old art historian just a little misty-eyed. After all—at some point in their life—everyone has a mother. (Excerpted from *Dr. Buckhardt's Art History for the Enthusiast and the Ignorant.*)

completely well and whole. The mother was sitting on the floor, bathing her daughter's feet. It was exactly the same scene Cassatt had been painting in her studio."

"Whoa. So she made the daughter better? Now, that's cool. Granny Custos made it sound like all they do is *influence* things."

"They do that, as well. Influence people and culture. Change the way they think or feel."

"That makes no sense."

"Well, think about this . . . Mary Cassatt infused all of her art with an aura of love and peace. She designed her paintings so that everywhere they are hung—even now, a hundred and fifty years later—they cast an influence of peaceful thought and feelings of goodwill. If you were to remove her paintings and bury them in the ocean, that influence would be gone and you would notice it. Violence and anger in the cities where those paintings hung would increase. The *Artisti* make a difference in the world—they are needed." Pim looked away into the desert. "How I wish I had followed that path."

Claudia brought her backpack up above her head to shield her eyes and thought for a while about Mary Cassatt. Finally she said, "Next question. Nee Gezicht has lived for so long because she sucks the life out of people's wills, right? Well, what about Granny Custos? I mean, you don't think she . . . sucks wills, too, do you?"

Pim's face glistened with sweat. "When I served Nee Gezicht, spying on one person or another through the window-paintings, she always had me searching for any sign of the Renaissance *Artisti*—the ones like her who created this world behind the canvas. I'd heard of Granny Custos, but I'd never seen her before we entered her house together."

"She didn't have any paintings in her house," Claudia said, thinking back to their evening with the old woman.

"Exactly. She knows there are threats that can emerge through a canvas, and she's careful not to expose herself to those threats." He wiped his face on his shirttail. "But in my wanderings, I heard rumors about *Artisti* who have separated themselves from their wills and hidden them here in the world behind the canvas. They are separated but remain tethered or anchored to their wills. Because things don't age here—at least not things from our world—their wills do not weaken or diminish. And therefore neither do the *Artisti*. It's just a rumor, but I suspect that is how Granny Custos has clung to life all these years."

"But if she can do that, why does Nee Gezicht need to reap wills? She could just do the same thing."

"Ah," Pim replied. "By separating yourself from your will, you lose your connection with magic."

"So you wouldn't really be an *Artisti* anymore?"

"You would not be able to access magic like an *Artisti*, no."

"But Granny Custos uses magic. She made the canvas-crossing ointment."

Pim smiled. "That wasn't magic. That was cooking. She just followed the recipe. Anyone could have done that."

"But . . ." Claudia's mental image of being sent to this world by a powerful magician deflated like a balloon. She was sent here by an eccentric chef who had hidden for ages from the roving eye of Nee Gezicht. If Granny Custos didn't have the guts or the power to take on Nee Gezicht, what did Claudia expect to do against the witch?

They marched on across the parched earth. Sweeping dunes

of sand (*Arabia,* she thought) intermixed randomly with stretches of red, hard-packed dirt (*Texas?*). They saw no sign of plants or animals until they came across a blindingly white cow skull resting freely on the ground. Several large, blossoming roses surrounded it, each cut at the stem and as white as chalk.[25]

Why hadn't the roses withered in the cruel sun? She bent low for a closer look. They appeared to be made of cloth, like something you would find at an arts and crafts store. She reached out to stroke the petals.

Pim's hand suddenly latched onto her wrist. "Let's not disturb that. Okay?" Pim pulled her forward and she reluctantly followed.

She glanced back at the mysterious arrangement. Did it mark a grave, the flowers placed by someone who cared? Or was it something else entirely? A warning, maybe, to those who were stupid enough to travel this direction.

They marched onward. Soon the tower—no, there were two of them—began to increase in size with every step. Enormous shadows stretched toward them across the sand like knobby fingers.

They were close enough now to make out details in the

---

25. GEORGIA O'KEEFFE (1887–1986). Some history books would have you believe that art has long been a man's game. There is no doubt that women artists are outrageously outnumbered in the opus of art history, but those women have had a definite impact through the centuries. And they haven't just created girly, lovey-dovey scenes with flowers and hearts and unicorns. In the seventeenth century Artemisia Gentileschi, for example, created a series of paintings of a woman chopping off the head of an evil general. In the twentieth century Meret Oppenheim created a virile, fur-covered cup and saucer for a Surrealist exhibition. And Georgia O'Keeffe, the Mother of American Modernism . . . well . . . okay, she painted flowers. Lots of them. And a few cow skulls. (Excerpted from *Dr. Buckhardt's Art History for the Enthusiast and the Ignorant.*)

towers. "The huge statues from the Dalí painting—back in Chicago. That's what they are, aren't they?" she said.

"Yes. *Archeological Reminiscence of Millet's 'Angelus,'*" Pim replied.

"They aren't any happier up close."

The towers took the forms of giant stone statues, decrepit and bowing slightly as if in prayer, just as she had seen in the Art Institute gallery. One had a long, thin neck and the other had no neck at all. They were featureless—not male or female, not young or old, void of faces—just outlines that suggested the human form. They were as tall as skyscrapers, and carrion birds circled their heads. It seemed ironic that figures bowed in prayer could send shivers down her back.

They came closer and closer until the structures loomed over them and the travelers plunged into the shadows. The relief from the sun felt good, but stepping into the ominous shadow made her skin crawl. At the base of the statues were other structures—arches and pointed domes—that might have been beautiful when they were first built. The stone was aged and crumbling, even blackened in some places, as if by fire. They passed through in silence.

At last they came to the base of the taller of the two towers, the one with the long neck. A wooden door was set into the stone. Like the towers, the door was weathered yet smooth from the windblown sand. A thick slope of sand was pushed halfway up the door, as though it was trying to keep the door from opening. As if it didn't want it to be discovered.

Pim stepped forward and grabbed a brass handle. It turned with a creak, but the door didn't move. He turned the handle again and this time threw his body against the door. It creaked louder but didn't budge. He stepped back for another go, and this time Cash charged at the door, too. They smashed into it together and it flew open, dust powdering the air. Pim and Cash tumbled into the opening.

Claudia hurried in and helped them to their feet. She looked around. The entryway opened into a small room with a stone floor and two sets of narrow stairs—one leading up and the other down. She carefully leaned over the wall of the twisted stairway going downward. The way became dark after the first few steps. But a faint light descended from the upward stairwell, illuminating the motes of dust hanging in the air. There was an eerie reverence about the place, like an abandoned cathedral.

Or a tomb.

"And I thought the Southern Forest gave me the willies," Cash muttered. He tucked his tail between his hind legs and flattened his ears against his head. "They got nothing on this place."

"Good," Pim said. "You can stay here and be the guard dog."

Claudia swatted at Pim. "You don't have to, Cash. You can come with us. It's okay."

"I'll stay. I like being where I can see the exit." Cash shot Pim a look. "I'll make sure no one tries to sneak out the back."

"Be more afraid of what might come through the other side of the door," Pim said. "If anything comes our way, let out a howl . . . or whatever it is you do."

"We'll be back soon," she added. *Maybe.*

Pim nodded toward the stairwell. "Up we go." He led the way and Claudia followed, glad they weren't taking the stairs heading downward. Somehow *up* seemed safer.

The spiral stairs, like the walls and the exterior of the statue, appeared to be carved from one enormous piece of brown stone. Thick veins of crystal ran through the walls, similar to the cave Claudia had come through the day before. Up she and Pim climbed without speaking, accompanied only by the sounds of their labored breathing and the grinding sand beneath their feet and . . . something else. A humming, like the wind or like people talking in the distance. And then they climbed a little higher, and it all made sense.

Window-paintings. Just like the ones in the cave. The first window they came to was dim, with barely enough light in the scene to make out a fancy living room beyond the etched image on the window. The second window showed the room of an ornate art museum, people filing by to stare at the painting. The windows lined the stone walls of the stairwell as far as she could see. An art gallery, a library, another art museum, a home. The muffled sounds of people and places on the other side echoed hauntingly through the stairwell.

Up and up they climbed. The window-paintings doused the stairs in multicolored rays of light, like a giant prism. Then Pim came to a stop and stared at a window-painting embedded in the wall. It was dark, like an empty well. Yet the canvas-textured glass had the faint etching of a woman with braided hair, holding what appeared to be a bowl of fruit.

No. A bowl of tomatoes.

"This is it," Pim said.

Of course it was. She felt it in the pit of her stomach before Pim even spoke the words. She reached her hand toward it but stopped short as something occurred to her.

"If Granny Custos doesn't have any paintings in her house,

why does Nee Gezicht?" she asked. "Isn't she afraid someone might, you know, come in and steal her staff or something?"

"She is indeed. There are two paintings into her manor. One hangs high above her fireplace. It's through that painting that I would speak with her when I . . . Anyway, that window-painting is found at the very top of this tower. You cannot appear in it without Nee Gezicht knowing, and it is protected—no one can enter with magic paste or otherwise."

"And this is the other? Why is it dark?" It was a question she wanted to whisper, but she raised her voice to be heard over the incessant ghostly murmurs from a thousand locations.

"The painting is buried away in her attic with mounds of other junk. It's been covered for centuries." The hope was plain on Pim's face. "I think she forgot about it a long time ago."

Claudia creased her eyebrows. "But it's not protected? It doesn't have an alarm on it?"

"She wasn't nearly as paranoid when she packed it away. She had fewer enemies back then. But I looked at it before I reclaimed my will—before I lost my connection to the magic. It was clean. We have to hope it still is."

The thought of being spit out of a dark painting with no idea of what's on the other side . . .

She brushed the window with her fingertips. Cold. Rough. This is what she had come for. To find what lay on the other side of this canvas. A flutter of fear ignited in her stomach and she tried to quench it. She had faced a dragon, the Fireside Angel, and two near-executions. There wasn't anything more to be scared of, was there?

"What if she's there?" she asked. "What if she's there in her house? What do I do?"

"She won't be. I looked through the other painting earlier. I've also made a few . . . inquiries with some old acquaintances. Nee Gezicht is traveling. Now's the perfect time."

"Old acquaintances?"

Pim smiled wryly. "The Cubists aren't the only ones with a good intelligence network."

"Right." *See? Nothing to worry about.* "Okay. A staff."

"Black walnut."

"Right."

"Gnarled. About a meter and a half long."

"Um . . . how long is that?"

"Four and a half feet."

"Right. Wait . . . won't she have it with her?"

Pim shook his head. "No, she used to travel with it but not anymore. Her *raccolta* keeps spells and enchantments in place— thousands of them. And each one adds weight to the staff. After a while, it just became too heavy to carry around. It's in her house. Somewhere. I think."

"Right." The house strangers aren't supposed to be able to enter. She opened her backpack and pulled out the mustard bottle. "Right." Why did she keep saying that? It sounded so stupid. And nervous. She twisted the lid and pointed it at her hand.

Pim placed his hand on hers and she looked up. She couldn't remember a boy ever putting his hand on hers before.

"If you don't wish to do this," Pim said, "even now I will gladly lead you back to your own window."

Her own window. Home. It would be easier that way. But she had seen too much. "Nee Gezicht can still hurt a lot of people, can't she?"

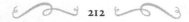

"Yes. She can."

"And there's no other way for you to escape."

Pim was silent.

His hand felt so warm on hers.

"Right," she said. *Ugh.* "I mean, I'm going in. Your job is to figure how to get us home when I come back."

Pim flashed a smile as warm as his hand. "Thank you, Claudia."

She squirted the cool paste onto her palm, carefully outlining her hand without using any more than necessary. There were still several trips in their travel plans.

Pim took the bottle and zipped it up in her backpack. She turned with a courage that she didn't really feel and faced the darkened window.

Then she gently placed her hand on the glass-canvas surface.

CHAPTER 20

CLAUDIA TUMBLED, turned, fell, and soared. Then with an intense warmth, a million little hands pushed her forward, out of the world behind the canvas. She found herself lying face-down on a cold, hard floor.

She gasped and dust filled her lungs, making her cough. But the dust on her tongue tasted like dust and not paint. Something large and light rubbed against her backpack and legs. She rolled over to find a large framed canvas practically on top of her.

It must have been facedown on the floor. That's why the window looked dark.

She pushed it up and came face-to-face with a fair-haired woman, practically life-size, painted against a backdrop of tomato vines. The woman was gorgeous—the shine in her hair and the perfection of her face were magazine model–worthy. But one eye was hard and cold, void of emotion. The other was covered with a black satin eye patch strapped to her head with a leather band. The silk-and-taffeta dress and the bowl of tomatoes placed the artwork immediately in Claudia's mind.

Pim's first story may have been a lie, but Verspronck's painting wasn't. This had to be Nee Gezicht, several hundred years ago.

Claudia stared into the painted eye a moment longer, trying to ignore the fear clenching her throat. Then Pim's face appeared in the background of the painting. He nodded encouragingly.

She scrambled to her feet and propped the painting against a wall. She looked around. Dusty wooden floors and a vaulted ceiling with exposed rafters made up an enormous attic the size of a school gym. It was like a warehouse crammed full of . . . everything. From an ancient spinning wheel in one corner to a grandfather clock in another, heaps of stuff surrounded her. The floor was completely covered—there wasn't a clear path to be seen. Dim light issued through several tiny circular windows near the ceiling on the far wall. Dusk or dawn, perhaps.

She looked at the mounds of junk again. "It could be anywhere. Where do I start?"

Pim chewed his lip in thought. "Not here," he whispered. "She would need to access it on occasion. Start downstairs."

"Right." She scanned the walls of the attic. There had to be . . . there. A door set into the far wall. "I'll be back."

She picked her way through wooden crates and furniture covered with drop cloths, stepping softly so as not to make a sound on the planked floor. Pim seemed certain no one was home, but still . . . She paused to glance at a horde of hideous gnomes with deformed faces cut from stone. A chill passed down her back. She climbed over an ancient printing press and bruised her shin against an anvil.

She arrived at the door, dust covering her hands and jeans. The wooden door was barely taller than she was, and the edges weren't square but came together at odd angles. A heap of junk pushed up against the bottom half of the door. She reached for the handle—an ugly brass gnome head with a tongue sticking out and eyes squeezed tight. Wincing at the thought of touching it, she took it in her fingers and twisted the knob.

The latch clicked and the door swung forcefully outward. Too late she realized that the weight of the rubbish by the door was leaning against it. She leaped to catch it, but a wooden crate toppled forward and crashed down the stairs, smashing glass plates and bowls in all directions. The echoing din faded to a tinkling as the pieces scattered down the wooden stairs and came to rest.

Claudia felt her heart stop. It didn't matter how big this house was—anyone, anywhere within its walls would have heard that. If Nee Gezicht was in the house, then the element of surprise had just been lost. Big-time.

Then she noticed she wasn't alone. At the bottom of the steep stairs, a few shards of glass surrounding it, was a cat. It was orange and enormous, with a sleek tail that whisked lazily from side to side. It looked up at Claudia with mismatched eyes, one white and scarred, the other green and glistening.

She hadn't seen it come into the stairwell. Had it been there before she opened the door? Or had her incredibly discreet entrance attracted it? Or did it just magically appear when needed to prevent intruders from coming and, say, stealing a staff?

The cat leaped to the first step, then the second. Scars gouged its beautiful coat in several places, and its spiked claws clacked on the wooden stairs.

Claudia hissed and flung her arms to shoo it away.

The cat tensed and growled low in its throat.

"Go on!" she whispered.

The cat snarled and leaped back. Then it turned and stared at her again with its wide, mismatched eyes before slinking around the corner.

She let the cat escape from sight before taking a deep breath and straining to hear any sound in the house below her. Silence. Pim said Nee Gezicht wasn't there—and he wouldn't be wrong about such a crucial part of the plan, right? She thought about the snarling cat again and her stomach twisted.

It's a cat, she told herself. She stepped forward.

Like the doorway out of the attic, the stairs were crooked—constructed at odd angles and varying sizes. It was like walking down a squarish, frozen waterfall. Her sneakers scuffed softly as they touched the wood, but the stairs didn't release a single creak.

The stairway led to a small windowless foyer. A pedestal rose up directly in front of her, topped by an old-fashioned black phone with a red lobster as a handset. The foyer branched off into three hallways with white walls and hardwood floors.

Walking past the bizarre phone (*Really? A lobster?*) she studied the hallways. They looked similar, and each angled off within a few paces, hiding their destinations. On the floor of the hallway to the left, however, were painted large blue human footprints.

Why footprints? Would they lead to the staff, or to someplace she didn't want to go? Or were they simply another oddity, like the uneven stairs and lobster phone?

At the moment, it was all she had to go on. She followed the footprints.

The hallway was dim, but there was enough light to see that

the walls and ceiling were covered in ink drawings. Complex murals with scenery and creatures and people that went on and on, stretching the length of the twisted hallway like tattoos on the flesh of the house. It finally opened up into a living room, richly decorated and crammed with furniture.

Claudia pressed herself against the wall of the hallway and scanned the room. There was no sign of anyone. Or the cat. She moved quietly forward.

A large fireplace mantel, much taller than Claudia, marked the head of the room. But a brick wall stood where the logs and fire should have been, and from the bricks protruded the front end of a smoking steam engine. The smoke dissipated toward the ceiling, lending a soft haze to the entire room. It looked vaguely familiar—maybe something from an art book. The term *Surrealism* came to mind. She didn't know much about Surrealism, except that it was even stranger than Cubism, if that was possible.

A painting hung high on the wall above the fireplace mantel, portraying a distorted laughing face amid a wash of color. Its frame was formed by rough wooden boughs, like something you might see in a log cabin. Two plush couches stretched out across from each other in the center of the room. One was shaped like a dark, full pair of red lips. The other took the form of a hot dog, complete with mustard and pickle relish pillows.

Other bizarre decorations filled out the room. Marble figures with rearranged body parts. A bicycle wheel stuck upside down on a wooden stool. A solid metal clothes iron with spikes protruding from its flat surface. An old-fashioned pot-bellied stove in the corner almost looked normal compared to everything around it.

And I thought the world behind the canvas was weird.

But there was no sign of the staff.

On the far wall hung a canvas in a glossy black frame. It held another portrait of Nee Gezicht, similar to the one in the attic but taller, almost touching the floor. Strange, since Pim had said there were only two paintings in the house. Claudia crossed the room for a closer look.

The detail and depth of the painting was incredible. Which master had painted this one? Perhaps Verspronck—Nee Gezicht looked about as young here as she did in the painting in the attic. Her golden hair was glossy and pulled up in intricate loops and braids around her head, each hair painted in fine detail. Her smooth skin had a soft glow, and her black silky gown flowed around her body like water. And the eyes . . .

Claudia gasped. The eye patch was gone. The witch's right eye was hard and cold and dark like the one in the attic painting. But the left eye was green, completely green, with a long slitted pupil, like a snake. Or a cat.

The cat on the stairs had eyes like that. Mismatched. There were others, too, weren't there? In the world behind the canvas? Yes . . . the Saint Bernard who had wanted to follow her and Cash. What else? The dragon? No . . . the bird, after the fight with the dragon. Its eyes were just like that. But why?

She stepped closer to the painting, transfixed by the eyes staring back at her in painted perfection.

The eyes blinked.

Claudia shrieked and stumbled backward. The painted Nee Gezicht grinned and swayed fluidly in the canvas. And then she stepped *forward*. Her black high-heeled boot passed over the frame, transforming from a painted canvas texture until it touched the floor. The other foot followed, and Nee Gezicht stood there in the flesh, her left hand clutching a straight staff of polished dark-yellow wood.

The staff came down to the floor with a cracking *thud*. The full gaze of her mismatched eyes turned on Claudia, who scrambled to her feet.

"*Goedemorgen. Welkom op mijn huis.*" Nee Gezicht spoke the words with a slight bow and a grin, like a Dutch spider might to a fly.

Run! Run! Run! Claudia's mind screamed the words. But to where? Could she really make it back through the attic before Nee Gezicht turned her into a . . . whatever?

"*Spreek je Nederlands?*" the woman asked, her grin spreading wider.

"I don't speak D-Dutch," Claudia stammered.

Nee Gezicht's eyebrows lifted slightly. "English. British?" She spoke with a strong accent and a condescending tone.

Claudia shook her head. "American." She was reining in her mind, tamping out her panic as she might a fire in the grass. She couldn't run, so she'd have to make do with what she had . . . which wasn't much. At least now she knew where the staff was.

Nee Gezicht nodded. "Good. And tell me, child, how I came to have the privilege of your unexpected visit to my home." The grin stayed on the woman's face.

"I . . ." Claudia forced a swallow. "I'm here on vacation with my parents. We're touring Holland. I thought this was a museum and just kind of let myself in." She cringed inside. Even on a good day that would have sounded lame.

"A museum? How charming. What is your name, dear?"

"Claudia." Again she cringed. Wasn't there something about not giving your real name away to a witch?

"And where are your parents?"

"Oh, they're outside. They're probably looking for me right now. I'm so sorry I came into your house without permission. I'll go now." If she could get away from Nee Gezicht, perhaps there was a chance. . . . She glanced around the room, but the only exit was the hallway she had come through. At the entry-way sat the large orange cat. It hissed a warning, and the hairs on the back of Claudia's neck told her to take it seriously.

I'm trapped.

Nee Gezicht finally dropped her grin. "Tsk, tsk, tsk," she chided with pursed lips. "You know, child, there was a time when all Dutch witches spoke only in rhyme to common folk and enemies, and in plain Dutch only to friends." She sauntered over to a rolltop desk and produced a key from within the folds of her gown. "It wasn't hard to do, because in Dutch everything sounds like you're clearing your throat, so most everything rhymes. But I never could quite get the hang of it in English." She slipped the key into the lock at the base of the tambour and turned it with a *click*.

"So tell me, Claudia, should I be speaking in rhyme with you?" Nee Gezicht lifted the handle of the tambour and rolled up the top of the desk.

There were eyes, lots of them. The desk held rows and rows of eyeballs, round and glistening, each sitting on a tiny saucer of fluid and lined up on racks like the spices in her mom's kitchen. As the tambour rolled back into the desk, the pupils collectively dilated.

Claudia choked on a cry.

Each of the eyeballs swiveled in unison in Claudia's direction. She had never felt so exposed before. Some of the eyeballs were distinctly human, while others were obviously from other creatures.

"Now, now, don't stare at our guest." Nee Gezicht waved her hand at the contents of the desk, and some of the eyeballs looked away. She reached up to her slitted green eye. "You must excuse me, but it gets tiresome having the same one in for so long. I'm sure you understand."

Nausea washed over Claudia and she stared at the floor. *Please don't throw up. Not here.*

A sucking sound was followed by a *pop*. Claudia involuntarily looked up to see the witch placing the eyeball in a tiny vacant saucer on the rack. Nee Gezicht glanced in her direction, one eye white and alert, the other closed and sunken. She turned back to the rack.

"Let me see . . ." Nee Gezicht's hand hovered over the rows of eyes, as though divining which would suit her best. Finally she selected one that was orange and wide, and she brought it carefully to her face.

Claudia looked away again.

"You will find it very useful, child"—*pop, squish*—"to be able to see things others can't. Vision is a glorious device."

Nee Gezicht blinked several times and flashed a smile at Claudia both sweet and malicious, like a poisoned kiss.

"For example," she continued, "even though I was a thousand miles away, I saw you step out of my attic."

The cat in the entryway hissed again. So Claudia's gut feeling about the cat had been right.

"Well, I . . ."

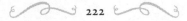

"This house is protected from the outside by a dozen different enchantments, making it impossible for tourists or anyone else to wander, break, or force their way in. And your hand holds the faint, glistening residue of canvas-crossing ointment, which, I admit, I haven't seen for decades."

Claudia glanced at her hand. Perhaps there was a faint shimmer.

"Now, the painting above the mantel cannot be crossed; I saw to that a long time ago. And my personal doorway"—she gestured to the empty painting she had stepped through—"can only be crossed by me." Nee Gezicht placed both hands on her staff and leaned gently forward. "So why don't you tell me, Claudia, how you came into my house. And why."

Claudia was at the end of her rope. However fast she ran, either the witch or the wild cat would get her before she could make it to the painting in the attic.

Despair filled her, as if the Fireside Angel were howling in her ear.

"Oh!" Nee Gezicht exclaimed. "My old portrait. You must have come through that old portrait. Is it still stashed away in the mess up there?"

Claudia's thoughts whipped through her mind.

What do you need?

I need to get that staff and get out of this house. If not through a painting, then at least through the front door.

What does Nee Gezicht want?

She wants wills. Other people's wills make her stronger. The wills of Artisti.

What should you do?

Be normal. Boring. Not a threat and certainly not interesting.

Dang it. You've never been any good at being normal.

Claudia focused again on the elegant woman in the black dress and cleared her throat. Her mind raced to recall what Cash had said about a poker face. Shoulders relaxed. Concentrate on your breathing. No nervous tics.

"Yes, you're right," Claudia said. "I have a friend. She says she's a kind of witch. She makes her magic through art. Or so she said. I didn't believe her. So she gave me this potion and told me to put it on my hand and then put it against a painting and it would take me to a whole new world. And it worked! It was amazing! I came back to find the painting I'd come through, and I thought it was the one in your attic. But . . . I guess not. I'm really sorry to bother you."

There. That was about as boring as she could make herself sound after having come through a painting.

She watched the witch's mismatched eyes.

Nee Gezicht held Claudia's gaze firmly, until finally the wicked smile reappeared on her face. "You're not a bother at all. In fact, I adore company. Why don't you stay for a cup of tea before you continue on your journey?"

"No. No, I really need to get going. I'm late enough as it is." Claudia tried to keep the panic out of her voice.

"Ah, but I insist. Besides, you've come to the right place. I would be delighted to help you return to your painting. I'm something of an expert in crossing the canvas, as you may have guessed." She waved toward the dark canvas she had appeared in moments ago. "Please. Stay for tea."

Nee Gezicht turned and glided over to the black stove in the corner of the room.

This woman was evil—Claudia's mind told her so.

Screamed it at her. But the witch's invitation . . . The words seemed to wrap themselves like webs around something deep inside Claudia and gently pull. There was a part of her that *wanted* to stay for tea.

The feeling terrified her. She had no idea where it came from. Still, staying for tea might be the easiest way to get out safely. "Okay. I need to go soon, though. My friend will be getting worried about me."

"Ah, yes, your friend." Nee Gezicht busied herself at the stove. "She does magic, does she? With art?"

"Uh, yeah. I suppose so."

"Good for her. There are so few of us these days who still practice. Perhaps you can introduce us. Is she a natural artist? Does she have an extraordinary talent for it?"

Claudia shuffled her feet. How far should she take her story? She couldn't let Nee Gezicht suspect that Granny Custos was involved. "Oh, I don't know about special. I mean, she's young, she's my age. But . . . she's just okay, I guess."

"And . . . what about you?" Nee Gezicht cast a sideways glance with her orange eye. "Do you practice?"

In other words, am I an Artisti whose will you can suck dry? "Me? Oh, no. No, no, no. I'm not that type." Claudia shrugged her shoulders and forced a smile, fighting the panic in her chest. "I'm just . . . normal."

"Well, you never know when hidden talents might float to the surface. Please, sit." She gestured to the odd couches.

Claudia walked slowly over to the couch shaped like a pair of red lips. She hesitated, unsure exactly how to sit on a pair of lips. She slipped off her backpack and lowered herself right in the middle of the couch.

Nee Gezicht had leaned her staff against the wall across the room. Claudia studied it longingly, knowing that there was no way to get out of the house with the staff now. She would be lucky to get out at all.

She glanced up to see Nee Gezicht watching her. *Does she think I'm an* Artisti*?*

"Did you decorate this house yourself?" Claudia said quickly with a glance around the room. "You must like art a lot."

Nee Gezicht carried a china cup and saucer over to Claudia and placed it on the coffee table in front of her.

"Most art I find repulsive. Vulgar. Void. Still, on occasion an artist will strike my fancy. Have you heard of Hieronymus Bosch,[26] for example? He painted scenes of people being thrust down to the fiery monsters of hell. Now, there was an artist with creative vision."

Claudia tried not to shudder.

Nee Gezicht sauntered to the stove and returned with her own cup of tea. She sat on the hot dog couch across from Claudia. The witch's cup and saucer—including the part that held the tea—were made entirely of fur.

Claudia suppressed a gag and looked away.

---

26. HIERONYMUS BOSCH (ca. 1450–1516). At first glance, you might mistake Bosch's works for those created by the Surrealists. Bosch, however, was painting bizarre beasts in baffling backdrops more than 400 years before those dilettantes. And Bosch's paintings were rich with religious symbolism and allusion. He is well-known for his triptychs, in which three paintings are hinged together like shutters on a window. The sprawling paintings often told a story, moving from happy and holy on the left to dark and devilish on the right, with plenty of frolicking and naughtiness in the middle. The moral of the story is clear: Be good in this life or a demon will swallow you whole in the next. So effective are the paintings that my mother didn't need to take me to Sunday school as a lad—she just stuck me in front of a Bosch once a week and I was puritanical for life. (Excerpted from *Dr. Buckhardt's Art History for the Enthusiast and the Ignorant.*)

"Please do try your tea. It's best when hot." Nee Gezicht sipped from the furry cup.

Claudia reluctantly picked up the cup and saucer. What was she going to do now? She'd always been told never to accept food and drink from strangers, and she was pretty sure that included will-sucking *Artisti* witches. Would Nee Gezicht have poisoned it? Did she even need to? If she wanted to do something to Claudia, couldn't she just cast a spell? Claudia wished someone had given a little more information on the whole *Artisti* thing.

The steam from the teacup held a woody scent. The liquid inside was a rich caramel color.

"What kind of tea is it?" Claudia asked.

"I make it myself. From trees in my garden. It's called witch hazel."

Witch hazel? That sounded familiar somehow. "It smells good. I'm just not much of a tea drinker myself. I have a weak stomach."

"I've never met a person who didn't like my witch hazel tea. And I assure you, it's very soothing on the stomach." Nee Gezicht's voice had a sudden edge to it. She sipped her tea.

The air was quickly becoming heavier. Claudia stared at the tea she held in her lap. The cat hissed from the doorway.

"Claudia, it is not wise to insult an old *Artisti* by refusing to try her tea." Nee Gezicht smiled, but her stare had hardened. Claudia felt as though she were sitting in front of a cobra that had risen to full height. "Taste it."

Again, the witch's words wrapped themselves around a piece of Claudia and tugged. A part of her *wanted* to taste the tea. Besides, poisoned tea or not, she was out of options. She lifted the china cup to her lips.

A tiny sip of scalding-hot liquid passed over her tongue and slid down her throat.

Nee Gezicht smiled.

"Claudia, stop!"

The familiar voice came from somewhere in the room.

Pim! Relief and terror washed over Claudia in torrents. Her gaze shot around the room, frantically looking for Pim. He had come for her! But that meant that Nee Gezicht would discover the truth.

There would be no escape now.

The witch was on her feet, staring at the painting above the fireplace. The painting of the grotesque face and—

Pim.

"Don't drink it, Claudia!" Pim shouted. "Not yet."

"Pim." Nee Gezicht's face showed pure astonishment. "I must say—you do know how to surprise a girl."

"She's not yours yet, Nee Gezicht," Pim said. His expression was smug, and his voice was thick with confidence. "Not until you hold up your end of our bargain."

"Bargain?" Nee Gezicht smoothed the immaculate black cloth of her dress. "It's been a while since we've spoken. You will need to refresh my memory."

Pim pressed his hands against the window-canvas. "You gave me your oath, old woman. You said if I brought you a young *Artisti*—someone to take my place—that you would let me go. You would release me from this world." His eyes shone savagely and flicked to Claudia. "Well, there she is. I've led her right into your living room."

The words sucked the air from Claudia's lungs, as if she had jumped into ice water. The cup and saucer fell from her trembling hands and shattered on the wooden floor.

How could this be?

After all she'd done . . . After all he'd promised . . . After all she'd trusted . . .

After it all . . . she had been played.

Deceived.

Betrayed.

CHAPTER 21

CLAUDIA'S MIND whirled, yet she stood motionless in the eye of the storm. She couldn't feel her limbs. She was vaguely aware of standing up, stepping forward. If there was a world around her, she was oblivious to it. Her only clear vision was of Pim, hands pressed against the window-canvas of the painting on the wall. Pim the liar. The deceiver. He wouldn't even look her way.

"An *Artisti*!" She heard Nee Gezicht's ravenous voice through the din in her head. "I suspected she might be. Another few minutes, of course, and I would have discovered it for myself."

"You'll need more than a cup of tea to reap her will," Pim said. "She's a strong one."

Still he didn't look at her. The tempest inside Claudia took form and shape and slowly began to aim itself at Pim. Less than two hours ago he had been baring his soul to her, telling her everything, coming clean. Now he was selling her to the witch. How could he do this?

"And so young," Nee Gezicht replied. "As young as you were, Pim."

"Yes. And *I* brought her here. You took an oath. And not even someone with a heart as black as yours would dare break it. Set me free."

Claudia had come here to help him fight against Nee Gezicht. It had been a trap all along.

"And just in time, too," Nee Gezicht continued, walking in a slow circle around Claudia. "My bones have ached ever since you left, Pim. But we're advancing on the Southern Tier in a week, and I'll need to feel fresh if I'm going to join in the fun." She paused and looked at Pim. "We could still use you, if you cared for a part."

Pim offered only a cold stare.

Nee Gezicht shrugged. "I'll honor the oath. But not until I reap her will. I need to prove the goods, boy, before I can pay for them."

"Then hurry up and do it. You'll need charcoal. And iron-weed, freshly picked."

Claudia's heart pounded. The witch was going to take her will. She would be a prisoner, trapped in the world behind the canvas, like Pim. She would never close her eyes in sleep. She would never taste real food. She would never see her family again.

Nee Gezicht leaned in close and Claudia jerked backward, ready to push, slap, scratch—anything she needed to do to get away from that evil woman. But with the witch's head turned, Pim finally locked eyes with Claudia. His wild, smug mask fell away, replaced by a look of terror and desperation. What did that mean? Was he afraid of the witch, too?

Nee Gezicht's words were low in her ear. "You have sipped my tea, Claudia. That means the reaping of your will has already started. You can't help but follow my every command. My command is this: Don't move from this spot until I return. And don't worry, dear. When this is all over, you won't feel a thing."

Claudia had sensed a tugging before when the woman told her to do something. But now icy fingers wrapped themselves around something inside of her. That something controlled her feet, and suddenly her feet wouldn't move. She tried to leap away, to run to the hallway and up the stairs and through the attic and out the painting—but her feet held fast as though superglued to the floor.

Nee Gezicht patted her on the head. Claudia didn't flinch— how was this happening? The witch turned to the wall behind her and grabbed the staff.

Winds of fear joined the storm in Claudia's head. She turned to see Nee Gezicht move toward the dark canvas on the wall. The witch looked at her cat, still in the doorway across the room.

"Keep an eye on them, Francis. I'll be back shortly." Then, staff in hand, she stepped through the canvas and was gone.

The storm inside Claudia broke the moment Nee Gezicht disappeared.

"How could you!" she yelled at Pim.

"Claudia—"

"I trusted you!" She picked up the furry teacup from the table and hurled it toward the painting. It fell short and scattered across the floor.

"Claudia, I—"

"No one else did, Pim. Nobody but me." She reached for a pickle relish pillow from the couch and threw it after the teacup.

"Listen to me!"

"No, you listen to me, you piece of . . . of . . . trash!"

"Claudia, shut up and listen!"

There was desperation in his voice. She looked around for something else to throw.

"I'm sorry. I'm so sorry. But I said those things just to get her out of the house. There was no other way." His painted blue eyes pleaded with her.

The storm inside her faltered but continued to blow.

"I don't know how to trust you anymore, Pim," she said.

"For now you just need to trust me more than you trust her." He pointed toward Nee Gezicht's darkened canvas. "How much tea did you drink?"

"What?"

"The tea, Claudia, how much did you drink?" he snapped.

"Just a sip."

"Then you have a chance. The tea is a temporary binder and it's weak. She thinks it will hold you, but she doesn't know how strong you are. I do."

The storm in her head was now a buzz of confusion. What did Pim know? He only cared about himself. About Nee Gezicht's staff, which had gone with her through the painting anyway. "My feet are stuck! I can't move my feet!" she shouted angrily.

"You still own your will, Claudia. Not her."

A fierce hiss came from behind. The cat bolted toward Pim's painting.

He glanced at the cat and spoke quickly. "Look inside your-self. Take control."

The cat leaped onto an armchair, then onto a stone statue by the fireplace mantel.

"I know you can do it," Pim shouted. "Get upstairs to the other painting."

Claws extended, the cat lunged in an upward arc and slammed into the painting. It hissed and snarled as fore claws slashed pell-mell, tearing at the canvas and rattling the frame. Within seconds, the picture hung in shreds. By the time the cat landed gracefully on the floor, it was obvious why Nee Gezicht had chosen it to guard her house.

The cat flexed its claws and hissed in Claudia's direction.

But her eyes sprang back to the painting. Or rather, the frame. It was made out of a dark, coarse wood, like thick boughs of a tree attached at rough corners. Except that one long side wasn't completely attached. The cat's slashing must have knocked it loose, because now it hung at a skewed angle. It was a slightly darker shade than the others, and one end seemed smooth and shiny, as if years of handling had polished it.

It was just the right size for a short walking staff.

A meter and a half.

And a dark wood.

Claudia didn't know what walnut wood looked like, but she didn't think it was yellow.

The staff in Nee Gezicht's hand had been yellow.

And longer than a meter and a half.

This was it. This was what they had come for!

No, this is what *she* had come for. Pim had come to help *her*. Hadn't he? He had made a bargain. He could have traded her for his freedom. But he hadn't. Her friend had come to help her.

And he knew she could do it.

I *know I can do it.*

She tore her gaze away from the staff on the wall. She strained at her feet, trying to force them to move, commanding her legs to take a step forward. She reached down and pulled at her knee, but the muscles in her leg kept the foot pressed tightly against the floor.

I am in control, she told herself.

She turned her attention to the icy hand holding on to something inside her—holding on to her will.

I am in control.

One at a time, she visualized prying back the fingers from the glowing blue orb inside her own chest. Her legs tingled.

I am in control.

She strained to peel back the last icy finger from the will inside of her, and she stumbled forward onto all fours. She scrambled to her feet, breathing hard with relief.

The cat stopped its pacing in front of the fireplace and hissed at her.

She grabbed the mustard pillow from the hot dog couch. "Back off."

The cat hissed again and charged, leaping through the air, claws extended. Claudia swung the pillow like a baseball bat and sent the cat flying into the couch.

She shot a glance at the fireplace mantel. The painting was high out of reach, but there had to be some way to scale up and grab the staff.

Twisting off its back, the cat jumped from the couch and

scampered to position itself between Claudia and the fireplace. It bared its teeth and grinned. And then the grin became wider.

And wider. The cat's entire head stretched lengthwise until it was twice the width. Wicked teeth filled its mouth like the smile of a demented Cheshire cat.

And it wasn't just the cat's head. Its legs grew longer until they looked gangly on the cat's body. The rear haunches thickened with muscular power. The claws extended into razor knives and its tail whipped in warning. Bones pushed against its skin as though now too long for its body. It looked like a baby tiger that had been twisted and pulled into a grotesque beast the size of a large dog.

Claudia couldn't believe it. This was the real world. Strange creatures existed behind the canvas, not here. What kind of bizarre magic was Nee Gezicht capable of?

She would have to fight it if she was going to escape. And if she was going to escape, the staff was coming with her.

She cast around for a weapon—something harder than the mustard pillow. Knickknacks and sculptures lined the room, but her backpack was the only item within reach. And it held nothing but nail polish and a book and—

The cat stepped toward her with a snarl.

She snatched up her backpack and retreated behind the couch.

Her small painting. The one Pim had appeared in. If only she could escape through it. But Granny Custos said it was too small. Her head would get stuck.

The beast crept toward her, keeping low as if stalking its prey.

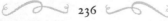

Where were the three Dutchmen when you needed them?

She frantically shifted to keep the hot dog couch between her and the cat. She was close to the wall now and she grabbed the spiked iron off a shelf, hefting it toward the beast. It was heavier than it looked and it fell short, smashing into the coffee table.

The cat bared its vicious teeth in a grin.

Then a crazy idea struck. What if it wasn't she who went through the small painting? What if it was something else?

She opened her backpack.

The monster leaped. Claudia yelped and scrambled to the side. It cleared the couch and closed the distance between them in a single movement. She ran, throwing down obstacles behind her. A chair, a sculpture, the stool with the bicycle wheel sticking out of the top.

There was the sound of clanging metal behind her followed by a snarl. The cat must have snagged the wheel. Claudia slid to the ground behind the lips couch and tore into her backpack.

The painting. The mustard bottle. She twisted open the bottle and squeezed a thin layer of paste quickly onto the painting, desperately hoping she didn't get sucked in by mistake. She dropped the bottle and held the picture frame with both hands.

The room was silent except for the metallic scrape of a slowly spinning bicycle wheel.

She waited, heart thumping. Still nothing. The silence was terrifying. Had it disappeared? Shrunk back down to normal size?

And then it was there, rounding the corner of the couch, jaws gaping, teeth bared, claws springing toward her.

She shrieked and held up the painting in front of her like a shield. The cat's deadly claw slammed against the canvas. Faint rays of light emanated from the painting as the cat crashed into her.

Claudia pushed the painting away and scrambled back. The cat twisted, writhing on the floor. One foreleg had disappeared completely into the painting. Its face pressed up against the frame as though something was yanking on its leg—only a head away from entering the canvas completely.

No time to waste. She snatched up the mustard bottle and backpack and tore off toward the fireplace.

She shoved the armchair closer to the fireplace and climbed up the back as the cat yowled. She teetered on top of the chair, fighting for balance, but gravity won and the chair tipped backward. She launched herself for the mantel. Her chest slammed into the edge of it, stealing her breath. She grasped the mantel with her arms, wheeling her legs to find purchase until her foot connected with the molding along the fireplace. Knickknacks scattered as she pushed herself up onto the mantel.

Her fingers pressed against the wall as she scooted along the narrow ledge. Then the shredded painting was in front of her. Up close it was easier to see that the askew part of the frame was a different color than the rest of the wood. She grasped it with both hands and pulled.

With a *crack*, the staff came away more easily than expected. The force of her pull and the weight of the staff carried her backward and she tumbled through the air, landing with a *thud* on the hardwood floor.

She groaned and forced herself to her feet. She wouldn't be sitting anytime soon, but nothing seemed broken.

Beside her lay Nee Gezicht's staff.

She bent down to pick it up. Pim was right—it was remarkably heavy, as though it was made from steel instead of wood. She lifted one end and held it tight.

She dragged the staff toward the hallway. Nee Gezicht's canvas on the other side of the room was dark and empty. The cat lay on the floor, its leg still in the painting but not as deep as before. Its other forepaw pressed against the frame and—bit by bit—it was pulling itself free.

Time to go.

She plunged into the long tattooed hallway. The heavy staff left a scraping trail on the blue footprints behind her. She ran through the foyer and started up the uneven stairs, straining to pull the staff up each stair.

Claws scrabbled across the floor in the distance. She looked back as she reached the top of the stairs. The cat tore into the stairwell—all four clawed feet free and threatening.

The cat hissed and leaped upward.

She tried to pull the attic door closed, but wooden crates blocked its path and the cat was moving quickly. She left the door and dived into the maze of attic clutter. The windows were dark now. The only light came from the doorway, and she squinted to make out the painting on the far side.

A violent growl. The cat was in the attic. She ducked low. She could try hiding, waiting it out. But cats could see in the dark, couldn't they? And Nee Gezicht would be back any minute. She had to keep moving, which meant climbing over things and dragging the staff behind her.

She jumped up and scrambled forward.

Another growl and the movement of claws. It had seen her.

Over couches and trunks, tables and crates. The sound of claws was closing in behind her. The staff slowed her down. She had to drop it to run. But she couldn't—this is what she had come for.

The painting drew closer. She fumbled with the zipper on her backpack as she ran, clamping the staff awkwardly under one arm, and grabbed the mustard bottle.

She risked a glance backward. The grotesque cat perched a few feet away, balancing on several stacks of books. It hissed and leaped, but the stacks fell with the motion, sending the cat tumbling to the floor.

She hurriedly squeezed an outline of paste onto her hand.

The cat regained its feet, claws scrabbling, closing the distance. She climbed, hands full and useless, over another bookcase and half lunged, half stumbled toward the painting. The single eye of the young Nee Gezicht watched her as she threw out her goopy hand and crashed into the canvas.

A maniacal yowl went up behind her and she braced herself for the claws that would tear at her neck and her arms and her backpack. But her hand was already as warm as a heating vent on a winter morning, and in an instant she fell, tumbling and turning, back into the world behind the canvas.

CHAPTER 22

THE WINDOW-PAINTING spit Claudia into the stairway like a watermelon seed. She slammed against the stone floor, rolling until the far wall stopped her. An echoing pounded her ears. She spun to face the window painting, head reeling. The cat tore at the painting in the attic with furious claws, just as it had the one above the fireplace. Ragged shreds flapped on the other side of the window with each terrible stroke. Then the window darkened and, with a sound like breaking ice, split into a web of hairline cracks.

Footsteps came from the stairs above and Pim rushed around the corner.

"Claudia!" It was easy to read the look of relief and concern on his face.

That expression was all she needed. Pim was her friend. He had the chance to sell her to the witch for his freedom, and instead he helped to save her. She would not doubt him again.

He ran and pulled her to her feet. The strain from the fear and dismay and anguish that had squeezed her heart over the last hour became acute now, and her tears started to flow. She pressed her face into Pim's shoulder, sobbing quietly.

It was embarrassing to cry like that in front of someone else. At home, all good cry sessions happened strictly in the privacy of her bedroom. But Pim's arms came up around her, and somehow that made it okay.

"Pim, she's awful," she whispered once she could breathe again.

Pim patted her backpack. "I'm afraid you don't even know the half of it."

"And then when you appeared and I thought you were . . . you had . . ." She choked on her words.

"I know. I'm sorry I had to do it that way. But it worked." He pushed her gently back so he could look into her face. "It *worked*, Claudia."

She quickly wiped her tears on her shirtsleeve.

"It's a shame we couldn't find the staff," he continued, "but it could have been a lot worse. To have Nee Gezicht appear—"

The staff.

Her heart leaped into her throat and she whirled around, eyes scanning the ground. Nothing. She stepped over to the broken window-canvas and put her hand up to the cracked surface. It must have fallen during her exit through the painting. She slammed her fist against the window. It had all been for nothing.

"Claudia, what is it?"

"I had it, Pim. I had the staff."

His face widened in surprise. "You did? Where is it?"

She played back in her mind the terrifying moments in the attic. "I had the mustard bottle in this hand. This other hand was goopy. I had the staff under this arm. It was so heavy. That cat was right behind me. I slammed into the painting. . . . It had to have come with me. Right?"

It was all a blur, that moment she came through the canvas. She couldn't see it clearly in her memory. But the staff obviously hadn't made it.

Unless . . .

She glanced up at Pim for a moment and then turned and rushed down the stairs.

Window-paintings flew by, the hum of the world rich in her ears. Her feet pounded down the spiral staircase. Before long the stairs spilled out into the foyer—

Cash sat on the stone floor, one paw on the fallen staff.

"'Bout time," he said. "Did you guys drop something?"

There it was. One and a half meters long. Black walnut. She stepped over and placed her foot on it next to Cash, hands triumphantly on her hips. She had done it.

Pim shot through the entrance and pulled up short, taking in the scene. His eyes grew wide. A grin spread slowly across his face. He threw back his head and laughed.

He rushed forward and lifted her off her feet, his arms around her waist. "Well done, Claudia. Well done indeed."

He set her on her feet and knelt down next to the staff. He ran his hands along the smooth wood. "This is it. This is really it." A voracious look sprang to his eyes. "Now we finish it."

Claudia nodded, her head still buzzing with triumph. "Together."

"Together." He stood, hefting the staff. "We need to hurry. She has other ways to enter this world, and other spies here besides. Let's do this quickly. Outside."

The thought of Nee Gezicht pursuing them with the

Fireside Angel in tow sent goose bumps along Claudia's arms, dousing the excitement of her victory. And it brought to mind something that concerned her even more.

"Pim," she said, trying to keep her voice even. "That thing with the tea and my feet. She said she had already started reaping my will. What does that mean?"

"She gave you witch hazel tea," he said, placing a hand on her shoulder. "If prepared correctly, it can temporarily make a person susceptible to suggestion. The closer the person's tie to magic, the more susceptible she is. Since you're an *Artisti*, one sip was enough to give her that control over you—to loosely bind your will to hers. She was trying to figure out on her own if you were an *Artisti* or not."

Claudia rolled her eyes. Of course she wasn't an *Artisti*. And yet . . . Pim thought she was. So did Nee Gezicht. Was it possible to have incredible talent without ever knowing it?

"What would have happened if I'd drunk the whole cup?" she asked.

"Then you would not be here right now. You would not have been able to break the binding. It would have held you long enough for her to prepare the ironweed and charcoal and to reap your will completely. She's desperate for someone like you, Claudia. Since I reclaimed my will, she has nothing to draw from but her own power. She will start to fade soon, and she knows it."

She shivered. "Will she still be able to tell me what to do, like she did with my feet?"

Pim's eyes filled with concern. "The effects of witch hazel tea take time to wear off. It's possible she can—and next time she won't underestimate your strength. Let's not give her the chance."

"Hey," Cash called. "We getting outta here, or what?"

Pim stepped cautiously to the doorway. "Have you seen anything down here? Heard anything?"

"Just whispers upstairs and water downstairs. This place is almost as creepy as the Southern Forest, I'll tell you that much."

"All right," Pim said. "Let's do it here and now."

Cash glanced up at Claudia. "You smell like cat."

"Yeah. I could've used your help up there. It was big and mean."

"Naw," Cash replied. "I'm allergic."

Pim rushed out into the sunlight and the others followed. The light filled Claudia's vision for half a minute before her eyes adjusted and she could make out the sandy horizon and the dilapidated architecture surrounding the towers. Pim pushed the sand away from a group of stone blocks next to the base of the tower. He laid the staff like a bridge across two of the larger blocks that sat several feet apart. Then he bent down and lifted a block the size of a large watermelon. Straining, he held it for a heartbeat over the staff and then slammed it down.

It hit with a *crack* right in the center of the staff.

And then the moan started. It emanated from the staff, low and rumbly at first, but then it grew louder and louder like a ghost with a megaphone until Claudia had to clamp her hands over her ears. Pim winced and let the block fall to the sand. Cash covered his head with his paws. The sound continued for nearly a minute, vibrating Claudia's bones, until it faded away.

"What was that?" she asked.

"I don't know," Pim said. "Some type of alarm, perhaps. Maybe it's calling to its master." He snatched up the staff and together they examined it.

No break. No dent. Not even a scratch.

Pim laid the staff back in its place on the stones and picked up the block, slamming it down again. The staff skittered a few inches across the stones but otherwise didn't even bend at the impact. And the terrible moan started once more.

This time Pim didn't hesitate. Sweat glistening on his forehead, he bent down to pick up the stone block again. Claudia reached down to help him, although it was much heavier than it looked. They held it high over the staff and thrust it down as hard as they could.

Still no mark.

They picked up the stone again, this time forcing it up above their heads before slamming it down.

The moan continued.

Again they picked it up, but Claudia's arms were already feeling rubbery. She and Pim barely lifted it two feet above the staff before letting it slip from their fingers.

Nothing.

Pim's face dripped sweat, and his eyes were wild and desperate. He lunged forward to grab the staff, knocking her to the ground. She scrambled out of the way as he hefted the staff high like an ax and slammed it down hard on the large stone block. In an instant it was above his head again, then down, then up again. He cried out with each blow, a sound so guttural and pained that it made her heart hurt for pity.

The staff was a blur as he rained down a series of blows on the enormous block until the stone was pocked and chipped and dust clouded the air.

The staff remained unscathed.

And the moan continued.

Cash stepped protectively to Claudia's side. She reached down and scratched behind his ear to let him know it was okay, although she wasn't entirely sure herself. Finally Pim dropped to his knees as his arms fell limp. His breathing was rapid, his face empty. The staff's moan faded and disappeared.

She put a hand on Pim's shoulder. "I'm sorry, Pim. There's got to be another way. Something else that can break it. Maybe if we get an ax or a saw. Or fire."

Pim rocked back and forth, mumbling to himself. "Fire might work. But she's had centuries to layer protections onto this staff. Centuries. It's a lot stronger than I expected. It's not going to be broken or destroyed by ordinary means. We need a solution that's unnatural. Or supernatural."

"Just gnaw on it for a while," Cash said. "Ain't never met a bone you can't suck the marrow out of if you just gnaw on it long enough."

"You'd break all your teeth, Cash," Claudia said.

"Well, *I* wasn't going to try it."

"No," Pim said. He slowly rose to his feet, looking at Cash. "The talking fur ball has an idea. And I know just the set of teeth that could do it."

Before Claudia could ask what he meant, a wail sounded farther out in the desert. It was distant but unmistakable.

"The Fireside Angel," Pim said, his own voice echoing the dread she felt.

"Spades and britches," Cash mumbled.

Pim stepped away from the base of the tower and shielded his eyes from the sun as he looked out over the sand into the heart of the desert. Claudia followed, hoping he was wrong. She and Cash had barely escaped that beast earlier. It was a long way back to the forest, and out here in the desert there was no place to hide.

Two figures dotted the horizon. One ran with a loping rhythm, arms and legs flailing wildly. The Fireside Angel. Next to it was a massive round creature that rocked side to side as it charged across the sand.

"Celebes," Pim said. "Why did she have to bring Celebes into this? If he's coming this way, she'll be with him." He dashed back to the stone blocks and picked up the staff.

"Who's Celebes?" Claudia asked, following. "And who's he bringing? Nee Gezicht?"

Pim nodded. "She's coming for the staff. And for you. We need to be fast. We'll take the Corridor."

Cash whimpered. "Not much of a water dog, myself."

"Then give my regards to the Fireside Angel," Pim said, lifting the staff and rushing back into the tower.

Claudia quickly scratched Cash behind the ears for comfort before they both followed.

"Where are we going?" she asked. "What's the Corridor? Like a canal?"

Pim shut the tower door firmly and pushed them toward the stairwell that led belowground. "You'll see. Faster. We need to hurry."

She scrambled down the stairs, Pim holding on to her elbow to both steady her and move her along. After descending several stories, she heard a steady roar coming from below.

Water. Lots of it.

The stairs let out onto a short beach of rocky, gray sand. The light from the stairway trickled down to illuminate the scene. It was dim and there was little to see. The narrow span of beach was blocked on both sides by smooth walls of stone. Beyond the beach hurried the white water of a river. The rushing noise of water that filled the cavern was intense and dangerous. The river was wide enough that the light didn't reveal the other side. Beyond it, everything fell into blackness.

It didn't look like much of an escape route.

"What, are we going to swim for it?" Claudia asked.

Cash whimpered again.

"There's a metal stake and chain buried in the sand," Pim replied. "Find it fast!"

Before Claudia could ask why, Cash leaped forward. He scampered across the sand, nose to the ground. Back and forth he paced. Then he stopped short of the waterline and began to dig furiously. Within seconds, a rusted metal stake appeared beneath his paws, wrapped by a length of chain that continued into the sand.

Pim jumped toward it and grabbed the chain. "Not bad, puppy dog." The chain broke through the sand and led into the water. Pim pulled. The chain snapped to the side and went taut, as though connected to something downstream.

Claudia stepped up beside him and pulled, the lapping waves soaking through her shoes.

A mass appeared from the darkness, floating on the water. They pulled it closer, against the current.

It was a small fishing boat, just big enough for several people. Its red surface was covered with plates of poorly fitting sheet metal, dented and rusted and anything but waterworthy. A thin mast rose up from the center of the boat. Pim reached out and hauled its prow up on the beach.

"We're going in that thing?" Claudia said. She was a decent

swimmer—in a swimming pool. But falling out of a boat into a moving river was something else.

"It's our best chance. This is the only boat here. They can't follow us this way." Pim moved to the boat and picked up the oars.

Claudia and Cash looked from the boat to each other, his eyes reflecting the doubt she felt.

"Well, come on," Pim urged.

Claudia huffed and climbed into the boat, annoyed more with herself than with Pim. After everything she'd been through the past two days, it seemed silly to be afraid of a river.

Pim handed her the staff, and she sat on the wooden bench in the back of the boat. "Cash!" she called.

The dog shivered on the beach and then ran and leaped into the boat, tucking himself between her feet.

"Hold on tight," Pim said, untying a thin rope that connected the boat to the chain. He huffed as he pushed the boat backward, scraping it along the rocky shore until it floated free in the water. Then he jumped aboard. He pushed the oars into place on the oarlock. "Here we go."

The current of the river picked up the boat and shoved it forward as if it were a leaf. Claudia knew her knuckles must be white as she gripped the sides, but she couldn't see them or anything else. They shot forward into darkness as the underground corridor swallowed them whole.

Yes, it seemed silly to be afraid of a river, she told herself. But careening down a river at terrifying speeds in the pitch black—that was something to be afraid of.

CHAPTER 23

IN THE complete darkness of the Corridor, the small fishing boat picked up more and more speed until the wind whipped Claudia's hair off her shoulders. She stretched her arms across the boat and gripped the sides with both hands. Pim grunted and struggled with the oars, trying to keep the boat even and moving in a straight line as the current thrust it forward.

A shriek echoed through the tunnel. The Fireside Angel. Claudia pictured him standing on the beach they had just left. Hopefully he didn't swim.

The boat crashed into something on the left and one of her hands jarred free. "Pim!" she cried.

"It's going to be rough for a bit. Hold on!"

Claudia squinted into the Corridor ahead, wishing for a glimpse of what they were heading into, but all was black.

The boat whipped to the right and immediately struck a rock or a wall on the opposite side. She tightened her grip and the boat bucked violently as they plunged forward into the spray. Wind and water slapped Claudia across the face and she gasped for breath. The roar of rushing water filled her ears. They had to be flying at an incredible speed—it was the feeling of riding on a roller coaster but without knowing whether you'll make it to the end of the ride.

The boat tilted forward and dropped suddenly, and her stomach was practically wrenched from her gut and left behind. They fell through the air, and Claudia held tight as the drop lifted her from the bench. They slammed again into the roiling river, water sloshing over the sides and flowing through her shoes. Images of rapids and waterfalls came to mind, with people flying down a river in rubber rafts with helmets and life vests and other things she didn't have.

Another drop, smaller, this time. And then the boat shuddered to a sudden stop, breaking Claudia's grip and sending her sprawling to the lower boards. The boat whipped around 180 degrees and was held in place at the base of the waterfall by something unseen in the darkness. The intense flow of the river forced the bow downward, and water came rushing over the side. It was cold and strong and Claudia's arms flailed, frantically grabbing for anything to keep from being washed overboard.

Her outstretched fingers brushed the staff tumbling in the water, and she latched on to it. Her other hand connected with the base of the mast. Water sprayed and coursed over her, and it was all she could do to keep her grip. Cash yelped.

"The painter's snagged!" shouted Pim.

She didn't know what that meant, and if he said anything else, she didn't hear it. The boat was flooded now as water poured in and over and out again in a constant cycle. The roar of the waterfall pummeled her ears, and water that tasted strongly of oil paint filled her mouth. She coughed and struggled to find air.

She was going to drown. Any second now, the waves would break her grip on the mast and pull her beneath the troubled water. She felt her fingers slipping.

Then the boat jerked and lunged forward like a sprinter off the line, forced onward by the torrent that had pounded them. They spun and dipped—water everywhere—and it was impossible to tell if they were sinking to the bottom of the river or floating on top.

"Almost out of it!" Pim shouted.

The boat twirled, dropped slightly one last time, and then the madness stopped.

The roar faded slowly behind them. The boat continued to rock, but it was gentle, bobbing.

"Pim?" she cried out, uncurling in the pool of water on the floor of the boat. "Are you there?"

She heard the creak and pull of the oars close by. "Yes, and you're sitting on my foot."

She scrambled onto the bench, still clutching the staff. She wrapped her arms around herself against the cold. The roar of the rapids seemed distant and almost innocent.

"Cash?"

"Still here," came his voice from the front of the boat. "'Bout as happy as a wet cat."

She sighed. It was a miracle none of them had ended up in the water. "You couldn't have warned us about that, Pim?"

"Sorry," Pim said. "It was closer to the entrance of the Corridor than I recalled. And the painter—the line at the front of the boat—must have gotten stuck in the rocks right when we took a dive. Fortunately the puppy dog's bite really is worse than his bark. He bit through the rope."

"You're welcome," Cash said.

"It wasn't too bad, though," Pim said. "Once we got past the rough bits."

"Yeah?" Claudia said through chattering teeth. "Well, next time I drive."

She clutched the staff and shivered. It would be so nice to get home and not be faced with life-or-death situations every ten minutes.

They knelt down and splashed water over the side with their hands until the boat seemed steadier in the water. She felt Cash weave his way over and curl up next to her on the bench. She petted his head. The oars creaked as Pim pulled on them. She looked around, searching for a pinprick of light in the distance, for shades of gray, for her hand in front of her face. But the darkness was complete and smothering.

At home, she never used a night-light, even when she was younger. Instead, she went to bed with the shades drawn wide. The night was always full of light. The moonlight, the streetlight, a passing car, the fireflies. She didn't need a light in her room when there was so much more interesting light outside.

But it was the darkness that made the light interesting. Like the darkened corners and crevices of a Caravaggio painting— the mystery of what they held and what they didn't. It was the way the street lamp cut a sharp line of brightness onto the asphalt. It was the way the full moon cast a glow on the world below her window so that you couldn't tell where the light stopped and the darkness started. The balance of light and dark—that was what she liked most about art.

Maybe that was why the pitch black of the underground river frightened her. It wasn't the darkness.

It was the lack of light, of balance.

Pim pulled regularly on the oars now, aiding the reluctant current. The boat bobbed and rocked, but it seemed like they were crawling along. She'd nearly drowned in the rapids, but at least those had some speed.

"Where does this let out?" she asked, as much to hear herself talk as for curiosity.

The oars creaked again. "Do you know Braque's painting *The Viaduct at L'Estaque?*"

"Braque[27]? He was a Cubist, right? So, no, I don't."

Pim laughed, and the laugh echoed eerily in the darkness. "That's right. I'm talking to the realist. Well, Braque's painting shows a huge viaduct—kind of like a bridge with columns that come all the way to the ground—that stretches over a canyon. This river comes out shortly before it passes under that viaduct. The quickest way to where we're going is to cross the viaduct."

---

27. GEORGES BRAQUE (1882–1963). Pablo Picasso supposedly said, "Good artists copy, great artists steal." Most artists prefer to think of this as "being influenced" by another's style, but the principle is the same. Braque is an excellent erudite example. He started out as a house painter while studying artistic painting on the side. His early works were influenced by the Impressionists, since they were the hot ticket in Paris at the time. Then he started using bold, emotional colors like the Fauves (which is French for "wild beasts"). Eventually he saw some of Cézanne's work on display, and for a time explored simultaneous perspective, just like Cézanne. Finally he began partnering with Picasso, and that led to the birth of Cubism.

The take-home message: Stealing is absolutely wrong. Unless you're an artist; then it's just part of the job. (Excerpted from *Dr. Buckhardt's Art History for the Enthusiast and the Ignorant.*)

"And where are we going?"

"To see Colossus."

"Is that a person or a . . . something else?"

"Kind of both."

"Well, he sounds big. Can he break the staff?"

"I don't know. When it comes to physical strength, there are two creatures that come to mind in this part of the world. Celebes and Colossus. Celebes, obviously, is not going to help us. So that leaves Colossus."

"And does Colossus work for Nee Gezicht?"

"Not exactly."

"Is he your friend?"

"Not exactly."

"Who painted him?"

"Francisco de Goya."[28]

"Oh, goodie," Claudia breathed nervously. She remembered his work from her art encyclopedia and other books in the library. His paintings often contained dark creatures and a bitter hopelessness.

"It's okay," Pim said quickly. "Colossus owes me a debt. He may not pay it willingly, but he'll pay it. If there is anyone or anything in this part of the world that can break the staff, it is Colossus."

"And if he can't break it?"

---

28. FRANCISCO DE GOYA (1746–1828). Goya was a Spanish painter who earned a handsome living through painting the portraits of rich people. But after losing his hearing due to a serious illness, he became withdrawn and introspective. His works became darker and darker, and to some he gave the caption, "The sleep of reason produces monsters." What a depressingly delicious dichotomy found in this artist—the creator of bright and regal portraits, and the designer of dreadfully dark depictions. (Excerpted from *Dr. Buckhardt's Art History for the Enthusiast and the Ignorant*.)

"Then we send you home."

"Don't be ridiculous. I'm not going home without you."

"I've already put you in great danger, Claudia. I don't think you realize just how much danger, even if you have stood up to the Sightless One face-to-face. There are other ways, perhaps, to break the staff. Maybe Granny Custos will know. But I could never forgive myself if you didn't make it home safely."

Claudia cleared her throat. She was suddenly glad it was dark because she could feel herself blushing, though she didn't quite understand why.

She racked her brain for something else to say. Cash wheezed quietly beside her in his sleep. "So what are you going to do when you get free? I mean, do you, like, have any . . . plans?"

The question was met with silence, broken only by the strokes of the oars, creaking in their oarlocks as the blades cut forcefully into the water.

"You could come and live with my family—at least for a while," Claudia suggested. "I mean, I'm sure my parents would love you— and especially my grandpa. It might be a little hard to explain, of course, but we'll think of something."

There was more silence and Claudia desperately wished she could see Pim's face.

"Yes," he finally said. "We'll have to cross that bridge when we come to it, I suppose."

It seemed like a strange response since they were talking about the goal they had worked so hard to accomplish. *Maybe after this long,* Claudia thought, *it's not something he lets himself think about.*

That thought was as sad as the Corridor was dark. Claudia

had a strong urge to move next to Pim and wrap her arms around him and put her head on his shoulder and whisper something encouraging. She shifted where she sat and almost moved forward. Almost.

Instead she wrapped her arms around herself and shivered.

CHAPTER 24

THEY RODE the river in silence, the Corridor amplifying the creak of the oars and the splash of their path through the water. Time was hard to hold on to in the darkness. It seemed that they had been on the river for at least an hour, but it was impossible to say for sure. The air grew warmer as they traveled, which at least stopped Claudia from shivering, despite her soaked clothes. She shifted uncomfortably from sitting on the hard wooden bench.

At last the echo of the water in the Corridor slowly changed. It sounded faster, as if the current now had a destination in mind.

"We're getting close," Pim said.

"Finally. I think I've had enough river to last me a while."

"Got that right," Cash mumbled, stretching his legs on the bench.

Within minutes, the darkness of the Corridor turned charcoal gray. She held her hand in front of her face and breathed a sigh of relief to see its outline appear against the dark. By degrees the darkness lessened, and the hint of colors returned as Pim continued to pull at the oars.

"We'll have to move quickly when we come to the bank," Pim said, his voice sounding strained and tired. "Our tracks won't be hard to follow. Nee Gezicht will know we came on the river. The Corridor only leads to one place, and she probably knows that, too. The question is how fast they can follow us over land. I think we'll come out ahead. But it will be close."

Claudia swallowed hard. "Good. Don't want to make this too easy, do we?"

A light gleamed up ahead, like a star in the dark fabric of the sky. It expanded as they continued, until she could make out the craggy outline of the wide exit from the Corridor. The light stung her eyes, but she forced herself to stare into it. She welcomed the pain, because the light restored the balance.

The current quickened, pulling the boat with it. Pim turned in his seat to face the bubbling white water ahead of them. It roiled over rocks that poked their heads above the surface.

Claudia gripped the side of the boat, staff in hand, preparing for another roller-coaster ride. Cash whimpered and jumped to the floor. Pim pushed at one oar, then the other, guiding the boat between the rocks. It dropped and spun slightly as water sprayed over the sides.

But that was it. The river leveled out, and a smooth path of water spread before them. Claudia let out the breath she had been holding. They passed through the wide rocky opening, giant boulders flanking the exit like sentinels.

A small cove with sheer, towering walls waited for them. It was open to the blue sky above, as though a canyon came to a dead end at the mouth of the cave. Pim again turned and laid into the oars, and they glided out of the cove and into the main part of the river.

On the left side of the canyon stretched a sheer wall that rose up more than a hundred feet above them. The right side provided a gradual slope away from the riverbank. The boat turned a bend and ahead of them stood what could only be the viaduct of L'Estaque.

"Whoa," she mumbled.

The viaduct crossed the expanse of the river with sandy-colored brickwork and three enormous columns reaching up from the water. It reminded Claudia of the trees in the Southern Forest—she could make out the general hulking shape, but the details of the structure were hard to focus on. It gave the suggestion of being a viaduct made out of bricks without really letting her see the specifics her eyes expected.

Pim guided the boat toward the bank on the right side, pulling hard across the current now that their destination was in sight. One final pull forced the fishing boat into the bank, sticking its prow in the mud and reeds. The sight of the viaduct made Claudia anxious to cross it, to get off the river, to keep moving. Cash leaped from the boat ahead of her.

"Let's go," Pim said, dropping the oars and jumping to his feet. He grabbed the staff and reached for her hand.

A trumpeting roar reverberated through the canyon so fiercely that Claudia's bones vibrated. She spun to find the source of the sound.

Several hundred yards upriver, on the other side of the viaduct, a hulking metal form rushed directly toward them with frightening speed. It looked like an enormous mechanical elephant crafted and welded out of a thick potbellied stove the size of a garage. Its two stout legs flashed through the water. A mechanical trunk extended from below wicked red eyes that flickered like flame, and long silver tusks glinted coldly in the sun. Its savage tail swayed as the beast ran, as thick and as long as a tree and ending with bull-like horns.

Smoke belched upward from ports in its side as it moved, swirling around a figure perched in a chair welded to the creature's back. Through the smoke, Claudia saw the hint of a black silk dress, and she didn't need to see any more.

She leaped from the boat, heart already racing.

Pim grabbed her arm as they scrambled together up the slope. "Cover your ears!" he shouted at her over another echoing blast from Celebes.

"What?" Did he think the noise from the beast would hurt her ears?

Then a voice echoed in the canyon—a woman's voice. The words were distant and unclear, but its owner unmistakable. The scene from Nee Gezicht's living room came to mind and Claudia knew what worried Pim.

She slapped her hands to her ears. She had sipped the witch hazel tea. Why on earth had she drunk the stupid tea? If the witch was close enough for Claudia to hear her command . . .

The soft dirt gave way as she stumbled on the slope. Pim half pulled, half steadied her. Cash skittered up and down the slope, muttering, "Come on, come on, come on."

They crested the hill, and Celebes disappeared from view as they charged along the dirt road that skirted a grove of trees and led to the viaduct.

From atop the hill she could see that the river canyon

widened in the distance, making room for houses built along the riverbank. She had only a moment to glance at the homes as she hurried forward, but it looked like some of the walls had been crushed into rubble. Perhaps a gift from the metal elephant's tail.

She turned to look back the way they had come, expecting to see Celebes charging over the top of the slope. There was nothing. Maybe it was too steep for Celebes to follow. Was there another path to the viaduct? Had Nee Gezicht not seen them?

And then they arrived at the viaduct, setting foot on the stone path, looking across to the other side of the canyon a hundred yards away. The path was straight and solid and offered a sense of hope. Masonry trowels and buckets and bricks were piled off to the side, as though recent repairs had been made.

"Go! Go!" Pim shouted, pushing her into a run.

They took five, six, seven strides when the elephantine roar filled the canyon once more, and this time it was followed by a crash of metal and stone, like a semitruck plowing head-on into an old brick building.

Boom!

The air around them convulsed. The viaduct shuddered and time seemed to slow as the smooth path split into hundreds of jagged cracks. Dust sprang into the air. The stone bricks beneath their feet were separating, pulling away from one another, sinking. Behind them, the entire section of viaduct they had just crossed was bowing like a wet towel. And then time resumed and down it went and Pim's hand was on her back and Claudia's legs carried her forward, flying over bricks that shifted and crumbled even as she raced across them.

The columns below the viaduct. That monster had just knocked out an entire column in one swipe of . . . what? Its tail?

She shot a frantic glance back at Pim, her eyes wide and filled with terror. His face held the same expression.

"Come on, kid!" Cash barked.

Boom!

The viaduct convulsed, this time more violently. Again they immediately found themselves scrambling forward over bricks and sections of stone that were separating and falling into the canyon below.

Pim slipped, and Claudia grabbed his elbow and hauled him upward as they ran. Cash bounded beside them.

That had to have been the second column.

There were only three.

Pim must have realized that as well, because he now pushed her forward with a frenzied force. The ground fell away behind them, and no sooner did they step on a solid, unmoving portion of the bridge than—

Boom!

The impact threw them both to the path. Claudia bashed her knees against the stone. Large segments of the path ahead of them ruptured and began to fall, but this time the brickwork beneath their feet stayed firm.

Pim yanked her upward and forward. A great fissure was opening ahead between them and the inviting green grass on the far side of the canyon.

And the remaining segment of the viaduct swayed beneath them.

An image flashed in Claudia's head of the nearly broken final column teetering on its base before falling like a cut tree to the canyon floor, taking the last portion of the viaduct path with it. They would have to jump for it.

White dust enveloped them. The path tilted forward and they climbed frantically uphill on the broken stone. She couldn't see. She couldn't breathe. Cash slipped and fell flat beside her. She scooped him up and tossed him forward with everything she had. He yelped and disappeared into the dust. Pim threw the staff after him.

She grabbed Pim's hand and they charged toward the top of the fragmented path as the column pitched forward. And they leaped.

CHAPTER 25

CLAUDIA FLEW through the thick cloud of dust as the last column of the viaduct crumbled beneath her. Pim's hand pulled away from hers and she wondered for the hundredth time since entering the world behind the canvas if this was the end. Then the base of the viaduct, attached to the lip of the canyon, appeared through the dust. It held the last few feet of path leading to the grass at the top of the canyon.

Claudia fell short. Her upper body slammed into the path, but her feet dangled along the side of the base where the bricks of the massive viaduct had broken away. Her hands frantically scrambled to find purchase on the surface of the path, fingers digging into the crevices between the bricks, armpits pushed painfully against the path's broken edge.

Something smashed into her, grabbing her ankle and yanking her downward. She cried out, digging her fingers harder into the crevices.

"Claudia! Hold on!" It was Pim, dangling from her ankle ten stories in the dusty air.

She couldn't answer. She focused every possible ounce of energy on gripping the bricks, willing her fingers not to let go. It felt like she was being ripped in half. How could Pim weigh so much when he didn't eat anything?

Below them, the remaining column thundered as it crashed into the canyon floor. A new wave of dust shot up.

She looked around for something—anything—more substantial to hold on to. The path ended just a few feet in front of her, but it may as well have been twenty feet away. A mess of bricks and masonry equipment lay to the side just off the path. Beyond them, in the green grass, was a white mound of fur.

"Cash!" she called out. The dog didn't move.

Suddenly the weight on her ankle lessened. "Pim!" she shouted, certain he had lost his grip.

"I'm here. I found part of a brick beneath my foot that will hold my weight," he replied, his voice taut. "For the moment." She could still feel his hands tight around her ankle.

She pushed with her forearms and elbows against the bricks. She could probably lift herself up to the path, just like getting out of a swimming pool. Then she could find something to lower down to Pim.

"I think I can climb up," she said. "Can you let go?"

Silence.

"Pim?"

There was reluctance in his voice. "The brick will hold my weight, but I'm at an angle. You're all I have to hold on to."

Without her, he would fall.

With him, she couldn't climb up.

Her fingers ached.

"Claudia," Pim said, "there are window-caves to the

northeast, on the other side of the forest. Run. Pick a window. You'll be safer in your world than you will be here. I'm sorry I couldn't do more."

What was he talking about? He couldn't really be thinking—

"Pim!" she shouted. "Don't be stupid!"

"Either I fall or we both do."

"We'll find a way. Just hold on!"

"Thank you for everything, Claudia."

"Wait! I see something!" She said it just to stall him, to break him out of his heroic determination. She looked around. A coil of rope lay in the pile of masonry trowels and shovels. One end was tied around the base of a nearby tree. Perhaps someone had used it to work on the side of the viaduct. "A rope. I think I can reach it."

She waited for a moment, and Pim's grip stayed firm. But her heart sank. There was no possible way for her to reach the rope. There was no way to save Pim.

"Cash!" she shouted again, but he still lay motionless.

Grasping the bricks tighter with her left hand, she lifted her right and stretched toward the rope. Her fingertips were still three feet away. She strained against the broken stone ledge, arm outstretched, trying not to kick the leg that Pim held.

It was useless, of course. She would never reach the rope. But it was all she had. Nothing else would save Pim and it was all she had.

So she stretched and fought back the tears welling in her eyes, wishing for Cash to be all right, wishing for the rope to draw closer, wishing for it to fly through the air into her open hand. She visualized it, saw it in her mind's eye, concentrating only on that because how could she think about Pim plunging into the canyon below? She stretched her fingers and concentrated, and wished without any hope.

The rope twitched. Just the end of it, lying atop the coil. There was no wind, and the ground had already stopped shaking. It had to be an illusion, but she didn't break her concentration, didn't withdraw her hand.

The rope moved again, the loose end inching toward her. She held her hand steady. What was happening? Could the rope be alive? Was it dangerous?

The thought made her hesitate, made her withdraw her hand a little, and the rope stopped moving.

She stretched out her hand again as far as it would go, wishing for the rope to come. It slithered across the stone path directly toward her hand.

Somehow *she* was controlling the rope.

And then it didn't matter because the end of the rope was close enough to snatch up. Gripping the stone path hard with her other hand, she grabbed the rope and tossed it over her shoulder.

"Pim!" She grabbed and tossed a dozen more times until the rope pulled taut against the tree. She yanked on it and it seemed firm. "That's it," she called down. "Grab the rope."

The entwined fibers of the rope creaked as Pim pulled on it. Then the pressure around her ankle disappeared and the rope snapped tight.

Now it was her turn. She pulled against the rope and pushed with her arm against the ledge. She twisted her body until she could swing one leg over the edge of the broken viaduct, hauling herself up and rolling over onto her back.

A grunt came from over the edge and she scrambled to her feet just as Pim's hand appeared on the stone path. She reached forward to help him up and caught a glimpse of the drop to the canyon floor below, still thick with dust. A wave of dizziness hit her but she tried to shove it away and focus on Pim.

She grabbed his wrist and pulled as he heaved himself up over the edge. They tumbled backward and sprawled on the grass.

Claudia lay there on solid ground, staring at the blue sky through a cloud of dust, waiting for the world to stop spinning.

"Thank you, Claudia," Pim said. "That's twice today you've saved my life."

"Yeah. Let's not make this a regular thing, okay?"

Her hand brushed something soft. She sat up to find Cash by her side. She stroked his fur and gently shook him. *Please be all right.*

Cash's eyes fluttered open and he raised his head. "We there yet?"

She laughed in relief and scratched behind his ears. "Are you hurt?"

"I don't think so. Heckuva dream, though. I was flying through the air."

"That was a nice throw, Claudia," said Pim.

Cash rose groggily to all fours. "Wait now—you *threw* me?"

"Sorry about that," she said. "I wasn't sure you would make the jump."

"Well, next time find a different way," Cash grumbled. "Nobody chucks this dog."

Pim smiled as he stood. "That's a shame. I was hoping for a turn."

Cash growled and Claudia reached over to kiss his head. "I'm glad you're okay."

An elephantine blast echoed in the distance. Claudia looked at Pim, who had found the staff in the grass.

"Do you think she knows we survived?" she asked.

"There was a lot of dust. She might not have seen us."

They both stared at the edge of the canyon and the broken remains of the viaduct. Nee Gezicht and Celebes had caught up with them so quickly. And the strength of that beast was terrifying.

"Who on earth painted that monster?"

"Ernst. A favorite of Nee Gezicht. Also created the Fireside Angel."

Claudia took a deep breath. The fact that they had almost plunged to their deaths was starting to sink in. Her hands were shaking. She folded her arms.

Pim seemed to notice. He knelt down beside her and placed an arm around her shoulders. It took her by surprise, but it was comforting. She leaned her head against him. After a moment her body stopped shaking, but she didn't pull away from him.

"Do you think they know where we're going?" she finally asked.

Pim bit his lip. "It wouldn't be hard for her to guess. She knows Colossus well. But without the viaduct it's a much longer route."

"She seems to get around pretty quickly."

"Then we'd better move."

Pim turned to Cash. "This is where we part ways, puppy dog."

Cash bared his teeth. "I stay with the kid. I've known pawn dealers I trust more than you."

"We're going someplace you can't follow," Pim replied.

"And where's that, exactly?"

"The window-caves," Pim said. "And beyond."

Cash took half of a step backward. "What's in them caves?"

Pim smiled knowingly. "You'll have to go inside one of these days and find out. But not today."

"I ain't leaving her alone with you."

"This is bigger than you," Pim said quietly. "And it's bigger than her. I need you to take a message to Rembrandt."

"Rembrandt?"

"He needs to know that the Sightless One will strike soon."

That seemed to take Cash by surprise. "Where?"

"Southern Tier. Within a week."

Immediately Claudia remembered Nee Gezicht's words to Pim in her living room. That was what she had meant. An attack here in this world.

"How do I know you're not still working for the witch?" Cash asked.

"Please, Cash," Claudia said. "It's true. I heard her say it. You need to tell Rembrandt. I'll be fine. Really." She hurriedly took his head in her hands. "Thank you for everything." She leaned in and kissed his white fur.

Cash backed up and brushed his face with his paw. "All right, all right. Don't get all emotional on me, then." He licked her hand. "Be careful."

He barked in Pim's direction. "Take care of her, Dutch boy,

or we'll have something more to settle later. And I'll be back for my dough, anyhow."

Then he turned and trotted off into the trees. It pulled at Claudia's heart to see him go.

She cinched down the straps on her dusty and battered backpack as they stood. "Hey, Pim?"

"Yes?"

"No more viaducts."

"Agreed."

"Or bridges."

"That's reasonable."

She took a deep breath. "Let's move."

Evening fell in earnest now as they hurried through the patchwork terrain beyond the canyon and the fallen viaduct. They followed a paved road for a time but then left it for a rough path that faded into the underbrush soon after they set foot on it. The land was forested but rocky, with craggy hills and ridges soon surrounding them on all sides. Some of the hills off to the left turned into foothills and rose up into a series of rocky gray mountains in the distance.

"Do you recognize those?" Pim asked, nodding toward the mountains backlit against a setting sun.

Claudia winced as she turned her ankle on a stone. "No," she replied with a heavy breath. "Should I?"

"The window-cave with the Rubens,[29] the one you came

29. PETER PAUL RUBENS (1577–1640). Rubens, one of the great Flemish masters, was a popular fellow. Loved by royalty across Europe, he painted portraits and scenes of history and mythology. In fact he was so adored by kings and queens that he was sent on various diplomatic missions—for several different countries. Remember that

through, is at the foot of those mountains. When we're done with Colossus, we head straight there—whether the staff is broken or not."

She was too tired and breathless to argue. The backpack slipped from her shoulder for the tenth time, so she dragged it by its top handle instead. One of the straps was hanging on by only a thread, and the zipper was busting open at the top. Their escape at the viaduct hadn't been kind to it—or to her aching fingertips. But at least nothing had fallen out. You never know when you'll need underwear or nail polish.

Their escape at the viaduct . . . She hadn't told Pim about the thing with the rope. She didn't know what to make of it. She hadn't imagined it, right? The rope really did move. It was almost like in old cartoons where a snake charmer makes a rope rise up out of a basket. But why had it happened for her? It had saved Pim's life—maybe even hers.

They hiked to the top of another rise, which looked down into a small basin surrounded by rocky hills. An enormous cave opening spread across the side of one hill, flanked by an array of unlit torches. Bones were strewn about the ground in front of it. Claudia didn't have to ask if that was their destination—it was obvious. Something lived in that cave.

Something big.

They descended the ridge into the basin and approached the cave. It was many times taller than Claudia, leading into the

when you're sitting in art class. You may be preparing yourself for a jolly good career in politics.

Rubens had significant skill at painting complex arrangements of people, twisting and turning in the midst of action. And he had a famous fascination for fleshy folks. He understood what so many artists today have forgotten: Real women have curves. (Excerpted from *Dr. Buckhardt's Art History for the Enthusiast and the Ignorant*.)

side of a hill covered with boulders and gravel and scraggy trees. While the window-cave she had stepped out of earlier had smooth lines carved into the mountainside, this cave seemed cobbled together without much thought on the part of nature—or the artist.

Claudia tried to ignore the bones scattered on the ground as she stepped around them. But even those weren't as unsettling as the pitch black that began just a few feet into the entrance of the cave. It was a darkness that hid secrets and didn't care if you wandered in because it could hide you, too.

She slipped a trembling hand into Pim's as they stopped a dozen paces from the opening.

Pim set his jaw and clenched the staff and stared with fiery eyes into the darkness.

"Colossus!" he shouted.

The name echoed over and over through the depths and eventually died out. The cave seemed to exhale and a warm stench flowed from the darkness that overpowered Claudia's senses, reminding her of decay and the worst kind of . . . disappointment. She wasn't sure if she wanted Pim to call out again.

"Colossus!"

He let the name echo and fade before continuing. "Colossus, you know this voice. You know what I did for you. I've never asked you to repay that debt. Until today. Come out. I am calling on your help."

The words were commanding and bold, and their force was surprising. It was a reminder that this twelve-year-old boy was anything but that. Yet when the echoes had disappeared, there was still only silence.

"Colossus, I need your help and I need it now. Come out and repay your debt!"

She felt the rumble before she heard the growl, but both shook her bones and her courage. The growl grew and became stronger. Something incredibly large moved in the darkness.

Pim squeezed her hand and spoke quickly. "Whatever happens, don't move. He won't harm you if you're with me."

That didn't help. Every part of her body screamed at her, *Run!*

Whatever monster hid in the darkness, it was coming toward them quickly. There were tremendous footfalls, a growl reverberating in her ears—

The torches at the sides of the cave sprang to life, orange fire burning hot as if it had glowed since their arrival.

And then a giant face, both man and beast, burst through the darkness as the torches flickered wickedly. Its jaws opened wide with easily enough room to stuff Claudia in whole, and it stopped in front of them as the growl turned into a massive roar.

Claudia squeezed her eyes shut as the foul stench of putrid oil paint and death—and, again, disappointment—washed over them. She grew light-headed, and the roar left her ears ringing painfully. Despite Pim's assurance, she knew she was about to be picked up and dashed against the boulders of the hill.

But the roar fell silent. When Claudia opened her eyes, a giant stood before her, almost as tall as the entrance to the cave. His bearded face was smeared with dirt, and his body was just as soiled and hairy. He was naked except for a large cloth that hung from his waist, revealing bulging muscles that any bodybuilder would have been proud of. The physical power of this giant was obvious.

Just the sort of power they needed.

Colossus set round eyes on Pim, ignoring Claudia altogether. "Curse you, boy," he said in a voice as deep and rocky as the hills. "Sadness follows you like shadow. Why do you bring it to my cave again?"

Pim returned the giant's gaze. "Your sadness was not my doing."

"Not your doing?" Colossus bared his teeth like a wildcat. "If it weren't for you . . ."

"I've come to collect the debt you owe me." Pim raised the staff in front of him. "You do this simple task and I'll take my sad shadow and never return. You have my word."

The giant stared at Pim for a moment longer and then sniffed, as though he knew something about the value of Pim's word. He noticed Claudia, seemingly for the first time. His face softened just slightly, and the fire dimmed in his monstrous eyes. She shuffled her feet nervously.

The gaze lingered and then reluctantly came back to Pim. "What do you ask of me?"

Pim let out the tiniest of sighs. "I can't break this staff. It's thick with magic. But I think you can do it."

Colossus crouched down and reached for the staff, which was shorter than his forearm. He brought it up before his eyes to examine it. He tapped it experimentally against a boulder. He stuck it in his mouth and bit gently. "Just wood," he mumbled.

Then letting out a cry that made Claudia jump, the giant took the staff in both hands and raised it above his head. He brought it down onto his bent knee with enough force that Claudia was sure it would have to explode into a thousand tiny splinters. But instead the giant howled in pain, dropping the staff to the ground.

Claudia stared at where it had fallen among the dust and gravel.

Whole and without a scratch. And it began to moan.

CHAPTER 26

T HE STAFF moaned louder this time, as though matching the size of the creature that had tried to break it. Claudia winced at the intensity of it. Pim picked up the staff. Colossus put his hands over his ears. And just when the instant couldn't get any more crowded, a flash of color at the edge of the forested ridge behind them caught her attention.

"Oh no," she mumbled. "Pim!"

The Fireside Angel came over the ridge, squinty-eyed and breathing hard.

It was a creature of flowing lines and gruesome features, the details of its body lost in ragged folds of colorful cloth. It was the size of a tall man with arms so long that its fingerlike claws scraped the ground. Its skeletal head was birdlike, except for the razor teeth and a ragged mane flowing down its neck. Its bowlegged stride ended in bulky boots that were spiked like vicious soccer cleats. Most grotesque was the beast attached to the Angel's leg, protruding as though it had grown out of the flesh of the larger monster. It had a jagged snout of its own and possessed a single foot with an array of claws, which it occasionally touched to the ground in an effort to participate in the hulking strides of the larger creature.

Pim turned and saw it, and without hesitation he grabbed Claudia's hand and pulled her toward the cave. She snatched one of the torches from its holder as they rushed in. The moaning of the staff echoed off the walls like a choir of zombies in a cathedral. Behind them, Colossus unleashed his roar on the Angel. The Angel answered back just as fiercely.

The evening light lingering at the entrance dimmed and disappeared as they ran farther and farther in. The torch gave a shadowy view of the cave, which reeked and was littered with bones and refuse.

Would Colossus fight to protect his cave? It didn't seem likely he would fight to protect *them*.

The immense cave stretched onward, bending and twisting and leading them deeper into the painted earth. Claudia glanced behind them and saw only darkness. In the distance, the howls of the two creatures continued.

Pim said something in Dutch that sounded like a curse. Claudia's head snapped around, but not in time to avoid colliding with Pim's back. She and Pim tumbled to the ground, the contents of her backpack scattering across the cave floor.

She'd bruised her knees again and her hands stung, but she immediately focused on something bigger. Thirty feet bigger.

The cave abruptly ended right in front of them. Boulder after boulder after boulder had been piled and stacked to create a wall that sealed off any chance of escape. It was thick and complete; not an open crack or hole to be seen. The moaning of the staff faded and stopped, but it left behind a ring of hopelessness in Claudia's ears.

Pim stumbled to his feet, his eyes wandering frantically over the wall of boulders. "This used to be a tunnel. It went north and connected with more window-caves, like the one you came through. Paintings." He closed his eyes. "That giant fool."

Claudia stood and grabbed the torch from the ground. She pushed on one of the boulders as if it might magically give way.

Solid. As a rock.

Pim's eyes were still closed and he stood motionless. He was out of ideas, she knew it. This was it. They had come to the end. Up until now she had relied on Pim to get her through this world—Pim, or Cash, Rembrandt, even the three Dutchmen. But now there was no one.

No one but her. *Ha! What good is that? I can't see a way out of this.*

Seeing. The odd refrain from the Cubists leaped into her mind.

The world can be different from how it appears . . .

But not this. They were talking about appreciating art, not life-and-death situations.

The world can be different from how it appears . . .

Claudia took a breath and closed her eyes. Then she slowly opened them, like the Venetian blinds her mother pulled up on the window every morning. *See differently,* she commanded herself. She thought vaguely of the Mona Lisa. This was the same thing.

Listen more quickly.

Open your mind.

See differently.

The walls of the cave surrounded her. Parts were rocky, parts were smooth. But the rocky parts were still solid; no cracks or crevices or holes. The smooth parts were large and wide and rose to the ceiling, like a canvas Rubens might have painted on. The floor . . .

No. The smooth walls weren't *like* a canvas, they *were* a canvas. Canvas and paint, just like everything else in that world. Canvas and paint that came alive because an *Artisti* had willed it to. Alive because an artist had touched brush to canvas. Magic channeled through art.

Vicious roars came from the distant cave opening—a battle between beasts.

Pim opened his eyes and turned to her. "Colossus roars, but he'll retreat as soon as the real fight begins. Claudia, we need to . . ."

She jammed the handle of the torch in between several large boulders to make it stick. There was an excitement boiling up inside of her now. Insight. Illumination. Inspiration. Of a kind she had never felt before. She scanned the cave floor where the contents of her backpack had scattered. There. She snatched up the package of Aunt Maggie's nail polish. She hurriedly dumped out the contents—twenty-four different colors and a plastic bottle of polish remover. Nail polish wasn't exactly oil paint, but maybe it would be similar enough. Either way, she had to try.

She grabbed a bottle of Promising Plum polish and stared at the smooth cave wall.

"What do we need?" she mumbled. Something fast. A car. But she had no idea how to drive a car. She turned to Pim.

"Can you ride a horse?"

He stared at her blankly. "Yes, but—"

She snatched up another polish bottle and tossed it to him. "Good. Let's do it."

Pim stared at her as though she'd tossed him a bottle of . . . nail polish. "Shall I start at the tail, then?" he said sarcastically.

"Yes, and hurry."

Pim remained still.

"Pim," she pleaded. "You tell me I'm an *Artisti*. I've got my doubts. But I'm going to try because we don't have any other choice. That wall is made out of paint and canvas. You know more about this than I do, so you tell me. Can we paint ourselves a horse?"

He stared at her a moment longer, and then the despair in his eyes transformed into something more solid. Faith or hope or friendship . . . it was hard to tell what. "Yes," he said quietly. "I think we can."

"Good. 'Cause I can't do it alone."

Pim smiled and stepped up next to her at the wall. He twisted open his bottle of Ravishing Raspberry. "Right, then. A horse."

They slashed the polish against the wall, using tiny brushes designed for fingernails instead of masterpieces. Claudia finished one bottle and moved on to another, and then another. Pim kept pace, creating a smooth line for the horse's back, wavy lines for the mane. Roars continued to echo in the distance. The ground vibrated. Claudia stroked on the legs and the hooves and the rounded underbelly. Within minutes they had formed the outline of a short but broad and powerful horse.

The two artists stepped back from the wall to look at their work. Despite the desperation and danger, there had been a quiet thrill in creating a piece of art in tandem with a friend. Art—as simple as it was—that came from within her, from her own dreams and imagination. But now that thrill faded hand in hand with her hope. Somehow she had expected the horse to magically leap off the wall when it was complete. But it remained noble, pink, and motionless. Claudia dropped the last empty bottle of nail polish to the floor.

And then in the distance they heard the trumpeting of Celebes joining the skirmish. Colossus was outnumbered.

"Now comes the hard part," Pim said. "You need to bring it to life."

"How on earth is that supposed to happen?"

"Remember that the art is simply a channel for the magic." Pim moved his hand from the horse on the wall toward Claudia. "There is a bond between what you've created and who you are. It's just as real as if there were a thousand threads connecting you and the painting of the horse."

Colossus howled in the distance. Then the laughter of the Fireside Angel echoed through the cave. It was coming.

"Find those threads with your mind, Claudia. And pull."

It sounded ridiculous. Absurd.

But the rope at the viaduct. Hadn't she done the same thing there? She hadn't found threads with her mind, but she had wished for the rope to come closer to her—was desperate for it to come closer—and it had. It had come because . . . she was an *Artisti*.

Claudia closed her eyes and took a deep breath, like the women in her mom's yoga class at the gym. She tried to open her mind, to feel around her with her thoughts.

And she found something. Pinpoints of substance, just out of reach of her normal senses. They felt so real, so tangible, as though she was touching them with her hands. She peeked through her eyelids but there was nothing there, and her arms were still at her sides. Closing her eyes, she quickly found them again. She pushed at them with her thoughts, followed them for a few feet, and returned. Just like Pim said, they were threads that stretched out in front of her. Intuitively, she knew that those threads were connected to the horse they had just painted.

She concentrated harder now, wrapping her thoughts around as many threads as her mind could hold, and pulling, pulling—

The wall cracked.

Claudia's eyes snapped open to see a fractured outline around the painting of the horse.

Loping footfalls echoed through the cave.

"Concentrate!" hissed Pim. "And hurry!"

She closed her eyes and continued pulling, yanking on the threads so hard that her head hurt.

The sound of breaking stone continued. "Yes, yes!" Pim shouted.

She couldn't keep her eyes closed any longer. She opened them but continued to pull with her thoughts.

Pebbles and dust were falling from the crack around the animal. Then the head of the painted horse tore itself from the stone wall, moving under its own strength. With effort, the horse wriggled and writhed, kicking and straining with its newly formed feet, shaking its head to gain momentum.

Claudia concentrated harder than ever, focusing on the threads that would pull loose individual pieces of the stone creature's body.

The horse shook free its torso, then its rear legs, and finally its tail whipped loose.

Between the lines of pink and purple and red polish, the body of the horse was filled with the stone of the cave wall. But it moved with the lithe fluidity of a natural creature. It stamped its feet on the ground and shook its head like a dog after a bath, releasing excess dust and gravel. Claudia stood in awe of their creation, life breathed into stone and canvas with the stroke of a tiny brush—and magic. Magic that had come from within her.

Artisti.

And then with a terrifying shriek the Fireside Angel was upon them, rushing toward them from around a bend in the cave.

Pim picked up the staff and turned to face the Angel. Claudia grabbed the torch and stood beside Pim. The Angel scared her down to the core—the powerful arms, the bone-white head. The creepy thing growing out of its leg, with snapping jaws and a single scraping claw. But she had just pulled a horse out of a stone wall. And that counted for something. She raised the torch.

The Angel charged. Pim swung at it with the staff. The Angel lithely spun and dodged the blow and struck Pim in the stomach with an elbow. Pim flew backward and slammed against the wall of boulders.

Claudia jammed the torch into the Angel's side. He shrieked and spun around as Claudia leaped back, brandishing the torch. The Angel looked at the flame, eyes wide. He raised his arms in front of his face.

Was he afraid of fire? With a name like Fireside Angel?

Claudia swung the torch back and forth. With each swing the Angel whimpered and backed away. Then she raised the torch like a flaming club and struck at his head.

The Angel caught the fire end of the torch in its massive claw. It grinned wickedly, flames licking through its grotesque fingers.

Not afraid of fire.

The Angel yanked the torch from her hand. He tossed it to the ground, scattering embers and flame.

Then Pim was behind him, raining down blows from the hefty staff on the Angel's head.

The Angel leaped to the side and roared. He circled for a moment and then lunged again. Pim brought the staff up in a vicious swing, but the Angel ducked and backed away. For a creature built like a bizarre, colorful gorilla, it was frighteningly quick.

The two of them circled each other slowly, crouching and shuffling their feet, Pim obviously trying to stay between the monster and Claudia. The horse whinnied and pranced by the cave wall.

Pim swung the staff and the Angel ducked the blow once again and backed away. He circled for a moment, and then the thin creature protruding from its leg gave a squeal of laughter and the Angel charged.

It came like a bull to the matador. It was done playing. There was no way they would come out of this fight on top. Claudia turned to the horse. They would have to run and hope for the best.

As the Angel rushed forward, there was the brisk sound of snapping plastic. Claudia turned to see the beast take another step, then another. Then it stumbled and fell with a roar. The speed from its charge carried it forward and it spun out of control on the stone floor, rolling with a crash into the cave wall.

Claudia sprang forward, avoiding Pim's reach as he grabbed for her. The Angel had stepped on and broken something plastic. It had to be something from her backpack.

Please, not the ointment. Without the ointment . . .

She scanned the floor for the yellow mustard bottle, retracing the path of the Angel. Instead she found the plastic bottle of nail polish remover. The Angel's heavy step had popped the top right off, cracking the neck of the bottle. Fluid had run out over the cave floor. But instead of forming a clear puddle—

"Claudia, now! Let's go!" Pim hauled her to her feet.

She looked over at the Angel, who was still on the floor, moaning in pain—and reaching for its foot as though it had stepped on the cutting edge of a knife.

"We need the ointment!" she said.

Pim dove for her backpack. He snatched a few of her belongings off the ground and shoved them in. "It's here! I have it!"

Claudia picked up the bottle of nail polish remover, carefully avoiding any of the fluid. She found the lid and used the edge of her shirt as she twisted it back onto the bottle. Some of the fluid soaked into the shirttail, and as she watched—

Just like the cave floor.

Pim shoved the backpack into her hands and she slipped the plastic bottle inside.

Then Pim lifted her quickly onto the horse, pulling himself up behind her, staff in hand. He cried out and kicked the stone horse with his heels.

Behind them, the Fireside Angel rose to its feet and roared.

They charged through the cave in darkness.

The putrid air of Colossus's cave whipped past her face.

Heavy hoofbeats echoed across the walls. The movement rattled Claudia's body, making it hard to concentrate. But there was something about what she had seen.

Back there on the cave floor, where the nail polish remover had spilled . . . And then again where it had touched her shirt . . . Claudia forced herself to think through what had happened.

There was a muddy puddle, but not one made out of dirt and liquid. It was the type of puddle you'd get by mixing a thick dab of paint and water and smearing it with your fingers. But the floor of the cave was solid rock. How could nail polish remover melt solid rock? And then behind the mess of melted rock—

Claudia gasped. Behind it she had glimpsed the unmistakable texture of canvas. Dirty and worn, but canvas.

She had found a way to break the staff

CHAPTER 27

THE NAIL POLISH remover. That was the answer and she'd had it with her the whole time. It was a solvent, it dissolved things. It made perfect sense—in a bizarre, mind-blowing way.

The stone horse charged through the cave with its two riders. A quick and powerful earthquake shook the cave walls, and Claudia's thoughts of discovery were pushed aside. Dust and shards of stone showered down on them in the darkness.

"Celebes."

"Yes," Pim said in her ear. "He's cutting off our only exit. They mean to trap us in here." He dug his heels into the sides of the stone horse repeatedly, urging it to move faster.

The ground and walls trembled again with a distant *boom*. The cave was brighter now and Claudia could make out the frantic bobbing of the horse's head. They turned a bend and the whole cave opened up before them in the light of the evening moon.

A great horned tail swung across the opening, crashing high on one of the inner walls. The cave shook again and chunks of rock tumbled in their path. A hedge of debris partially blocked their exit. One more good swing and they would be trapped.

"Hold on!" Pim shouted. Claudia crouched low over the stony mane. The horse charged forward, crushing smaller stones with its hooves and deftly leaping over debris in its path.

Forty feet from the exit. Twenty.

Celebes's horned tail swung again, slamming into the cave wall. The terrible sound of breaking stone took Claudia back to the horror of the viaduct. But this time the stones were raining down in front of them and around them and all but upon them as the horse leaped through the opening of the crumbling cave.

The great metal elephant was already rearing its tail for another strike as they touched the ground. Pim pulled the mane of the horse to guide it, but it was unnecessary. The horse swerved mid-stride and tore off past the beast toward the tree line at the top of the rugged terrain.

But the elephant's trunk! It swung as they passed, clipping a hind leg of the horse. The stone beast stumbled and fell and Claudia flew off its back. The ground slammed the wind from her lungs as she tumbled through the undergrowth.

She forced herself to her feet, head spinning. The horse was already up, prancing, as if waiting for them to get on its back. Pim was scrambling a few feet away, shouting something, staring at the ground by the elephant's advancing feet.

The staff.

Before the beast reached it, the staff rose into the air as if drawn upward by a string. Celebes came to a halt. Then the staff shot off to the other side of the basin—and into the outstretched hand of Nee Gezicht. Her mismatched eyes shone triumphantly in the torchlight.

"No!" Pim shouted. He would have charged forward, but Claudia lunged and caught his arm. She pulled him toward the horse. "No!" he cried again, and there was heartbreak in his cry.

"Let's go!"

Pim hesitated, his face twisted and pained. Then he mounted the horse and hauled Claudia up behind him.

"Claudia!" Nee Gezicht called out across the basin.

Claudia dug her heels into the side of the horse and it sprang forward. Holding tight to Pim, she couldn't cover her ears, and she braced herself for what Nee Gezicht might say next, for a command that would make Claudia's body betray her own will.

Then Celebes trumpeted, and Nee Gezicht's words were lost in the thunderous noise. The horse charged up the ridge and into the trees.

Fresh evening air whipped past Claudia's face, a welcome sensation after the stifling cave.

But her heart was in her throat and she couldn't breathe. They had been so close. They had stolen the staff from the witch—and Claudia had found a way to break it. *She had found a way.* She should have stopped Pim back in the cave and destroyed it once and for all, Fireside Angel or no. They would never have that chance again.

So close.

She squeezed Pim tight. He would never escape. He would never get to redeem himself. He would never stop Nee Gezicht from enslaving the people of this world.

It was all for nothing.

They rushed through the trees. Claudia and Pim had drawn the horse well—it moved so swiftly that clinging to its back was both thrilling and terrifying. Claudia strained to hear sounds of pursuit—the rumble of Celebes or the shriek of the Fireside Angel. Did the Angel even escape from the crumbling cave? Did it matter? Nee Gezicht had reclaimed the staff.

All Claudia could hear was the pounding of the horse's stone hooves and the rush of leaves and wind. The trees began to thicken and they plunged deeper into the forest, where the light of the late-evening sky didn't follow. Darkness surrounded them. Yet the horse veered around trees and leaped over obstacles as though daylight reigned, never slowing, never missing a step.

They rode until Claudia's backside became sore and, in the random thoughts that passed through her despondent mind, she wished they had drawn a saddle. She considered telling Pim about the nail polish remover, but decided against it. Discussing it would only drive home how close they had come to succeeding, and how impossible that was now. She couldn't get the picture out of her mind of Nee Gezicht holding the staff once more, a look of triumph on her face.

"Where are we going?" she finally shouted over the wind, although she already suspected the answer.

"To the window-caves. We're taking you home."

"There has to be another way to beat her."

"We had our chance," he said bitterly over his shoulder. "We lost."

As if to accentuate his point, the shriek of the Fireside Angel rose in the distance. Even from far off, it still laced her heart with despair. There was another sound, too—the beat of hooves, perhaps. Or was that just an echo?

"Do you think they're following us?"

Pim nodded. "Nee Gezicht won't just let you go."

Claudia glanced behind them, half expecting to see Celebes come crashing through the trees. But there was only dark foliage.

They continued in rapid silence until Pim pulled at the horse's mane. They slowed to a stop in a rare patch of moonlight that escaped through the canopy above. The echo of horse hooves faded quickly in the forest. Pim looked around carefully, straining in the darkness.

"What's wrong?" she asked.

Pim continued to search. "I haven't been through this forest for a long time. I think we've been heading in the right direction, but I'm not entirely sure where we are."

"We're lost?" Claudia's heart rose into her throat. She again looked behind them. This wasn't good, not with Nee Gezicht in pursuit.

Leaves crackled in the darkness off to the left. Pim tensed, clutching the horse's mane.

A twig snapped ahead of them. Another off to the right.

Claudia readied her feet to kick against the flanks of the horse, mentally bracing herself for the Fireside Angel to come barreling toward them.

There was movement in the darkness directly ahead of them and something emerged from the trees. But it wasn't the Fireside Angel.

It was a horse and rider dressed in a black cloak and a broad feathered hat.

"Balthasar? Is that you?" Claudia gasped.

The rider urged his horse slowly forward. The paltry moonlight filtering through the treetops glinted on the blade of the sword he extended toward them.

"If you have harmed a hair on this lady's head, witch-son, I will run you through without a second thought."

Claudia let out a sigh of relief. "It is you!"

There was movement off to the left, and Hendrik, also on horseback with sword drawn, stepped from the trees.

"Let her go, boy."

Claudia slid off the horse and placed herself between the Dutchmen and Pim. "Stop it right now! Whether you like it or not, Pim is my friend. He's helping me—helping all of you. He's fighting against Nee Gezicht. Against the Sightless One. You have to trust me."

The tip of Hendrik's sword dipped slightly. "The canine was right?"

Claudia made the connection right away. "You talked to Cash?"

Balthasar nodded slowly. "Not but an hour ago. He said you had stolen something valuable, something powerful from the witch. And that the boy Pim was fighting on our side."

"Yes, but—"

Hoofbeats came from behind them, along the path they had traveled. The third rider broke through the trees and came to a stop. Cornelis took in the gathering with a single sweeping glance, his eyes lingering on Pim.

"The Fireside Angel approaches," he said urgently. "It has picked up their trail. You have a matter of minutes, if that."

"And the metal beast?" Balthasar asked.

"I've seen no sign of it, not since we heard it earlier."

"The canine's story rings true, Cornelis," Hendrik said, nodding toward Claudia and Pim.

"The Sightless One is after her," Pim said. "I need to get her to the window-caves, the ones close to where you first found her. Get out of the way and let us go. Please."

"If that is your destination, then I would wager that you are lost," Balthasar said quietly, eyes on Pim.

"Then help us," Claudia pleaded.

Cornelis approached, towering over Pim. He drew his sword and placed it against Pim's neck. "We will help you, my lady. But I cannot assure you that my sword will not wander in the heat of battle, and land where it has so longed to strike."

Pim swallowed. "If that is the price of recompense, then I will pay it. But not until she is safe."

The sword lingered for a moment, and then withdrew. "Well, then, my lady. It appears you have the service of our swords once more."

"Huzzah!" shouted Hendrik. He immediately shrank under Cornelis's gaze.

Balthasar dismounted and bowed in front of Claudia. "With permission." He lifted her at the waist and set her back on the stone horse.

"You cannot outpace the Angel," Cornelis said. "Even with your curious steed, it will overtake you. Ride on. We will wait here and meet the monster."

"Can you beat it?" Claudia asked, suddenly concerned. It didn't seem likely it could be held with ropes, as the dragon had.

There was a flicker of doubt in Cornelis's face. "I have always wanted to try," he said grimly.

The Fireside Angel shrieked. It sounded close.

Pim grabbed the horse's stony mane.

"Wait!" Claudia said. They didn't know if they could beat it. It was quick and powerful, even with a wounded foot. She didn't need them sacrificing themselves for her—this time to something fiercer than a dragon.

Again the image of the dragon lying bound in the forest clearing sprang to her mind. And with it, an idea.

"You don't need to fight it, just slow it down."

"That is how we slow down such a creature, my lady," Hendrik said.

"But what if there's another way?"

"What do you mean?" Balthasar asked.

"Has Saint George come to pick up his dragon yet?"

It took a moment, but the eyes of the three Dutchmen grew wide.

It turned out that Saint George hadn't come to claim the dragon yet. A short and furious ride brought them to the clearing from the previous day. Here the moon shone brightly as the trees opened up, revealing the leaf-strewn ground.

And in the center, the dragon. Its feet were still bound and Claudia's shoelaces were tied in a bow around its neck.

Even as they rode into the clearing, the wicked cry of the Fireside Angel sounded in the not-so-distance.

The riders leaped from their horses. They would have to work quickly.

"You have rope?" Claudia asked.

"Do we have rope?" Hendrik said, digging into his saddlebags. "Ha!"

"Tie one around me," Cornelis ordered.

"No. Around me," Claudia corrected.

"But . . ." Pim said.

"I'm the lightest and you're the strongest. There's no time to argue, just do it," Claudia said.

Reluctantly Cornelis began busying himself with the other rope.

Balthasar gently looped the rope under Claudia's arms and tied it firmly. "Where does your courage come from?" he asked quietly.

Claudia looked over at Pim, who was tossing the ends of the ropes over branches high above. "From synergy."

"Hmm. Synergy. There's a song in there somewhere, no doubt." Balthasar handed Claudia a knife with a leather handle. "It is sharp enough to split the ropes with a single thrust."

She nodded, swallowing hard. "Right."

They were ready in less than a minute, and the others scattered farther into the trees with the horses.

The dragon looked up at her with large, adoring eyes, attempting to scoot its body closer to her.

"It's too bad. I kind of like you this way," she said.

She focused on the edge of the clearing. The Fireside Angel would be tracking them, following the same path they took. She listened carefully, but the night was silent. Just the panting of the dragon. A soft whinny from a horse.

She looked back at the others, but they were lost in the darkness of the forest.

And then a sound of tearing branches. There was no doubt what it was.

She knelt down and thrust the knife against the rope binding the dragon's hind feet. The rope fell away and the dragon came alive with excitement, scrabbling on its scaly claws to get closer to Claudia.

"Down, boy, down!" she whispered.

She pushed the knife against the front rope, freeing the dragon's front paws as well.

Immediately it leaped on her like a giant, friendly Great Dane, knocking her to the ground and licking her face over and over.

"Claudia!" she heard Pim cry out.

Her face soaked with drool, she pushed back at the dragon's head. "Down! Sit! Sit!"

The dragon backed off and sat. Claudia wiped the slobber from her face with her shirttail and stood up, wondering how the dragon knew the command for *sit*. Then she noticed the dragon was staring at the edge of the clearing.

And the Fireside Angel was staring right back.

In an instant, the Angel charged. He ran on all fours, favoring the foot that had stepped on the nail polish remover. But, if possible, he was quicker and fiercer in his movements than before.

Claudia grabbed the shoelaces around the dragon's neck and slipped in the knife. "Good boy," she whispered.

She thrust the knife back, slicing through the shoelaces. "Now!"

The rope around her torso went taut and she snapped backward and upward, the Fireside Angel just steps away. He leaped after her, gnarled claws outstretched, sailing higher into the air than she would have thought possible.

But the territorial dragon had sprung to life the second the shoelaces fell. It snarled and spun, once again lithe and power-ful, and larger than Claudia remembered. Its gaping jaws snapped at the Angel's leg, catching him and pulling him to the ground in a wild cry of pain.

Claudia flew into the trees, completely unnoticed by the dragon. A second rope had been attached to redirect the first, and now they lowered her while taking the second rope in, drawing her to them on the ground.

As her feet touched the earth, she looked up at the melee in the clearing. The Angel had freed itself from the jaws of the dragon, and the two now grappled and snapped in the most ferocious wrestling match imaginable.

"Well done, once again, my lady," Balthasar said as he lifted her from the ground and onto the stone horse. "And on we go."

Once more they were hurtling forward through the trees on horseback, the mild thrill of a tiny success surging through Claudia. Minutes passed and there was no indication of pursuit. But the thrill quickly faded. As they rode, they could hear the thunder of crashing rock in the distance. Like a deep bass drum, resounding and ominous.

"No!" Pim finally shouted as they left the cover of the forest.

The sounds of destruction, of course, came from Celebes. As Nee Gezicht perched in her seat on its back, the potbellied monster crashed its tail against what remained of the entrance to the window-cave Claudia had exited the day before. The overhang and the outer walls had fallen, blocking the cave and the Rubens painting inside with debris and leaving only the smallest of openings at the top.

Nee Gezicht whirled in her seat to face them. She shouted

something at them—at Claudia, perhaps—but they were still out of earshot.

Pim kept the horse moving at full speed but veered it sharply to the side. "There's another cave!"

The Dutchmen didn't waver from their original course. They charged Celebes, swords drawn, barreling down at full speed.

Claudia turned to watch as they met the elephantine beast. They swerved and ducked, but it caught Cornelis hard with the blunt of its tail, and he flew from his saddle. The others scattered, but even as they regrouped, Celebes broke off the fight and charged after Claudia and Pim.

"Here they come!" she shouted.

The horse tore along the foothills of the mountain, crushing the gravel beneath its feet into powder. Ahead of them was an opening into what looked like a canyon. They turned sharply. It had cracked, stony walls topped with boulders and tall trees far above. It was narrow, but plenty wide for Celebes.

Claudia looked back as they turned. Celebes trailed close enough that she could see the beast's fiery red eyes and Nee Gezicht perched on top, silhouetted in the moonlight. The Dutchmen were still in pursuit.

"Almost there!" shouted Pim.

Claudia looked back again to see Celebes enter the canyon. No sooner had he done so than Nee Gezicht lifted her arms. Dust fell from the walls above her, and then more than dust. Stones tumbled, followed by rocks and boulders, and finally a tall pine tree that cracked in half as it fell, slanted, into the canyon.

Though dust and darkness obstructed her view, the result

would be obvious. Nee Gezicht had blocked off the canyon, shutting out the three Dutchmen.

But how? Celebes hadn't even twitched his tail.

"Ride on, my lady!" came a distant shout from Balthasar. At least they were all right.

"There it is," Pim said. "Get ready!"

She gripped the straps of her backpack.

As they approached a shadowy patch in the side of the canyon wall, Pim hauled back on the horse's mane.

"Whoa!"

The horse slowed and Pim slid off its back, pulling Claudia after him. She turned and slapped the horse on its rump. It leaped away without any further encouragement—the metal elephant was closing in quickly.

They ran toward the craggy stone wall. Claudia almost hit it before she saw that, buried in the shadows of the moonlight, a vertical crack stretched upward, just big enough to squeeze through. Not big enough for a horse, and definitely not big enough for a metal elephant.

Roughly, Pim hurried her into the crack and closely followed. It was a tight fit and at an odd angle, but after several feet she was through. It opened up into a large tunnel, the walls of which were erratically striped with thick veins of crystal. The veins glowed eerily with a light of their own, like some sort of Halloween spiderweb decoration.

Pim still hadn't wriggled out of the crack when trembling footsteps from outside ended with Celebes's tail crashing against the outer face of the wall, once and then again.

The walls of the cave shook. Pim's foot seemed to be wedged against something, and he struggled to get it free and pull himself from the entrance. Claudia reached in and grabbed for his hand.

"No!" he cried. "Go now!"

"Hold!" shouted a voice from the outside.

Claudia caught Pim's hand and threw herself backward. Pim pulled free from the entrance and they tumbled to the floor of the tunnel.

The pounding stopped. They both turned and watched for just a moment—a moment too long. The mismatched eyes of Nee Gezicht, bathed in moonlight, peered through the crack.

"Claudia," said the Sightless One. "Come to me."

CHAPTER 20

THE EFFECT was immediate and it was powerful. No sooner had Nee Gezicht spoken the words than Claudia's strongest desire was to push herself back through the crack in the cave wall. All other thoughts became blurred and elusive, like reaching for sunbeams in murky water.

She stepped toward the crack.

Someone's hand clinched her shoulder in a flash, jerking her back into the darkness of the cave. Someone her own height—a boy, maybe—slapped a hand over one ear and smothered the other against his shoulder, and then pulled her deeper into the tunnels. They hurried through one passage and then veered down another, then another.

The tunnel was dim without the moonlight. Only the soft glow of the crystal veins remained. But light or dark, it didn't matter. This wasn't right. She was supposed to be somewhere. Somewhere back the way she had come. She needed to go. To go now.

Go now!

She whirled her fists up and around, striking at whomever held her. The person cried out and released the grip just enough for Claudia to slip out and tear away into the darkness.

Back the way I came. Back the way I came.

The person who had held her called out from behind. "Claudia!" The cry echoed through the tunnels. That was her name. How strange for that person to know her name.

Back the way I came. Back the way I came.

It was hard to see straight despite the glow surrounding her. She felt for the wall and found it, cool and rough. Footsteps echoed in the distance. There was an opening on the right, a sharp turning in the wall, and she took it. Immediately there was another turn and she took that one also.

She had to get back to . . . to what? Why couldn't she remember?

The crystal veins thinned and the light dimmed as she continued, and before long she moved in the dark. On she rushed, frantic now because everything was black, even her mind, and she knew it. No light, nothing familiar.

But what about Pim? The thought came upon her unexpectedly. *Pim!*

"Pim!"

The shout leaped from her lips, and the image of Pim's smile emerged through the fog and wavered at the front of her thoughts.

Yes! She had been with Pim. They had come to this cave together. Where had he gone? Why did she want to leave so badly?

"Claudia!" It was Pim's voice, faint and remote.

Another shout was on her lips, but it died when a different voice filled the dark tunnel like thick smoke. It echoed across the walls and through the air, piercing Claudia's mind.

"Sun, moon, withering star,
How foolish little children are.
They run and think they can be free,
But in the end they'll come to me."

Icy fingers. There were icy fingers wrapping slowly around her will, pulling at her heartstrings, making her feet shuffle forward again. She had to move, back the way she had come. She wanted to get back to the cave entrance. Wanted it so badly that her ears hurt, a sharp, stabbing pain. Her thoughts spun—like particles of paper and goop in an ancient blender she had once seen on a dining room table. Somewhere.

She was supposed to meet someone at the cave entrance. Someone important.

Is it Pim?

Pim! Where was Pim?

Her shoes pounded the ground as she tore through the darkness in a mental blender of her own, now slamming into walls where the tunnel turned, now tripping and crunching her knees into the ground.

"Pitter patter little feet run;
Now strikes the witching hour.
All they do shall come undone
When met with greater power."

Again the voice rang across the walls and into her head. Rhyme. The voice was speaking in rhyme. Speaking to the witch's enemies. The mental fog gained a red tinge and a burst of anger rose in her throat like bile.

And why should she care about Pim anyway? She'd shown him friendship. She'd never reached out to anyone before, not to a friend. And what did he do? Put her in danger. Tricked her. Lied to her. For all she knew, he was still lying to her. Like that deception in Nee Gezicht's house—

No. That anger wasn't hers. It came from someplace else, somewhere outside of her. She had drunk the tea. Why had she drunk the tea? The icy hand was grasping her will, gripping, crushing. And, oh, how her ears hurt!

But she had pried the hand off her will before, hadn't she? She could do it again.

Mentally she pulled at the fingers, but they burned at the touch and barely gave way. It was stronger than before. The Sightless One must be desperate. Nee Gezicht was putting everything she had into bringing Claudia back to her. She knew Claudia—the *Artisti*—was about to slip through her grasp. And she suspected that Claudia knew . . . what? Claudia had figured something out. What was it?

Curled into a ball on her knees, in the darkness, she cried out again. "Pim!"

Her ears rang with a flash of pain. Stars danced before her closed eyes. And footsteps, there were footsteps.

Someone was suddenly kneeling before her. A hand brushed her cheek gently. "Claudia," Pim whispered, "you can do this. You beat her before, you can do it again."

"No," she moaned. "Not this time. It's too strong."

His hands were on her shoulders, shaking her. "Focus, Claudia. You can do it! She can't take your will completely unless you give it to her. Fight back!"

Claudia took a deep breath and inwardly pried at the icy fingers once again. But the fog in her thoughts grew darker, more dense. She had no strength left. If she got to her feet, they would take her back to Nee Gezicht and it would be over. All she could do was crouch on the cold painted ground and wait for fate to find her.

"I'm so sorry," she breathed. She watched the black fog roll into the crevices of her mind and waited for Pim's footsteps to echo away from her, waited for the approaching *swish* of the Sightless One's black silk gown.

But instead she felt Pim grab her arm and yank her to her feet.

"I'm sorry, too, that I ever brought you here. But it doesn't end like this."

He turned and plunged back through the tunnel, dragging Claudia with his hand firmly clamped on her arm.

All of her thoughts were obscured by the black fog in her mind and she didn't know what to think and so she thought nothing. But her body fought back. Her feet refused to move and her arm jerked in resistance to Pim's pull.

But his grip was solid and he pulled her along swiftly through the tunnels, turning right, then left, then descending a grade so sharp that they had to run to keep from falling over. In the back of her mind she heard other footsteps, not far behind.

And then without warning they turned and burst into a narrow passageway bathed in the soft glow of a hundred different locations.

Window-paintings generously lined the walls, arranged carefully as though in a museum gallery and not deep beneath a mountain. The murmur of noises from around the world filled the tunnel. Veins of glowing crystal once again wormed through the stone walls around the window-paintings.

Claudia's body still struggled against Pim's hold, her fingers clawing clumsily at his grip and straining to break away. But the sudden plunge from constant darkness into light stirred the thick fog in her mind like a gust of wind, allowing a few rays of clarity to shine through.

"Paintings," she whispered. She had sat for hours and hours staring at paintings and drawing them. That was before—

"Pim!" Her body involuntarily lunged away from the boy who held her tight.

"Almost there," he said, moving swiftly with her in tow, glancing briefly at each window-painting. "We'll get you home, but we need to do it before Nee Gezicht catches up with us. She can't know where you've gone."

Nee Gezicht. Claudia was supposed to meet her, wasn't she? Back the other way. Why was she letting this boy pull her around? She had to get away, had to break away.

The tunnel opened up into a cavern with a high ceiling and wide, rounded walls like a circular gymnasium. Rough stone pillars stretched from floor to ceiling, interspersed with massive stalactites hanging from above.

"There it is!" cried Pim, dragging her toward a window-painting on the far side.

A familiar voice sounded once more. It seemed close, although Claudia couldn't tell if it echoed from the walls around her, or only in the walls of her own head.

"As hope descends with every breath,
Ne'er again shall it be risen.
For here's a fate far worse than death,
In this, your canvas prison."

A vision came out of Claudia's thick mental fog. The Sightless One would reap her will—she had already begun—and neither Claudia nor Pim would be able to stop her. Pim she would destroy, and Claudia she would keep there behind the canvas, slowly feeding on Claudia's will for hundreds of years. It was inevitable.

The dark fog in Claudia's mind congealed into fear and then hardened into hopelessness. There was nothing she could do but take her place beside Nee Gezicht—and she was coming. She was almost there.

Pim was rooting around in her backpack with one hand, the other still holding tight to her as she strained against him. He pulled out the yellow mustard bottle and spun Claudia around, clutching her wrist.

"I'm so sorry, Claudia." His voice wavered as he squeezed the paste onto her hand, outlining her fingers. Her body tried to tug her hand away, but he held firm.

"I'm sorry it turned out this way. I never wanted you to get hurt." Paste spurted onto her last finger. "After you go through the painting, run. Get out of sight. I don't know how long she can keep her hold on you, but the farther you are from a painting, the better."

She was hitting at him now with a curled fist, trying to wring her other arm free.

"Good-bye, my friend."

He pulled her wrist over toward the painting with the hand outstretched, ready to touch paste to canvas.

Behind the fog and fear and hopelessness, Claudia glanced up at the window-painting. On the far side was a gallery, dark but familiar, with a large cushy bench in the center. And etched into the canvas-glass were three men in wide-brimmed hats and rapiers drawn.

The three Dutchmen. She had come full circle. She had first seen Pim in that painting.

Pim.

Granny Custos. Cornelis. Hendrik. Balthasar.

Rembrandt.

Cash. The Lady. Pablo the Cubist. Colossus.

Pim. Dear Pim. She had come to save him.

Her friend.

Her goopy fingers inches away from the canvas-glass, Claudia wrenched her wrist from Pim's grasp.

Pim, my friend.

The icy hand around her will no longer had fingers but had slowly become a case of solid ice. It constricted tighter, pulling against the sinew of her muscles and the threads of her thoughts and the very roots of her will.

I came to save him.

Her will flexed, pushing outward in all directions with an explosive force. The icy hand cracked and then burst into shards that instantly melted.

The dark fog in her mind suddenly became raggedy, as rays of light—insight, inspiration, illumination—came pouring in.

And my will is mine! she shouted in her head. A thrill of excitement shot through her veins because she knew it was true.

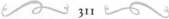 311

It was her will that had brought her there, her will that had driven her forward, and her will that would save Pim.

And she knew how. *She knew how.*

She turned and threw her arms around Pim.

"Claudia—" he exclaimed.

"It's okay. It's me. She's not going to take my will without a fight."

"You need to go." Pim pushed her back.

"I came here to save you, Pim. And I know how." She tore the worn yellow backpack from her shoulders.

Laughter rang from the stone walls. Nee Gezicht passed through the low entryway into the cavernous gallery, her staff tapping against the floor. "Save Pim? That's so precious, child. You can't even save yourself."

Pim whirled around. "Go now, Claudia!"

Nee Gezicht grimaced and swung her hand across her body. Pim flew off his feet and slammed into the cavern wall like a doll. His head knocked against the stone and he crumpled to the ground.

"Pim!" Claudia leaped in his direction, but she was caught mid-stride by an invisible force snatching her left wrist and holding it firmly in the air.

"Let's clean you up a bit," Nee Gezicht hissed.

The ointment Pim had placed on Claudia's hand now rapidly peeled from her skin. It hung suspended in the air for a moment, like oil in water. Then Nee Gezicht flicked her fingers and it, too, smashed into the cavern wall, bursting into a fine mist.

The force released Claudia's wrist as her backpack slid violently away from her feet and skidded across the cavern floor.

It spun, her cell phone and art history book flying through the broken zipper. It came to rest at Nee Gezicht's feet.

There was no sign of the nail polish remover. It was still tucked away.

Good. Claudia was going to need it.

She locked eyes with Nee Gezicht.

The Sightless One brought her hands together as if in prayer. "Your mistake, Claudia, is that you placed your trust in a fool." She glanced at Pim.

Claudia followed her gaze. His chest still rose and fell.

"A fool who was as greedy as he was blind," the witch continued. "Great power does not a man make. And now he is a weakling. A shell."

Claudia's thoughts raced. She needed the staff. She needed the nail polish remover. She needed to keep Pim safe. She needed to not get killed.

Nee Gezicht's eyes returned to Claudia and she smiled tightly. "It's time we got to know each other better, child. Come to me."

Claudia braced herself, waiting for a tug in her mind or fingers around her will. But she felt only a stifling breeze coming from the direction of Nee Gezicht, and that was all. Her will was her own.

Nee Gezicht's eyes widened. "Come to me." Her commanding voice rang through the cavern.

"Not this time," whispered Claudia.

The witch grinned. "An *Artisti* so young, so ignorant and untrained. And yet so powerful. This is too delicious."

Nee Gezicht had connected with objects—the backpack, Pim, Claudia's wrist—pulling their threads to make them move, just like Claudia had done with the rope at the viaduct and with the stone horse. Maybe she could do the same here and now.

"Who says I haven't been trained?" Claudia said. She began to probe through the cavern with her mind, looking for threads that connected to something, anything.

"Well, for one thing, you drank my tea."

"Okay. Maybe. But you're not the only Renaissance *Artisti* still around, you know."

Nee Gezicht's smile flickered. "Renaissance *Artisti*? Don't tell me you've met one. Who would it be? Custos the hag? The lovesick Spaniard? Impotent fools who cower in houses without paintings. Come with me, Claudia, and I can teach you the real meaning of power. Power over lands. Power over people. Power over magic."

Claudia felt a force moving toward her, groping and invisible. Nee Gezicht was reaching for the threads that connected to her. The witch would throw her against the wall like she did Pim, or drag her back through the tunnels.

The force lunged for her, and Claudia swung her arm and mentally batted it away. It backed off and then charged again. She swung again, almost feeling something tangible as her mind connected with it.

The invisible force retreated. Her focus frantically bounced around the cavern, searching for another attack. She found the staff in Nee Gezicht's hand, but doubtless the witch would sense her mental probing just as Claudia had. She needed something that Nee Gezicht wouldn't expect.

"Remarkable world, isn't it?" Nee Gezicht hissed. "Everything that enters succumbs to the synergy of paint and canvas. And that, in turn, succumbs to me."

A low rumble emanated from the cavern ceiling. One of the enormous stalactites directly above Claudia cracked across the base that secured it. It plunged toward the ground and Claudia leaped forward, barely escaping the pointed tip that smashed just behind her. Stone shards scattered and dust surged into the air.

The rumble continued and, with another *crack*, a second stalactite fell from above. She tumbled forward and then again, aware that a third was already falling.

She's driving me toward her. She quenched the panic rising in her throat and looked up as a series of *cracks* rang out. The remaining stalactites on this side of the cavern were now falling toward her. Behind them, the veins of crystal ran through the stone ceiling and down the walls, like ropes holding up the cavern.

Like ropes.

She ran and leaped.

The stalactites smashed into the ground behind her. The earsplitting noise still thundered on when she felt a force wrap around her midsection and lift her from the floor. She was only paces from the eager gaze and outstretched arms of Nee Gezicht.

Claudia didn't strike at the force that held her. Instead she reached out with her mind to the walls of the cavern, collecting all the threads she could find that attached to the veins of crystal.

Nee Gezicht's invisible grip tightened and she drew Claudia closer.

Claudia spread her arms and *pulled*. Pulled like she had with the nail polish horse, but this time without the hesitation, without the doubt. She was an *Artisti*, and while she didn't know everything that meant, in that moment it meant she was going to save Pim.

The veins of crystal sprang from the walls of the cave with a grinding *crunch*. They floated in the air like ribbons in the wind, one end still attached to the cavern wall.

At a pull from Claudia's thoughts, they shot from all directions toward Nee Gezicht. The Sightless One cried out in surprise as strands of crystal ribbons twirled themselves around one arm, then the other. They spun and looped, raveling into a mess that pulled tighter as Nee Gezicht struggled. Another ribbon twisted itself around Nee Gezicht's mouth, silencing her cries.

The force around Claudia's torso released and she dropped to her feet. She directed all her energy into the crystal ribbons. They continued to swirl and tighten, but Nee Gezicht was fighting back, trying to peel them away and untangle herself.

Sweat broke out across Claudia's forehead. She had to keep the ribbons in place. Nee Gezicht had overcome her surprise and was pushing back against the ribbons. The staff was still in her hand. Claudia didn't see how she could grab the staff without breaking her concentration.

And then someone was running past her toward Nee Gezicht.

Pim!

He flew by and wrested the staff from Nee Gezicht's hand. It left her grasp, but still Pim struggled to pull it away, as though it was drawn to her by a powerful magnet. Claudia forced the ribbons even tighter. The staff came away and Pim stumbled backward.

Stars danced in front of Claudia's vision as she strained to keep the ribbons tight. "Pim . . . bottle . . . backpack."

Pim snatched up the backpack and rummaged inside, emerging with the yellow mustard bottle. He held it up and stepped over to Claudia.

"Other . . . bottle," she murmured desperately.

His hand dived back in, drawing out the bottle of nail polish remover. He twisted off the lid and looked at Claudia, obviously confused.

Boys.

Cinching down one last thrust on the ribbons, she dropped her concentration and spun to face Pim. The release was dizzying and she almost toppled over. Nee Gezicht thrashed violently against the ribbons.

Claudia snatched the nail polish remover from Pim's hand and grabbed one end of the staff, holding it out between the two of them. She looked into Pim's trusting eyes.

Then she emptied the bottle onto the staff.

Nee Gezicht freed one hand, which tore away the ribbons from her mouth. "No!"

The liquid splashed onto the staff in the dead center of its length. It glistened and trickled. It seeped and dripped. And the paint that looked like wood began to run.

The moan rose from the staff once more. It lifted and echoed off the walls of the cavern, higher and louder, rising in pitch and volume until it was so shrill that Claudia thought her eardrums would burst.

And then with a mighty *crack* the moaning cut off, leaving only piteous echoes on the stone walls. Silence reigned for a moment as everyone stared at the staff, cloven through the middle.

Break the staff. Break the curse. Break Nee Gezicht.

Claudia looked up until her eyes locked with Pim's, which

overflowed with hope. Together they tossed the pieces of the staff aside. Nee Gezicht howled and rushed toward the remains of the staff, but one hand was still tangled in the crystal ribbons. She struggled against them, tears plunging down her face.

Pim snatched up the mustard bottle and outlined Claudia's hand once again with paste. Then he passed the bottle to her, and she outlined his hand, squeezing until only air came from the nozzle. She hoped it would be enough. They rushed over to the window-painting of the three Dutchmen. Claudia snatched up her art history book as they passed over it.

She glanced back at Nee Gezicht, who had finally broken free from the ribbons. She cradled the remains of the staff in her arms, vainly attempting to force the broken ends back together.

Claudia looked at Pim and gestured to the painting. "Age before beauty."

Pim shook his head. "You first."

"No. I want to make sure you go through."

Pim hesitated, an argument on his lips, but he turned and stared at the window-painting. Carefully lifting his hand, he placed it on the canvas-rough glass and was gone in an instant.

Claudia smiled brilliantly. She glanced back at the Sightless One, who was now rising to her feet, eyes fiery and wicked. She wished she had some witty rhyme of her own to retort in this moment of victory, but instead she simply said, "Good-bye."

Then, hand extended, she left the world behind the canvas.

CHAPTER 29

C LAUDIA LANDED next to Pim, her feet firmly set on the floor of the Florence Museum of Arts and Culture. Her museum.

Pim was studying his hands, rubbing them together, stretching his fingers. His face shone with wonder as if he noticed for the first time that he had hands.

Claudia had the sudden sense that they weren't alone. She spun to the painting of the three Dutchmen. There in the upper corner—the same place she had first seen Pim—was the face of Nee Gezicht. Her eyes were wide with fury, but also fear. Her fist banged against the window-painting like a child throwing a tantrum.

"I will find you, Claudia," hissed Nee Gezicht. "You will never be out of my reach."

"I already am," Claudia said. She had the strong suspicion that Nee Gezicht had no way out—that the severed staff also broke her connection with magic. She was trapped in the same prison she had made for Pim. Claudia hoped it was true.

She grabbed Pim by the arm and pulled him from the room. Nee Gezicht shouted her name behind them, but soon the sound was lost in the depths of the galleries.

They came to a stop in the large atrium at the center of the museum. The wide skylight above them revealed a silver moon, full and round, in a bed of stars. Between the glow of the moon and the soft security lights along the walls, she could clearly see Pim, and she marveled at how real he looked. His face no longer held the shimmery gleam of paint, or the rough texture of canvas, but instead was soft and lifelike.

Pim placed his hands on her shoulders and smiled gently. "There is nothing I could ever say or do to show you how grateful I am."

A thrill of delight and relief ran through Claudia and she couldn't help but giggle. "Anytime." She took his hands and held them in hers. "I can't believe we did it, we actually did it! There in those tunnels I thought it was all over, but we did it. Did you see how I fought her—and how I pulled that crystal right out of the wall to tie her up? I really am an *Artisti*, aren't I?"

She let go of his hands and spun around, bubbling with excitement. "This is amazing. We made it out. You can come live with my family. We have a spare room and you could come with me to school and you can go to the supermarket any time you want. And we can come here to the museum together to—"

His sad eyes brought her to a halt.

Pim shook his head. "You have freed me from my prison, but you have freed me so that I can rest." He took her hand again and squeezed it tightly. "Thank you."

Something was wrong. There was too much sincerity and

depth and finality to that *thank you*. Tears lined Claudia's eyes and she had no idea why. "I don't know what you're talking . . ."

Pim stepped back, eyes closed. And then she saw the change.

He was growing taller, so much taller than the twelve-year-old Pim. And there were subtle changes to his face, his hands, the hair on his arms. And then they weren't so subtle anymore, and in an instant a fully grown Pim stood before her, handsome and strong, and stretching out the clothes he wore.

The changes continued. His face began to wrinkle. His hair, now long, turned gray, then white. His back developed a rounded curve. His fingers became bent and gnarled.

And as quickly as Pim changed, Claudia understood. Pim was more than three hundred and sixty years old. His body had been suspended in paint and canvas for most of that time, but now that he had returned to a world where time mattered, his body was catching up.

A numbing cold replaced the excitement that had run through her veins just moments before. Tears ran freely down her face. She tried to speak but only choked out a strained, "No, Pim, no."

She was losing him.

Before her stood the boy she knew, her first real and best friend, white beard descending toward the floor, skin wrinkled and sagging, so old that she ached to look at him. His back bent terribly and he had to crane his neck to look up at her. His eyes opened, bold and blue and unchanged, and locked with hers. Those eyes that had seen so much across hundreds of years. Those eyes that had had been filled with laughter, and longing, and remorse. Those eyes that had seen her as a friend, even when she doubted.

A smile spread across his ancient lips. Then Pim closed his eyes one last time, drew in one last mighty breath, and sighed.

As though a wind had blown across a sandy beach, the sigh scattered his body into millions of tiny particles. The particles swirled and twisted in the air like a long, thin strip of silk. They playfully twirled once around Claudia and then rose upward, higher and higher, until they reached the domed skylight, and she could no longer tell which was star and which was Pim.

Chapter 30

It was a week later when Claudia finally found the courage to return to the Florence Museum of Arts and Culture. She hesitated at the entryway, took a deep breath, and stepped inside.

The afternoon was warm, and the air-conditioned galleries felt welcoming and familiar. She meandered by the paintings in the first room. They were obscure, painted by artists who probably didn't even appear in her art encyclopedia (which had been dented and soaked and was a little worse for the wear). Had she seen any of those people on her journey through the other world? Had she walked in those particular fields?

And whether they were obscure or not, she understood those paintings better than she had. Not in a textbook kind of way. In an *Artisti* kind of way that she didn't have words for. There was a connection there, like there had been between her and the horse on the cave wall. It was real and it was strong and she didn't know what it meant—yet.

Open your mind. See differently.

She passed by the purple cushy bench she had slept on that night after Pim left. She didn't even remember lying down to sleep, but Mr. Custos had found her there the next morning when he turned on the museum lights.

"Good morning!" he said. "Looks like someone has been off adventuring." He didn't ask any questions but brought her a cup of cocoa and some crackers. She was relieved to find they didn't taste like paint, and that they took the edge off her raging hunger.

Mr. Custos watched her eat in silence. When she finished, he asked, "And your friend in the painting?"

Claudia looked up at the skylight. "He made it out. Tell Granny Custos that he made it out."

Mr. Custos nodded in satisfaction.

"And," Claudia continued, "tell her that we have a lot to talk about. *A lot* to talk about."

She had made her way home after that. She told her mom a series of lies—which she again swore would be her last—about coming home early on the bus and forgetting to call and she was so sorry but what a great time she had at Aunt Maggie's. Her backpack? And her cell phone? Oh. She must have left them on the bus. . . .

Now in the museum she wandered through the galleries and finally stopped in front of the portrait of the three Dutchmen sitting around a small wooden table. Their swords were still drawn, their faces still stoic, and their eyes still twinkled with adventure. Claudia now understood why.

The blank area of the painting, in the background between

Cornelis and Balthasar—she knew their names now—was empty. There was no sign of Nee Gezicht. Hopefully she had moved on to . . . who knows where.

Claudia's thoughts turned to the other face she had seen in that painting. A boy. And a friend. She pictured Pim sitting patiently in that enormous cavern, staring out of the window-painting, watching her.

It was hard to be sad for Pim. He was free from his prison, free from his suffering. And they had broken Nee Gezicht, which, perhaps, made up for some of the wrongs he'd committed in that world.

But she missed him.

After a time, she turned away and let her eyes roam the gallery. Several patrons milled about, and directly in front of her, sitting on the center square bench, was Megan Connell. Her elbows dug into her knees and her chin rested in her hands. Her eyes stared at the gray carpet and she sighed.

Claudia studied her for a few moments. Her impulse was to walk away, to find a corner nook where she could draw undisturbed. Instead she took a few steps forward and sat beside Megan on the cushy bench.

"Hello," Claudia said quietly.

Megan glanced at her. "Hey, Claudia."

"Doesn't look like you're having much fun."

Megan rolled her eyes. "My dad made me come." She pointed to a man on the other side of the room, deep in conversation with Mr. Custos. They were gesturing to a painting on the far wall.

"Ah. Gotcha. And you don't like art?"

The girl crinkled her nose. "They're just a bunch of dumb pictures."

Claudia swung her feet gently against the bench for a few moments. She glanced up again at the painting of the three Dutchmen—and breathed in sharply. The familiar face of a white bulldog had been added to the scene, in one of the lower corners of the painting. Claudia grinned, and the bulldog winked at her. Apparently Cash had overcome his fear of the window-caves. She winked back, thrilled to still be connected—even in a small way—to the world behind the canvas.

Claudia turned again to Megan. "Do you see that painting in front of us? With the three men and their swords?"

"You mean the guys *without* blue eyes?" She flashed Claudia a smile.

Claudia smiled and nodded. "Yeah. But you know who they are, right?"

"I don't think so."

Claudia stopped swinging her feet and stared at her in mock surprise. "You've never heard of the Three Dutchmen?"

Megan's eyes widened ever so slightly, and she shook her head.

"How they fought a doomed battle with Saint George's dragon?" Balthasar wouldn't mind if she embellished a bit.

The girl's eyes widened more and she shook her head again.

"And how a ferocious heroine with magic in her fingertips swooped in to save the day?"

Megan shifted on the bench to face Claudia.

Claudia made herself more comfortable and looked into the painted faces of the three Dutchmen and the white dog beside them, stretching across the broad canvas.[30] "Well, have I got a story for you. . . ."

---

30. CANVAS. Ah, canvas. There is nothing more thrilling than to look on a fresh, untouched canvas. The poetic brick and mortar of the art world. A painter takes a piece of canvas fabric and lovingly stretches it over a rectangular wooden frame. A thin glue, called gesso, is applied. The artist then has a surface sufficient for satisfying his creative vision. The vision will live in perpetuity on the surface of the canvas, in the imaginations of the viewers . . . and who knows where else? (Excerpted from *Dr. Buckhardt's Art History for the Enthusiast and the Ignorant.*)

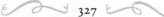

ACKNOWLEDGMENTS

The original thought for the book you just finished came from a painting my dad brought home from Holland before I was even born. It was of a Dutch boy in a funny hat who stared out of the canvas with parted lips. I spent a great deal of time as a kid staring back.

The thought became a goal with the encouragement of a beautiful wife and four kids who are the best excuse in the world to not sit down and work.

The goal became a story with the help of the Middle Critters Critique Group. Even a reclusive author needs friends.

The story became a book with the help of my agent, Jennifer Weltz, and the wonderful support of the Jean V. Naggar Literary Agency.

The book found its way into your hands in all its artistic glory with the help of Liz Szabla and the talented team at Feiwel and Friends.

Finally, of course, where would we be without the indomitable Dr. Buckhardt, art historian extraordinaire? The only thing bigger than his ego is his mustache. He is one of the few people who know that the world behind the canvas really exists.

And now, my friend, so do you.

Alexander Vance